BILLY BUCKHORN

AND THE RISE OF THE NIGHT SEERS

BILLY BUCKHORN

AND THE RISE OF THE NIGHT SEERS

Gary Robinson

7th GENERATION
Summertown, Tennessee

Library of Congress Cataloging-in-Publication Data available upon request.

Front cover art by Chevron Lowery, chevronlowery.artstation.com
Cover and interior design: John Wincek, aerocraftart.com

7th Generation
Book Publishing Company
PO Box 99, Summertown, TN 38483
888-260-8458
bookpubco.com
nativevoicesbooks.com

Printed in the United States of America

ISBN: 978-0-9669317-5-4
eBook ISBN: 978-0-9673108-1-7

29 28 27 26 25 24 1 2 3 4 5 6 7 8 9

DEDICATION

I want to thank my best friend and significant other, Lola, for her ongoing support in all things. I couldn't do this work without her. She has been by my side for many years, and no words printed here could ever express my true gratitude.

NOTE TO READERS

Osiyo (hello). As I noted in book one of the Thunder Child series, this is a work of fantasy fiction. Elements of Native American cultures and histories have been blended with fictional tribal cultures, religions, and histories to achieve what I hope is compelling storytelling. In these pages, reality and fantasy come together in a unique way.

To learn more about the actual Cherokee language, history, and culture, I recommend the following online resources:

The Cherokee Nation's language website:
http://language.cherokee.org/

Cherokee Word of the Week YouTube channel:
https://www.youtube.com/watch?v=6jiK-5bJbKc

OsiyoTV YouTube channel:
https://www.youtube.com/c/OsiyoTV

Wado (thank you).
Gary Robinson

CONTENTS

PROLOGUE

Sixteen-year-old Bryan Johnson was convinced that nothing interesting would take place on this family winter vacation to the Great Smoky Mountains National Park. *What makes it so great?* he thought. *Absolutely nothing, as far as I can see.*

The weather seemed worse than usual, even for this time of year. A relentless wind howled through the trees, sounding every bit like a pack of hungry wolves. Occasionally, an odd, mechanical-sounding squawk rang out, echoing across the mountains. It all made the teen's skin crawl.

The Johnson family had been making this annual "pilgrimage to nature," as Bryan's parents called it, since before he was born. Mr. Johnson had researched the family's genealogy and discovered they had a Cherokee ancestor mixed in among the mostly German Americans in the family tree. He was proud of that little fact.

The Smokemont Campground, near the Oconaluftee River, was a favorite destination spot for countless numbers of families from Tennessee and the Carolinas during the winter school break. It was located less than ten miles north of the Eastern Cherokee reservation in North Carolina. That was one reason Bryan's parents liked coming to these campgrounds.

Sounding much like a travel brochure, Bryan's father often said he loved the park's breathtaking mountain scenery, panoramic views, rushing mountain streams, and old hardwood forests that stretched to the horizon. Coincidentally, Bryan did indeed trace those exact words back to the park's printed guide.

Bryan's ten-year-old brother, Jessie, apparently still found the annual trip exciting and interesting, and he was having a great time. But the boy had a tendency to spend many of his waking hours entranced in some make-believe fantasy involving magic and warlocks or dungeons and dragons.

That was why it was no real big surprise to Bryan when Jessie came running into the campsite early that New Year's Eve morning, screaming at the top of his lungs, "A giant bird just kidnapped Corky!"

The young boy was near tears and panicked out of his mind at the loss of the family pet. "Good acting," Bryan said with a laugh. "That was an Oscar-worthy performance!"

The boys' parents emerged from their tent.

"I'm not acting!" Jessie responded angrily. "I saw it happen with my own eyes!" He buried his face in his mother's embrace and began sobbing.

"What kind of bird is big enough and strong enough to pick up a thirty-pound cocker spaniel?" Mr. Johnson asked as he scanned the sky.

"I don't know what kind of bird it was," Jessie replied, still sobbing. "But his feathers looked like they were made of metal, and his claws were big enough to pick up a cow."

"You mean you guys are buying this story?" Bryan asked in disbelief. "He's obviously in the middle of one of his fantasies, or he lost Corky somewhere along the trail and had to make up a story so he wouldn't get blamed."

Jessie let go of his mother and ran toward his older brother.

"I'm not making it up!" the boy said as he took a swing at Bryan. "You don't know what I saw!"

Their father, who'd been scanning the woods around them, stepped in between the boys and took hold of Jessie. Squatting down, he turned the boy so they were face-to-face.

"What do you say we get on over to the ranger station?" he said. "We need to report this incident to the park authorities immediately and then do a thorough search for Corky along the trail. Maybe the bird dropped him somewhere."

"Good idea," Mrs. Johnson said. "Bryan can stay here and watch the camp." She eyed her eldest son sternly.

Jessie stopped crying and nodded his approval of the plan.

So, the three Johnsons marched the two hundred yards to the Smokemont Ranger Station, which had just opened for the day. Fifty-year-old Joseph Saunooke, a Cherokee ranger who'd worked for the Great Smoky Mountains National Park the last ten years, had just finished raising the American flag on the pole next to the station when the Johnsons approached.

The Cherokee man gave them a warm welcome, noticing that the boy was quite distressed. Once they were inside Saunooke's office, Mr. Johnson tried as best he could to describe what Jessie had reported to him without sounding *too* out there. It was a balancing act for sure.

"Jessie, describe the bird in as much detail as you can," Ranger Saunooke said in a sympathetic tone.

"It was bigger than any bird I've ever seen!" the boy said excitedly. "Its feathers were about the same color as a penny. I could tell it was hungry because his head was moving back and forth, you know, like he was looking for something on the ground to eat."

"What else?" the ranger asked.

"Corky started barking his head off and jerked the leash out of my hands." The boy began to tear up again. "That's when the thing saw him. Corky ran toward the bird, barking at it up in the sky. I heard a clanking noise coming from the wings as it began to swoop down toward my dog."

After a pause, the boy wiped his eyes, then turned serious.

"The giant claws opened up, and Corky yelped as they closed around him." Jessie took a deep breath and finished his story. "It flew off upriver with a loud squawking sound. I could see Corky's leash dangling from the claw. I watched the bird turn toward some cliffs, and it looked like there was a cave near the top. The thing took Corky inside the cave, and that was the last I saw of them."

Exhausted from recounting the event, the boy blew out a big gush of air and slumped back in his chair.

Hugging his son and winking at the ranger, Mr. Johnson said, "Quite a tale, isn't it? Who's ever heard of a giant bird with metallic wings?"

Joseph Saunooke, for one, had heard of such a bird all his life—the Tlanuwa, his people called it—but he wasn't about to admit it to this family of Anglo tourists.

"I'll file a report about the missing dog and the bird sighting today" was all he said. "Why don't you folks go on back to your campsite, and I'll organize a little search party for your dog. Hopefully, we'll find him hiding out somewhere near the trail."

Satisfied with that response, the Johnsons headed back to their campsite.

After they were gone, Joseph immediately placed a phone call to his aging uncle Bucky Wachacha. The Cherokee elder and medicine man had spent a lifetime gathering the legends, songs, and cultural practices of their people. He said he was a member of some intertribal group of medicine people from different parts of the country.

Recently the old man had been carrying on about some ancient prophecy that was about to be fulfilled. The prophecy foretold of a time when the old stories would prove to be true, a time when the legends would come to life.

No one had reported seeing a Tlanuwa in two hundred years, at least. The copper-feathered creatures were known to fly up and down the Oconaluftee and Little Tennessee Rivers, grabbing goats, dogs, and even small children and taking them back to their nests inside caves located high up on cliffsides along the waterways. They'd terrorized the Eastern Cherokee for centuries.

Was today the day the prophecy came true? Joseph hoped to find out.

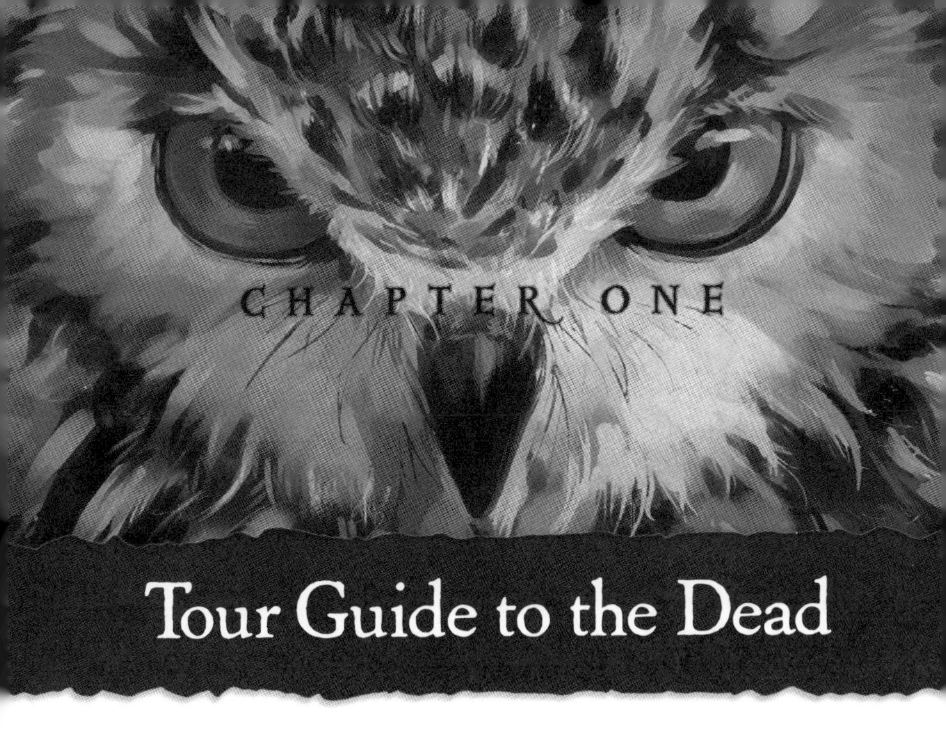

CHAPTER ONE

Tour Guide to the Dead

Since the gathering of the Intertribal Medicine Council—also known as the ITMC—on the first day of autumn last September, reports of possible "Chosen One" candidates had come to Cecil Lookout from Native American communities via phone, letter, email, text, and tweet.

However, the eighty-year-old head of the council didn't do emails, texts, or tweets. His teenage grandson Cody, who lived with him, handled those reports. Every one of them had to be investigated and followed up on. Finding and preparing this future spirit warrior for their upcoming role was vital, not only for the sake of the Native American population but for all the people of Turtle Island.

One of those calling in to report to Cecil was his granddaughter Lisa, who told him of a Cherokee teenager, the grandson of a medicine man, she'd been reading about in newspapers from the area where she lived. The boy, Billy Buckhorn, had been struck by lightning, had miraculously saved a busload of kids from certain death, and had died himself and come back from the dead with enhanced abilities.

Last fall Lisa told her grandfather, "I plan on tracking him down so I can talk with him. Maybe you and Dad can come to Tahlequah to meet with him sometime soon."

"It sounds like this boy might be a real contender, if the news reports are accurate," Cecil replied. "And if the boy isn't pulling off some kind of hoax just to get attention."

On the most recent winter solstice, the members of the Medicine Council had gathered again to review and evaluate the most likely candidates. Three people, all from recognized families of Native healers, had been put on the short list.

The winter solstice, falling on December 21, was the seasonal turning point and beginning of the new year for traditional Native peoples. It was coincidentally also Lisa Lookout's birthday.

During the afternoon, while the ITMC was holding its sacred winter solstice proceedings, all those in attendance felt it—the unmistakable signal that a profoundly significant supernatural event was taking place. The signal rippled through the group as the most psychically sensitive perceived it first, and then others gradually recognized it.

The point of origin of the subtle signal seemed to be southwest of their location, but only one person, Cecil, was able to narrow that information down to a specific region—somewhere in eastern Oklahoma. He could also sense that the event, whatever it was, involved the first activation of the Fire Crystal since its disappearance almost a thousand years ago. That was a significant development for sure.

From Lisa's reports, Cecil and his son Ethan knew that eastern Oklahoma was home turf for Billy Buckhorn. Was the supernatural signal related to the boy, or was it merely a coincidence? This would have to be investigated sooner rather than later.

Cecil, Ethan, and Lisa didn't know that at that precise moment, the Paranormal Patrol had successfully recaptured the Horned Serpent in a cave near the Oklahoma-Arkansas border.

The facetiously named Paranormal Patrol had been made up of Billy; his best friend, Chigger; Billy's father, James; and university archaeologist Augustus Stevens. The group's sole task had been to recapture the Horned Serpent, which had been thought of, until recently, as mere Cherokee mythology.

Now, ten days after that solstice, just after dawn on New Year's Eve, an early morning freezing fog was interfering with Billy Buckhorn's ability to focus. Fog and frost were both common for Oklahoma winters, but not usually at the same time.

Through years of experience in woods and wilderness, along with his grandfather's traditional Native teachings, the Cherokee teen had become finely attuned to his natural surroundings. At the moment, he was trying to follow a set of fresh, barely visible deer tracks through dry underbrush in the woods just north of the Brushy Mountains in the Cherokee Nation of Oklahoma.

Bowhunting for deer was Billy's favorite winter sport, following an ancient tradition of his Cherokee people. In fact, the sixteen-year-old's well-preserved recurve bow had been handed down from his aptly nicknamed great-grandfather Bullseye Buckhorn.

Hunting deer with a bow and quiver of arrows was far more challenging than hunting with a rifle. That was why Billy liked it. And because the young man could easily imagine himself a hundred or two hundred years ago doing the same thing.

These days, a sixteen-year-old Cherokee was qualified to receive a bowhunting license good for hunting on several different tracts of land within the Cherokee Nation boundaries. And this time of year, the end of December, was among the final days of deer hunting season for archers.

Like Cherokee hunters of old, Billy had purified himself in a small temporary sweat lodge before undertaking this hunt. That ritual not only allowed for the opportunity to pray for success but also cleansed him of his human scent so as not to alert the prey to his presence.

The sudden crack of a breaking twig a hundred feet ahead caused Billy to stop dead in his tracks. The gentle rustling of leaves in a soft, cold breeze was all he heard for the next few seconds. Then he heard a second twig break in the distance. Ah, his prey was closer than ever now.

With one eye on the deer's tracks and the other on the path ahead, Billy moved silently forward. Careful not to step on any twigs himself, the young hunter skillfully crept along. A few minutes later he saw that the deer's trail rounded a large boulder. Using the rock for cover, Billy peered through the trees until he spotted the animal. The young buck had stopped to take a sip of water from a nearby stream.

Now's my chance, Billy thought.

Nocking an arrow, he pulled the bowstring taut. Then, taking aim at a spot just behind the creature's front shoulder, Billy whispered a prayer asking for the animal's forgiveness.

At that exact moment, the deer turned his head and looked straight at Billy. The animal's eyes locked on to the hunter's.

"Shoot if you must," the boy heard in his mind. "I do forgive you."

Shocked by what he'd heard, the archer froze. Had the animal just spoken to him?

The bowstring remained taut. The arrow remained nocked. Billy's eyes remained locked on the deer's eyes, while the deer's gaze remained firmly fixed on Billy.

"What'll it be, young medicine man?"

Billy aimed the arrow up and away from the deer. Upon its release, the projectile flew harmlessly into the forest's upper canopy. The animal motioned his approval with a nod of his head, then turned and calmly ambled away.

"What just happened?" Billy asked out loud.

He'd become more or less accustomed to strange things happening in his life, beginning with the lightning strike on Labor Day and continuing with his near-death experience over the Thanksgiving holiday. Each incident had been followed by strange phenomena, like his ability to read people's minds, sleep on books to learn their content, predict the future, and talk to the spirits of the dead.

And thanks to the thousand-year-old spirit of the Sun Priest, Billy could now see energy fields around people and understand the Cherokee language.

Billy was also experiencing painful physical growth spurts. Not the normal bits of growth a typical teenage boy might experience. More like abnormal growth that the gigantism disorder might bring on. At first Billy thought his imagination was just running wild, but the periodic bouts of pain were undeniable. And when his mother complained about having to let the seams out of all his clothes, he knew it must be real.

And now this—he'd actually heard the thoughts of a wild animal. Sure, Cherokee legends were filled with tales of animals and people talking to one another, but those were symbolic, fanciful myths, weren't they? Of course, he had repeatedly told Chigger that all Native legends had a core of truth based on some reality from the ancient past. Billy realized that concept had been proven with the appearance of the Raven Stalker and the discovery of the Horned Serpent, which had slithered out of the crystal cave back in November.

What was it the spirit of Billy's grandmother had told his grandfather during the Labor Day stomp dance? Oh yeah. "Strange changes are afoot."

All this swirled through his mind as he headed back to his campsite. Chigger had declined his invitation to join him on this hunt, saying mysteriously that he would be hunting something larger and more significant. Billy hadn't pushed it, sensing that his friend was becoming more and more interested in pursuing his own path. That was okay. In fact, it was best for both of them. It was high time the faithful sidekick moved out from under Billy's shadow.

Back at the campsite, Billy stowed his bow and arrows behind the seat in his pickup, started a small blaze in the firepit, and put a pot of coffee on to boil. He was in no hurry; he had all day to pack up and drive to Live Oak ceremonial grounds in time for the winter spruce dance that would begin after dark.

Several hours later, the teen continued to review the recent past as he drove toward the stomp dance grounds. The dance was once held yearly on the night of winter solstice, but ceremonial leaders had shifted the time to New Year's Eve because more people had time off work for the holiday.

He'd had plenty of choices for where to spend New Year's Eve. He could have opted to spend a quiet night at home in Park Hill with his father, who would be in his upstairs study while his mother made some extra money working the night shift at the Tahlequah Indian hospital. Or he could have hung out with Chigger at his family's mobile home. They'd probably watch the ball drop in New York City on TV. He could have even gone to a party some of his school friends were having at a classmate's house while his parents were away. That party would involve guzzling as many kinds of booze as they could scrounge up.

But Billy had chosen to continue the tradition he'd begun with Grandpa Wesley three years earlier: participating in the stomp dances at Live Oak. There was nowhere else the teen would rather be than sitting beside his medicine man grandfather in his Red Paint Clan's arbor on New Year's Eve. Or dancing around the sacred fire to the cadence of the call-and-response songs and the *shh-shh-shh* percussion of the turtle shell leg rattles worn by the women.

No billboard or neon sign advertised this remote eastern Oklahoma event. No radio DJ or television news announcer broadcast the time or whereabouts of this private ritual. It was only for those who belonged there. And Billy knew he belonged there.

There had been times recently when he'd questioned his involvement in what his grandfather called the "medicine path." But he'd resolved the doubts that had dogged him and vowed to remain on the path.

So he calmed his busy mind and focused on the night ahead. It seemed as though his pickup knew the way to the ceremonial site so well it could steer itself there. Like it somehow had its own sense memory, through the feel of tires on familiar ground, the recognized pattern of left and right turns of the steering wheel, or the accelerations and decelerations of the old Chevy engine.

As the trip progressed and the road transitioned from a paved two-lane highway to a one-lane dirt affair, it symbolized the mental journey Billy was taking away from his modern, everyday life to a more remote state of mind.

Making the final turn, the forest-green Silverado moved down a gravel-covered back road that wound its way through the dark, silent woods. Ahead of the teen lay a return to a distant yet vibrant past.

Grandpa Wesley had recounted the history of these dances many times over the years. Cherokees had brought all their ceremonies and traditions with them on their forced migration from Georgia and North Carolina to Oklahoma Territory. The journey, taken in the 1830s, was known as the Trail Where They Cried, or simply the Trail of Tears, because of the pain, suffering, and death experienced by the Cherokee people. One-quarter of the Principal People died on the march, supervised by armed United States soldiers.

Meant for believers and practitioners of the old Indian religion, these stomp dance rituals had descended from tribal ancestors who lived hundreds, if not thousands, of years ago. So far, Wesley had only hinted at the deeper mysteries behind those stories, songs, and dances of old.

Deeper understandings were yet to come.

As Billy steered the truck off the dirt road, its headlights swung in an arc, illuminating flashes of chrome mixed with dust and mud on two dozen cars and trucks crammed into a dirt parking lot at the edge of a clearing.

A light turnout, Billy thought as he pulled up and parked next to his grandfather's red-and-white Ford pickup. The low chatter of Cherokees reached his ears as he climbed out of the cab of his own truck. Orange-yellow light from the ceremonial fire danced in the teen's eyes as he made his way toward the circle of arbors that surrounded the central square.

A remembered moment flashed in Billy's mind. It was from the last dance he'd attended, during Labor Day weekend. While in a trance in the middle of the night, he saw a ladder with thirteen rungs. In the vision, he was standing on the third rung, ready to take the next step upward. But as he attempted it, he slipped and fell. That fall woke him from the vision, the meaning of which his grandfather said would eventually be revealed. And it was.

Other monumental moments from that fateful weekend flooded into his mind uninvited, including the lightning strike that coursed through his body, creating the spiderweb pattern of burns permanently scarring the side of his neck and the back of his hand. Touching the neck scar, he told himself it would be time to update his personal medicine journal after tonight's ceremony.

The ceremonial leader's first call to the dancers brought Billy back to the here and now. The man's voice resounded through the clearing, and the teen quickly headed for the Red Paint Clan arbor, where his grandfather would be waiting.

Seven brush arbors encircled the dance grounds that, in turn, encircled the sacred fire. The fire that burned within the sacred square was said to symbolize the center of the universe. Four logs set the perimeter of the fire, each aimed at one of the four cardinal directions. Thanks to Wesley's teachings, Billy knew the fire also symbolized the spirit within each person who would take part in the ceremony, as well as the fire of creation that brought the world into being.

"On Indian time, as usual," Wesley said with a smile as his grandson took a seat on the bench next to him.

"Not a minute too soon, not a minute too late," Billy replied, returning the smile. "You taught me well."

The second call went out to the dancers seated in the seven arbors. Native adults and children began moving toward the center, falling in single file behind the leader, alternating male and female in the line. The head man began his slow counter-clockwise rotation around the fire. The turtle shell rattles worn by the women on their lower legs began their familiar rhythmic impersonation of falling rain.

"Maybe we'll both get a visit or a message from your grandma tonight," Wesley said as he rose from his seat to join the dance.

Stomp dances at Live Oak were known for providing spirit connections to departed loved ones. Wesley looked forward to his visits with the spirit of his deceased wife, Billy's grandmother Awinita, that often occurred during the night-long ceremonies. Wesley considered himself lucky and blessed if she appeared to him even momentarily at some point during the all-night affair.

Billy was silent as he followed his elder toward the fire. The teen fell in behind a woman as the line of dancers spiraled around the blaze. In the past it had taken him at least an hour to reach the state of mind dancers strove for, that twilight condition somewhere between waking and sleeping that allowed for subconscious communication or trance visions.

This time it was only a matter of minutes before the familiar humming vibration came over him. His whole body quivered as a translucent scene presented itself, superimposed over the physical setting. Concentrating as best he could, Billy attempted to continue following the woman in front of him.

The vibrational energy intensified and increased in speed until a circle of invisible sparks shot out from him in all directions. Losing consciousness, the boy collapsed on the ground, and nearby dancers moved out of line to pick him up. Four men carried him to the Red Paint Clan arbor and laid him out on a bench. It was a common experience during the ceremonies.

Within Billy's own reality, however, something quite different was happening. His nonphysical energy body rose above the fire, the dancers, and the brush arbors. The boy had left his body before, usually with the assistance of helpers of the Sun Priest—except for that one time he died on the hospital operating table.

Maybe my body is dying again, Billy thought to himself. *Maybe I'm actually going to cross over this time.*

"Stop being so dramatic," a voice inside his head said. "You're not dying. You're just going nonphysical again."

There was something familiar about the voice, but Billy couldn't place it. "Who said that?" Billy responded, looking around his immediate nonphysical environment. The only thing he could pick up was a small bright spot of light that flitted back and forth just above him. The being seemed like an insect or a hummingbird that couldn't sit still. Then, gradually, the bright spot dimmed until it became a recognizable figure.

"Little Wolf, I should've known."

"Surprise, surprise!" the diminutive Cherokee said.

As one of the legendary Yunwi Tsunsdi, or Little People, he stood about two feet tall. He had first appeared in physical form when Billy was a boy, then again in the hospital during his recovery from the lightning strike. Long before those instances, however, the little man had served as a medicine helper to Grandpa Wesley.

"How am I seeing you now in nonphysical form?" Billy asked. "I thought you were a physical being."

"Ah, you think you know so much, and yet you know so little," Little Wolf said with a deep sigh. "We Yunwi Tsunsdi are multidimensional. How else do you think I could appear and disappear in your hospital room?"

"Okay, got it. But what are you doing here now, and where's Grandma Awinita?"

"Your grandmother is busy with a visitation to your grandpa tonight. But she left me specific instructions on what to do as your tour guide."

"Tour guide? Why do I need a tour guide?"

"The nonphysical dimension is a vast, multilayered thing. If you're going to be connecting the living with the dead, you have to know where to find the dead, right?"

"I guess so. I thought they'd just come to me."

"Sometimes they will, but it's not that simple. We'd better get a move on while your body is safely resting under the arbor."

Little Wolf pointed with his lips toward the Red Paint Clan's arbor. Billy looked that way and saw himself resting on the bench.

"Two places at the same time once again," he said to himself.

"You'll get used to it," Little Wolf replied. The small man made a circling motion with both hands, which created an energy bubble that enclosed the two of them. "First stop on the tour—the cemetery."

The pair zipped away in their energy bubble. At first Billy experienced a blurring effect as his physical surroundings whizzed by. But very quickly they arrived at a spot high above a military graveyard that held row upon row of neatly aligned white gravestones.

"Why come here?" Billy asked.

"To show you where you rarely find the spirits of the dead," Little Wolf replied. "Most people think graveyards are filled with ghosts, but that's not necessarily true. Ghosts are self-imprisoned spirits who can't let go of some part of their physical lives, so they're usually hanging around other places."

Little Wolf guided Billy down closer to the ground, stopping in front of one particular grave. The words engraved on the headstone said *Franklin Buckhorn, US Army*. Billy knew this was an uncle on his father's side of the family.

"You unexpectedly met your mother's deceased brother, Luther, last year because he had some unfinished business to tend to with your uncle John, the preacher," Little Wolf said.

"Yeah, Grandma Awinita brought him to see me."

"But you don't see your father's brother Franklin hanging around the cemetery here, do you?"

Billy looked around and didn't see any spirits lurking about.

"That's because most people killed in the midst of battle get stuck somewhere near where they were killed, like on the battlefield," Little Wolf continued.

"I see what you're getting at."

"And there are plenty of people who don't even really realize they've died, because they're so focused on still trying to fight the battle they were in the middle of fighting when they died."

Billy remained silent a moment as that idea penetrated his mind. "Is that where my uncle Frank is?" he asked.

"Bingo!" the spirit replied.

Billy and the diminutive Indian immediately zipped across some indescribable space and came to a stop just above a desert valley dotted with short bushy trees and large boulders. A battle raged between two opposing forces: a row of camouflage-uniformed soldiers in the middle of a dry riverbed who faced lines of Middle Eastern men with beards who attacked from both sides.

Billy recognized one of the uniformed soldiers as his father's brother Franklin, known to those closest to him as Frank. He was engaged in hand-to-hand combat with one of the bearded men. The only problem was that neither man was making any progress in harming the other because their blows failed to strike any solid flesh. Both were merely energy forms—spirits—with no physical body to hit.

"What, they're dead and don't know it?" Billy blurted out.

"Bingo again."

"How long have they been like this?"

"How long ago did you get the news that your uncle was killed in action?"

"I'm not sure—ten years, maybe." The reality of the situation dawned on Billy. "They've been stuck here doing this for ten years?"

"Some spirits keep it up for centuries. Think of haunted castles and such. Time's not really a hard-and-fast factor over here, so you don't sense how much time has passed."

"Can we help get him unstuck?" Billy asked.

"That's what we're here for. Others have tried. Now it's your turn."

Billy floated closer to the action. "Uncle! Uncle!" he shouted. "It's me, Billy, your nephew!"

Frank didn't seem to notice, so the teen moved in closer and took up a position within his uncle's line of sight.

"Franklin Redpaint Buckhorn, look at me!" he shouted more loudly and forcefully. He waved his arms while whistling and yelling until his uncle finally noticed him.

"Get back!" Frank responded. "They'll kill you!"

The man continued his fruitless combat maneuvers.

"He can't kill me," Billy said. "He can't kill you either, because you're already dead. In fact, you can stop fighting because he's dead too."

That got Frank's attention. He stopped struggling and stood still.

The Middle Eastern man continued his efforts to strike his opponent, to no avail. His blows passed right through Frank's translucent form. Finally, the bearded fighter stopped trying to damage his enemy. Looking around, he blinked a couple of times, saw Billy, and exclaimed, "Allah be praised!"

The man fell to his knees before the teen and bowed his head to the ground in worship. He began a fervent prayer chant.

"He thinks you're a god or something," Frank said. "Are you?"

"No, I'm your nephew, Billy Buckhorn."

Billy realized that the last time his uncle had seen him, he was a young boy of about five or six years old.

"But how are you here?" Frank asked. "And where is here?"

Just then some sort of opening appeared above them, and a bright light spilled on them. Who appeared in that doorway but Billy's great-grandfather, Bullseye Buckhorn. He called to his grandson Franklin, who looked in his direction.

"Grandfather, is that you?" Frank asked as Bullseye floated toward him.

Bullseye sort of winked at Billy as he escorted his grandson through the opening and disappeared.

The Middle Eastern man witnessed the same sequence of events Billy had seen and stood up with a puzzled look on his translucent face.

"I am also dead?" he said.

Billy merely nodded.

"What am I to do now?" the man asked.

A thought appeared in Billy's mind. "I'm not sure, but I think you're supposed to just wait here, and someone you know will come and find you."

The man blinked as he digested the idea. "*Inshallah!*" the man exclaimed. "If God wills it."

Momentarily, an opening appeared nearby like before, and a man wearing flowing tan robes stepped through it. The Middle Eastern man seemed to recognize the visitor and followed him back through the opening, smiling at Billy before disappearing.

After that the scene fell silent. The teen looked around but couldn't detect Little Wolf's presence, and so he just floated, realizing that his tour, or whatever the heck it was, must be over.

As he closed the eyes of his energy body, he thought of the Red Paint Clan arbor at the stomp grounds. He pictured the stomp dance grounds clearly, seeing the circle of dancers, hearing the call-and-response of the songs, even smelling the smoke from the central sacred fire.

In a matter of a few seconds, he felt the familiar stretching sensation, and in the blink of an eye, he detected the denseness of his own physical body around him. He opened his physical eyes and blinked a couple of times. There was no sign of Little Wolf, Bullseye, or his uncle Frank. He spent a few moments absorbing what he'd just experienced, but once again his mind filled with questions—questions he doubted could be answered by his grandfather or anyone still in the flesh.

Traditional Cherokees believed a person's soul hung around for four days after death and then traveled westward to the land of the dead, Billy remembered. And according to Uncle John, churchgoers believed the souls of the dead slept—that is, rested in peace—until Jesus returned to take them to heaven one day, but only the true believers.

The experiences he'd just had didn't line up with either of those beliefs. He'd have to talk to *someone* about it all very soon.

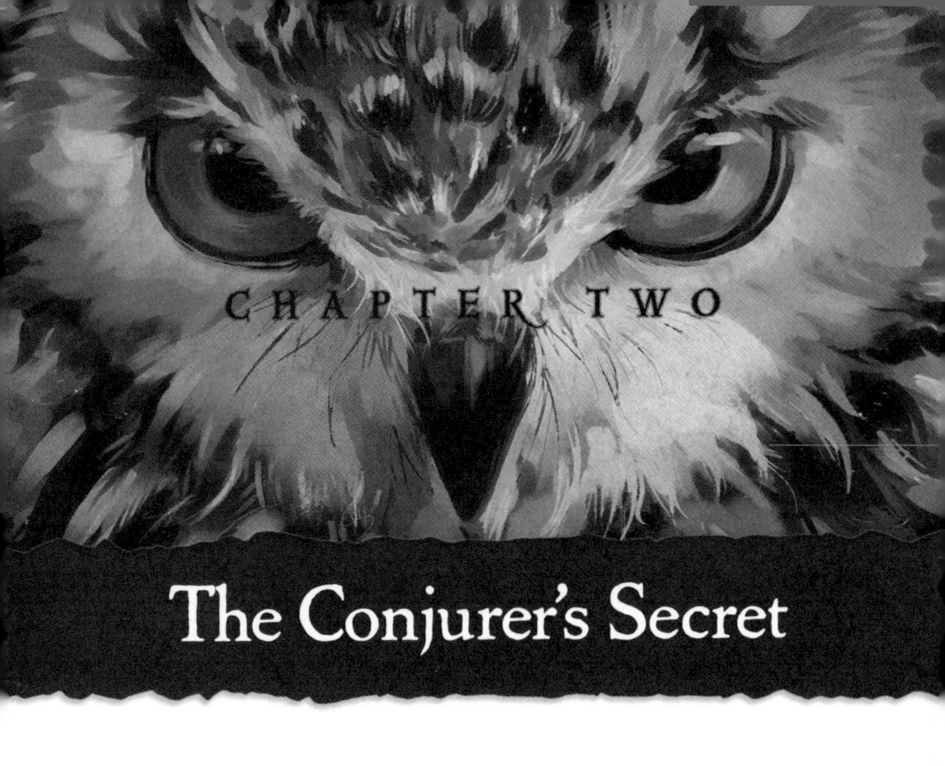

CHAPTER TWO

The Conjurer's Secret

Later that night in another wooded part of eastern Oklahoma, an unexpected blast of frigid air forced Charles Checotah Muskrat to turn up the collar on his well-worn winter coat. The Cherokee teen, known to most as Chigger, was on his own mission in the middle of the night. His objective: Bigfoot. His companions on this quest were a handful of members of the Oklahoma Bigfoot Research Association, most of them white men in their fifties and sixties.

Chigger was pleased with himself because he'd never before ventured into the woods at night unless he was with Billy. But now the boy felt it was time to move out from under his friend's shadow. In fact, he felt the move was long overdue. No one in the Paranormal Patrol took him seriously, but he knew he could become famous on his own. He just had to venture out and make it happen.

"Hold up!" the lead Bigfoot tracker said in a loud whisper. "I think I just heard somethin' a coupla klicks to the east."

The intrepid band of monster hunters froze in place, barely breathing. Chigger, trying hard to feel brave while in the woods in the dead of night, heard nothing but the raspy breath of one of the men in the group who smoked too much.

After about a minute of silence, their leader whispered, "Okay, keep moving."

Chigger tried to stay in about the middle of the group. He didn't want to be up front in case they actually did encounter one of the large, hairy creatures. But he didn't want to bring up the rear for fear of getting lost or being left behind in the dark. The middle of the pack was the safest place to be.

An image of Billy momentarily flashed in Chigger's mind, reminding him of previous adventures in the dark with his friend. The pair sometimes did some late-night fishing on one of the many lakes in the area. Or they'd camp overnight in the mountains while collecting the special plants and herbs Billy's grandpa Wesley needed for his traditional doctoring.

Since Chigger had been part of the Paranormal Patrol, which had successfully recaptured the Horned Serpent and trapped him in the hidden cave, it was time to gain some notoriety on his own. It made perfect sense. Hadn't it been Chigger himself who had come under the spell of the Uktena creature and been physically and mentally tortured by the power of the dark crystal?

Now Chigger would make a name for himself as a Bigfoot researcher/hunter. The Cherokee people both in North Carolina and Oklahoma, as well as other Native American tribes, had long believed in the existence of the creatures. The mythological Raven Stalker and the Uktena had both turned out to be real, so didn't it make sense that Bigfoot would too?

Chigger ran these arguments through his mind over and over again as the ragtag Bigfoot bunch traipsed through the dark wilderness. He was so immersed in these thoughts that he failed to notice he was now walking alone through an uncharted section of forest.

He swept the immediate area with his night vision goggles, looking for his companions.

No one else was in sight. How had he lost track of them? He looked behind him along the ground to see if he could pick up his own footprints. There were no tracks to be found in the bed of fallen leaves.

Just then a mournful, not-quite-human-sounding cry rang out through the bare trees, a noise like nothing Chigger had ever heard before. A jolt of fear shot through the boy's body, momentarily paralyzing him.

Almost immediately, however, another sort of jolt coursed through him. It was warm and invigorating, reminding him of the times he'd secretly taken a swallow of whiskey from the bottle his father kept out in the shed behind their mobile home.

"You can do this" was the message that immediately came into the boy's mind. Feelings of courage and confidence rushed up his spine and into his brain as well.

Where were these sensations coming from? He wasn't sure, but it felt good. Suddenly, a mental image of the purple crystal from the lower cave appeared in his mind. The gem almost seemed to call to him once again, pulling on him like a magnet.

Then a voice began speaking to him. Whether it came from inside his mind or from somewhere outside of him, Chigger couldn't tell.

"You and the dark crystal belong together," the voice seemed to say. "Together you can do great things."

Immediately, the teen tried to cancel the idea.

That's impossible, he argued in his mind. *The purple crystal must remain on the pedestal at the bottom of the cave to keep the Horned Serpent imprisoned.*

He searched his brain for other objections to the absurd suggestion.

Let's not forget that it burned my skin and turned me into a monstrosity when I took it home with me.

A fluttering sound from nearby drew Chigger's attention. He focused his night vision goggles in the direction the sound came from just as a great horned owl landed on a nearby tree branch. It was the largest owl the teen had ever seen.

"I can keep the crystal from burning you or turning you into a monster," the voice continued.

Chigger realized the owl was the one talking to him, using a woman's voice.

"Is someone about to die?" the boy asked the bird, speaking out loud. "Old Cherokees always say you owls are the messengers of death."

"That's not all we're good for."

"Are you a *skili*?" Chigger asked. In the Cherokee language, the word *skili* means both "owl" and "witch."

"Yes and yes," the owl replied.

At that point Chigger didn't know whether to run or scream or continue the strangest conversation he'd ever had.

"Can you keep a secret?" the owl asked. After rotating her head a full 360 degrees to make sure no one else was near, she continued. "I'm not supposed to show this to anyone, so I need to know if you can keep a secret."

Chigger was hooked now. He had to stay. "Of course, I'm the best at keeping secrets," the teen said. "I haven't told *anyone* about the Horned Serpent or how I helped capture it."

As soon as those words escaped Chigger's mouth, he realized he'd just broken his sworn silence regarding the creature. The owl noticed the boy's reaction.

"Don't worry. I already knew your secret, and it's safe with me. Now I can share my secret with you."

Spreading her wings, the owl lifted herself from the tree branch. But instead of flying away, the bird began a transformation as she eased herself to the ground. Within seconds, a very old Indian woman stood before Chigger.

"You *are* a *skili*!" the boy exclaimed. "That is the coolest thing I've ever seen!"

"I prefer the term *conjurer*," the woman said. "It's a well-respected profession among our people."

In the darkness, even with the night vision goggles, Chigger could barely make out the tattooed lines on the elder's face. One line ran diagonally from the hairline above her left eye, down across the bridge of her nose, and along the cheek, ending on the right side of her jaw. A series of small stars followed the line. The narrow point of a sideways V began on the left side of her mouth, widening and extending across the left side of her face. Chigger remembered seeing a similar tattoo pictured on the sketch of a Cherokee warrior from the 1700s.

"Whatever," Chigger responded with his usual flippant attitude.

"But you must keep it a secret," the woman continued. "Otherwise, I wouldn't be able to continue my special work."

"So you help people, like Billy's grandpa Wesley does?"

"More or less—and I'm looking for an apprentice."

The woman was pleased to see Chigger's eyes light up at the idea, because she knew he would take the bait.

"What about you, young man? Aren't you tired of playing second fiddle to that Billy Buckhorn boy? I mean, look at you, out here in the woods in the middle of the night hunting for Bigfoot."

Uncanny, the boy thought. That was exactly what he'd been thinking right before the owl showed up.

"My name's Carmelita Tuckaleechee, by the way," the old woman said. "I live up near Buzzard Bend on Route 10."

She extended her wrinkled brown hand.

"Charles Checotah Muskrat," the boy said, extending his own hand to hers.

As they shook, Chigger began to feel a strange tingling sensation in his arm. The woman's hand seemed to be generating a mild electrical current that he felt all the way up in his brain. He pulled his hand back quickly and rubbed it with his other hand.

"What was that?" he asked.

"Your first test, to see how compatible your energy is with mine. It's one of the ways we'll work together, but don't worry about it now. You passed."

Just then, Chigger heard footsteps and yelling coming his way. "Here he is, over here," a man called from a distance.

The teen looked in the direction the sound was coming from. His night vision goggles revealed the troop of Bigfoot hunters tramping through the underbrush.

Quickly, he looked back to see how Carmelita was reacting to the appearance of the intruders, but she had vanished. Then he heard the hoot of an owl coming from high up in the nearest tree.

"Donadagohvi," the old woman's voice said in his mind. "Until we meet again."

Chigger scanned the branches one last time, looking for the owl, before rejoining the Bigfoot search team.

Standing behind a large tree not twenty-five feet from the boy was an eight-foot-tall hairy member of what Cherokee elders called "the Secluded Tribe." Only the conjurer had been aware of the Bigfoot's presence, but she was sworn to secrecy regarding the whereabouts of any of their species.

CHAPTER THREE

The Girl with the Spider Tattoo

It was the afternoon of New Year's Eve, and Lisa Lookout wondered why she hadn't heard from Billy Buckhorn. It had been more than ten days since she'd surprised him on his front porch and given him her phone number and email address. It seemed pretty clear that she wanted to hear from him, not for herself so much but for the potential role he might play within the Intertribal Medicine Council.

As the seventeen-year-old Osage girl drove her Honda Shadow Spirit 750 motorcycle toward St. Louis on Interstate 44, she imagined how the spider tattoo on the back of her hand might look up against the spiderweb scar on the side of his neck. *What a perfect match,* she thought and then caught herself. *Where did that idea come from?*

She felt herself blushing a little as her cell phone rang. The full-face Bluetooth helmet she wore allowed her hands-free access to phone calls.

"Can you hear me?" the male voice on the other end of the call said. Lisa recognized the caller.

"Loud and clear, Dad," she answered.

"How far away are you?" Ethan Lookout asked from his location in St. Louis. "Your grandfather wants to start by five."

"I'll make it. I'm just passing Springfield, about three hours out."

"Good. I'll let him know. Drive safe."

Lisa clicked off the call and increased her speed a couple of notches. Another click on the side of her helmet turned on her traveling playlist: powwow songs by the Black Lodge Singers.

She loved these trips back home. The open road gave her time to think, time to remember how she fit into the big picture, at least according to her Osage grandpa, Cecil.

Family oral history told her she came from a long line of Osage medicine people known as Keepers of the Center. The Osage are descendants of the Original People who inhabited the lands around the convergence of the Mississippi and Missouri Rivers for more than a thousand years. They were among the ruling class during the golden age of Solstice City, now known as Cahokia, when thousands and thousands of people inhabited the city that stretched out for miles.

In the 1870s, the tribe was forced to relocate to a reservation created in northern Oklahoma, centered around the town of Pawhuska. Most of the tribe lived there now. But the lands around St. Louis along the Mississippi and Missouri Rivers had been the traditional homelands of the Osage for countless generations.

Lisa's own immediate family had its own history of relocation. She and her mother, Lucinda, had relocated several times over the years, following her father, Ethan, from one archaeological dig to another. As one of the few Native American archaeologists in the country, he was obsessed with learning all he could about the Mississippian Mound Builder culture, which meant participating in as many digs at those far-flung sites as possible.

All the traveling and long periods of time away from home became more than Lisa's mother could stand. Mother and daughter moved to Kansas City, Missouri, Lucinda's birthplace and home to many members of her own Wichita tribe.

Lisa often said she felt like a yo-yo as a kid, being bounced from Kansas City to Pawhuska to St. Louis to spend time with various family members. But, for reasons she couldn't explain, Grandpa Cecil's house next to the Sugarloaf Mound on the bank of the Mississippi seemed more like home than anywhere else.

Even before Lisa pulled her motorcycle into her grandfather's driveway on Ohio Street, she had seen smoke rising from the firepit south of the earthen mound. She knew her father would be tending the fire there as fire keeper for the sweat lodge her grandfather would lead.

After parking the bike beside the garage, she rushed toward the pillar of smoke. Rounding the back of the mound, she saw the dome-shaped sweat lodge covered with various-colored tarps and canvases stretched over a frame of curved willow branches. The eastward-facing doorway to the lodge was open, awaiting both people and hot stones for the ceremony.

Large enough to hold all thirteen members of the ITMC and attending assistants, the lodge had been the site of the New Year's Eve sweat for as long as Cecil had been the head of the ITMC.

"Dad, I made it!" Lisa called.

Pitchfork in hand, Ethan was beside the firepit, busily moving burning coals off the stones that had been "cooking" for the past two hours. The tall brown-skinned man with a single braid looked up in time to see his daughter coming toward him, grinning from ear to ear.

"You're just in time," he said. "Grandpa is ready to begin the sweat."

Father and daughter hugged briefly. He smelled of woodsmoke and burning sage. "I'll change clothes and be right back," she said. "Is Grandpa in the house?"

"He and the council members are waiting in the living room," Ethan replied as he resumed his fire-keeping duties.

Entering her grandfather's house through the back door, Lisa first encountered her cousin Cody standing in the kitchen wearing swim trunks and wrapped in a towel. Lisa's aunt Josephine was tending two large cooking pots on the stove, no doubt filled with buffalo stew, corn soup, or some other hearty dish to be consumed after the sweat ended.

After bumping fists with her cousin and hugging her aunt, the girl headed to the bedroom to change clothes for the sweat. As she took off her street clothes and put on the ankle-length dress she kept in the bottom drawer of a dresser, she could hear the elders chatting in hushed tones coming from the front room of the house.

Finding a large beach towel covered in tropical designs, she wrapped it around her waist and headed toward the living room. The elders, each wrapped in a towel, had already begun streaming out the back door. The men wore swim trunks or cutoff shorts, while the women wore full-length dresses similar to the one Lisa had on. All were happy to see that Cecil's granddaughter would be joining the ceremony.

Cecil, the last to exit the living room, was dressed as the other men but also carried an eagle feather fan and a rattle made of deer bone attached to a carved hollow gourd.

"Ah, my granddaughter Spider Woman, I'm glad to see you here," he said in a soft voice. "I believe you and I will have much to talk about after we receive the spirit message in the lodge today." He took her hand in his, saying, "Walk with me."

Hand in hand, the pair made their way out the door to the sweat lodge entrance.

Everyone else had already crawled into the structure and taken their seats on the ground in a circle around the central sunken pit. Lisa's father stood ready to begin the process of carrying the heated stones on his pitchfork from the firepit and placing them in the lodge.

After the elder and his granddaughter crawled inside, Cecil signaled his son, and the ceremony began. Seven stones came into the lodge and were sprinkled with sage, sweetgrass, and cedar as Lisa's grandfather began singing the first round of traditional songs. Another signal from Cecil prompted Ethan to close the lodge flap, plunging the participants into darkness. The red glow of heated stones provided the only light.

Lisa scooped the first ladle of water from a bucket near the door and poured it over the sacred stones. Instantly, a hiss of steam escaped from the red globes of heat, saturating the lodge's interior with moist, superheated air.

Each of the ceremony's four rounds would have an important purpose to fulfill, including prayers for the physical, emotional, and spiritual healing of the participants, their loved ones, the ancestors who'd gone before, and the young ones yet to be born.

But the fourth and final round would be the main event, for that was the round when the spirits were invited into the lodge. For most sweat lodge leaders and participants, this phenomenon—the visitation of spirits—was mostly invisible. It had to be taken on faith that this was actually happening, because most people lacked the spiritual sight to know for sure this was taking place. The more sensitive medicine people who led sweat lodges in Native communities might experience a few sensations or physical cues that actual spirits were present, but that wasn't always the case.

But the Intertribal Medicine Council was a collection of the most adept and supernaturally sensitive Native people in the land, so the infusion of spirit presences within the ceremony was sensed and recognized by all.

Lisa's grandfather began the first song of the fourth round as she poured another ladle of water over the stones. The familiar hiss of steam escaped from the Stone People. Lisa's father had just finished placing the final stone, the twenty-eighth, in the center of the lodge and closed the flap. The stones were at their hottest. The air in the lodge at its thickest. The energy level at its highest.

The ancient words and melody Cecil sang had been memorized and passed down for many generations, an incantation given to humans from the ancestor spirits themselves for just this occasion, for just this purpose. After the last syllable and note had been uttered, the drum fell quiet, and the melody ceased. A dense silence overtook the womb-like space. Everyone waited.

The faintest *swoosh* sound accompanied the entry of the first spirit. Appearing as Little Wolf had looked to Billy, this tiny spark of light, the spirit scout, entered the lodge to make sure all was in readiness. The dot of light flitted from one side of the lodge to the other, from the high point of the dome to the space in front of Cecil. Satisfied that everything was as it should be, the other spirits made their appearances.

Lisa counted a total of thirteen white pinpoints of light descending from the center of the dome. After circling the stones in a clockwise direction, the points of light spread themselves out, taking up spots floating in between the physical bodies already in the lodge.

The sound of multiple whispering voices vying for attention was the first signal that a message was about to be delivered from the spirits. After a few seconds, the voices fell into unison, sounding like a single whispered voice followed by a slight echo. The Whisper spoke the first few words in Osage, Cecil's tribal language, telling him that a message of rebuke was to follow.

“We are not pleased with your lack of progress,” the Whisper said in English, heard and understood by all in the lodge. “The timetable of events has accelerated, so you must quicken your pace. Otherwise, a thousand years of waiting and watching will be for naught.”

“On behalf of the council, I offer my sincerest apologies for our slowness of action,” Cecil said. “We offer no excuse other than we are old and feeble.”

The Whisper continued. “The five pieces of the Sky Stone must be reassembled on the next summer solstice, complete with the Fire Crystal inserted in its central place to assure its full activation.”

This news produced a collective gasp from the sweat lodge participants, who indeed recognized this pronouncement as a foreshortening of the previous schedule.

“But, Holy Ones, we just learned of the missing piece of the Sky Stone and the discovery of the Fire Crystal,” Cecil replied on behalf of the ITMC. “How can we be expected to secure these elusive items?”

“It is not we who require this of you,” the Whisper said, beginning a progressive increase in intensity. “It is your brothers and sisters of Turtle Island. It is all the dwellers of the Middleworld who are in danger.”

As the volume of the Whisper’s statement continued to rise, the final message ended in a deafening crescendo.

“It falls to you—however old, feeble, and tired you feel—to lead the way to Mother Earth’s salvation. Maybe you’ve forgotten what’s at stake! Failure is not an option! A-ho!”

With that, the thirteen points of light circled the interior of the lodge, increasing speed until, after the fourth rotation, they rose in unison out of the top of the dome. Their exit extinguished any heat remaining in the once-glowing stones.

Left in total darkness, the congregants sat in stunned silence for a moment. After a pause, Cecil shook his rattle and began singing, tentative and weak at first, the sweat's closing song. As everyone's mind returned to the present reality, each took possession of a new sense of urgency and a renewed sense of finality.

The cosmic clock was ticking, and according to the ancestor spirits, less than six months remained on the dial!

After the ceremony, as other members of the ITMC gathered and ate inside the house, Cecil met with his son and granddaughter near Sugarloaf Mound.

"The three of us must travel to Tahlequah as soon as possible," the elder said. "You heard the spirits. We have to identify and train the Chosen One quickly, immediately."

"I'll make the call, Grandfather," Lisa replied. "I'll set up a time to meet Billy."

As the trio planned the details of the trip, a worrisome thought nagged at the back of Lisa's brain. Would the reclusive Cherokee teen take on the challenge he'd be asked to accept if he truly was the Chosen One? Would he be willing to rise above his station as a mere Native teen and adopt the mantle of a spirit warrior?

That night the girl dreamed a troubling dream starring none other than Billy Buckhorn. In it, the youth was being chased by a dark entity. They ran through the thick underbrush of a wooded valley as thorns tore at the boy's flesh. Blood trickled from the many shallow cuts caused by the brambles, and sweat clung to his fear-filled face.

Lisa didn't know it, but Billy's condition in the dream matched his physical condition when the bats battered him as they flew out of the crystal cave last November.

But in the dream, Lisa wanted to know who or what was chasing him. So she injected her own will into the dream, forcing her view to change. With great effort, almost like moving a large, heavy camera, she pivoted around to face the dark pursuer.

What Lisa saw was the oscillating image of a shape-changing creature, one moment an enormous owl, the next moment an elderly Native woman with a diagonal scar across her face. What didn't fluctuate between the two were the round yellow eyes with dark black centers.

At first, the eyes were intently focused on Billy as he ducked and weaved his way through the tangled brush, determined not to allow the boy to escape. But in a very short time, the creature's eyes shifted focus, trying to see who had shown up within the dream. Lisa suddenly realized she'd become visible to the sorceress and forced herself to wake up.

Sitting up in bed and breathing heavily, Lisa proclaimed, "Tomorrow I have to call Billy."

The next morning, New Year's Day, Cecil led the Medicine Council in a sunrise ceremony, and then the group got down to the business of making plans to save the world.

Four items on their agenda were marked *URGENT*. First was the matter of locating the Chosen One. Second, locating the missing piece of the Sky Stone. Third, tracking down the whereabouts of the Fire Crystal. All were crucial to the success of their mission. And fourth, replacing the deceased Choctaw medicine man, Elmore Proctor, with a new member of the Intertribal Medicine Council.

After much discussion, it appeared that a trip to Oklahoma might address all four priorities.

CHAPTER FOUR

Cold Moon

Billy slept much of New Year's Day, recovering from his night of stomp dancing. At around six, Grandpa Wesley arrived to share a dinner with the family to kick off the new calendar year and celebrate the Cherokee month of Cold Moon.

The family always ate traditional Cherokee foods at this time to honor and remember tribal customs. The meal included corn, beans, and squash, commonly known as the three sisters, along with dried berries, dried deer meat, roasted turkey, and corn bread. Billy loved all of it, not only because it tasted great but because he fondly remembered his grandmother Awinita preparing some of these dishes.

The Cold Moon meal was also a time when Billy and Wesley compared the experiences they'd had during the previous night's winter spruce dance. After dinner was finished, the two settled into a couple of Adirondack chairs sitting on the Buckhorns' front porch.

Wesley went first.

"I had a most disturbing experience during the ceremony," he said. "I'm not sure I should tell you about it, because speaking of it might empower it, manifest it."

Billy remained silent, allowing his grandfather space and time to come to his own conclusion about recounting the experience.

Finally, Wesley spoke. "I saw a vision of you wrapped in some sort of cocoon," he said. "It's like you were in some sort of prison and unable to move about freely."

Billy sat quietly for a moment as he allowed his mind to absorb the information. "What else?"

"You were struggling with all your might to break free," the elder answered.

"Could this be a symbolic image? Maybe I'm figuratively trapped?"

"I couldn't really see that."

Billy just nodded.

"There's a little more," Grandpa said.

Billy remained quiet. Wesley waited, but his grandson didn't reply.

"Grandma told me that someone called Spider Woman is to be considered an ally," Grandpa said. "Her presence will be helpful to you in the near future."

"Spider Woman? Who is Spider Woman?" Then an answer to this question popped into his mind, and he smiled. *Lisa?*

"One last thing," the elder added.

"Okay."

"You are ready to take on more than you're willing to admit," Wesley said. "Grandma's going to be showing up less often so your abilities and powers can grow, so you will learn to rely on yourself instead of her."

Upset by this news, Billy stood abruptly. "Why would she do that? I'm going to need her more than ever! How am I supposed to carry out what's expected of me on the medicine path?"

"She said you already know enough to get started, and the rest you'll learn along the way."

Billy began pacing back and forth on the wood-plank porch and proceeded to tell Wesley about his own visionary experience during the spruce dance.

"So you rescued your uncle Franklin?" the elder said after hearing the story. "That's incredible! That means you *are* ready to begin your medicine work."

"But you always said the spirits of the dead hung around for four days before heading west to the land of the dead."

"That's what the traditional Cherokee teachings say," Wesley replied. "So do the traditional teachings of a lot of other tribes. Those understandings have been handed down for generations, often based only on someone's brief glimpse of the spirit world."

"So a lot of the Cherokee religious teachings are just mythology," Billy said, ending his pacing. "I guess my dad's been right all along. You can't necessarily trust what the stomp grounds teach. Or what any religion teaches, for that matter, I guess."

Wesley stood up and faced his grandson. "Until you came along, I'd never met anyone who could actually do spirit travel," he said. "I mean, I'd heard of medicine people who could do it, but no one seemed to talk about it much. You're exploring uncharted territory, revealing unknown secrets. It seems to me you are becoming the teacher, and I am the student."

Billy did not like the sound of that. He'd always relied on his parents and his grandparents to guide him in this world, to know what to do or at least how to keep things in perspective. Now, he was supposed to throw all that guidance out the window and act on his own experiences and intuition.

Feeling overwhelmed, the teen opened the front door and stepped inside the house. He'd planned on escaping to his room, but his father was standing there holding something.

"I'm glad you came in," James said. "I wanted to give you this before you went to bed." He handed the object to his son. It was a brand-new cell phone.

"What's this for?" Billy asked, almost angry.

"You're maturing so fast and out on your own so much," Billy's father replied. "Your mom and I thought it was silly for us to prevent you from having a cell phone any longer."

Instead of getting a thanks from his son, James watched as Billy took the device, darted toward his room in the back of the house, and slammed the door closed.

"Teenagers!" James said and headed out the front door to see if Wesley could shed any light on his son's unusual behavior.

Meanwhile, in his room, Billy had an idea. He unboxed the smartphone and plugged it into the charger. *Perfect timing,* he thought. *I've got to talk to somebody outside this family.*

With the charging cable still plugged into the wall, he dialed Chigger's house phone.

Mrs. Muskrat answered after the third ring.

"Is Chigger around?" Billy asked.

Mrs. Muskrat called her son to the phone.

"Guess what?" Chigger immediately asked after taking the receiver. "You're not the only one who's an apprentice to a Cherokee medicine man . . . uh, person."

"What are you talking about?" Billy said.

"A medicine woman named Carmelita Tuckaleechee asked me to be her apprentice. I'm going to her house tomorrow to begin training."

Billy didn't reply.

"Soon you won't be the only one who can heal people and perform miraculous stunts."

"Chigger, not all medicine people are who they say they are. Some are frauds and others are downright dangerous."

"Well, Carmelita is the real deal. I saw her change from an owl to a human and back again."

Billy was now very alarmed. "That's not necessarily a good thing, Chigger," he said.

"You're just jealous because your grandfather can't do that!" After a brief pause, Billy's friend continued. "And I'm not Chigger anymore! From now on I will be known as Checotah, after my great-grandfather."

With that, Chigger abruptly ended the call.

The whole interaction was shocking to Billy. He'd never heard his friend talk or act like that . . . except when he'd been under the spell of the purple crystal.

Sitting in silence in his bedroom, another idea popped into Billy's mind. Opening the drawer of his nightstand, he rummaged around until he found what he was looking for: the piece of paper Lisa Lookout had written her phone number on. Noticing that the area code was not from eastern Oklahoma, he assumed it was her cell phone. Without hesitation, he punched the numbers into his new phone. She answered on the fourth ring.

"I don't recognize this number," Lisa said in the way of a greeting, speaking loudly over background noise. "I don't usually answer calls from unknown numbers, so consider yourself lucky."

"This is lucky Billy."

Lisa was surprised and delighted. "Hi, Billy. I wondered if you would ever call. Hang on just a minute."

Lisa excused herself from the mini-powwow that was taking place in her grandfather's backyard as the drum group vigorously pounded out a song. She stepped inside the back door and found a quiet spot in the living room.

"Are you at the school?" the boy asked. "I thought I might come see you."

"Sorry, I'm in St. Louis at my grandpa's house. We're having a kind of big ceremony."

"Oh, that's too bad," Billy replied. "I was sort of in the mood to talk, finally."

Lisa was silent a moment. "I'll be back in Tahlequah in two days. It would be great to see you."

Billy was suddenly nervous about seeing her. "Well, I'm . . . uh—"

"I'll come to your house," Lisa said with a pleasant tone. "We can sit on the front porch and talk. How about that?"

"Sounds good," Billy replied with relief. He felt he could handle that okay.

"See you then," the girl said in a bright voice and ended the call.

Feeling better about things, Billy stepped into the living room, where he found his mom, dad, and grandpa huddled in deep discussion. They obviously changed the subject and altered the tone of their conversation when the teen entered the room.

"I want to apologize for my attitude earlier," Billy said. "I don't exactly know what that was about."

"I think I do," his mother said. "Big things have been happening to you the past few months, and you may not be ready to permanently step into the new, bigger phase of your life."

Billy was silent.

"It's only natural to feel unsure of what the changes may mean," she continued. "I say there's no big rush. Take your time."

Billy nodded. "You're probably right, as usual, Mom."

"Since you still have a few more days before returning to school, do you feel like coming over to my house to work with me?" Wesley asked.

"Sure, Grandpa, I'll be over in the morning. For now, I'm going to turn in."

"Be sure to bring with you the crystal you brought back from the upper room of the crystal cave."

"Why?"

"You'll see," Wesley replied. "Please just bring it."

Billy shrugged, said okay, left the three in the living room to no doubt talk about him some more, and went to bed.

At about three in the morning, Billy woke up for no particular reason. Having promised to practice spirit travel, the teen thought he'd give it a try. He knew he needed to learn how to do it all on his own with no help from anyone, so this seemed as good a time as any.

Lying in the middle of his bed, he began humming the chant used to separate from his body while clearing his mind of any thoughts about his daily life. The vibrational energy reached a steady plateau, and after hearing what sounded like two pieces of Velcro separating, the teen rolled out, then floated up from his body.

After he'd remained suspended in silence for a few moments, a dense gray fog rolled in and surrounded him. Or maybe it was the other way around. Maybe the fog had been stationary, and he'd floated into it. Either way, he now found himself immersed in grayness with no sense of place. There was no sign or hint of anyone else within his perception, and really no sign or hint of anything else—at first.

The middle of nowhere was the thought that drifted into his mind just as the sound of murmuring whispers reached his ears. Within a few seconds, the intensity of the sound increased until it became the annoying sound of hundreds of people whispering in a loud dissonance.

In an attempt to get oriented, Billy reached out with his nonphysical hands and unexpectedly felt hard, curved, almost metallic surfaces at his fingertips. Shortly afterward, his feet came to rest on a hard floor. He was no longer floating but rather standing on a firm surface. He raised a hand over his head, and it, too, touched a hard, curved surface.

"You're inside a smooth sphere, Buckhorn," the teen said. "How'd you get here?"

The gray fog began dissipating, revealing the correctness of his conclusion. Checking all parts of the seamless surface, he confirmed there was no doorway or opening of any kind. He tried pushing on the enclosure in various places, with no results. A slight sense of panic began to overtake him.

Where the hell am I?

His growing feeling of panic led him to try another approach as he attempted to shoulder his way through the spherical barrier. He slammed into its curved walls several times in several different areas, with no result.

He screamed in frustration and fear.

Suddenly, someone slammed into the barrier from the outside, startling Billy. Then another "someone" slammed into another part of the sphere from another direction. Then another, and another. Each one mirrored the panic that Billy was experiencing. Each one screamed in fear.

Soon the teen was surrounded by a horrifying sea of trapped and panicked souls who were pounding, clawing, and screaming to get out. Seeing the futility of trying to escape, Billy closed himself into a ball on the floor.

Then, in his relaxed state, he heard a thought in his mind.

"Remember your spirit travel lessons near the crystal cave at winter solstice. Controlling your movement is purely a function of thought. Simply thinking of your destination and picturing it in your mind takes you there."

He pictured his own bedroom in his mind, and within seconds he found himself hovering above his own physical body as it lay in bed. *What a relief!* After merging back with the flesh, the boy sat up in bed and looked around his room. Nothing seemed out of place, and he fell back on his pillow and went back to sleep.

The next morning, as Billy had experienced most recent mornings, his pajamas felt tighter on him. This in spite of the fact that these pj's were a size larger than the ones he had worn just ten days earlier. At breakfast he showed the problem to his mother, who seemed to have other things on her mind.

"And my shoes!" he added. "I can't even fit my feet into them anymore. This just isn't natural."

Her mind clearly focused elsewhere, Rebecca found her purse, opened her wallet, and handed Billy fifty dollars. Maybe her son didn't want to admit he just wanted a new pair of shoes.

"Go to Walmart and buy yourself a new pair. We can talk more about this when I get home from work."

"Thanks," he said, not sure how long the next pair of shoes would fit before he'd have to replace them with the next larger size.

The typical collection of Grandpa's Cherokee patients greeted Billy when he arrived at Wesley's house an hour later. Working his way through the crowd, the teen let himself into his grandfather's house. Wesley wasn't anywhere in the house, so he helped himself to a cup of coffee in the kitchen.

After a couple of sips, Billy was pleased to see Wesley step into the kitchen from out back, carrying a couple of freshly harvested herbs.

"Good—you're here," the elder said. "I see you brought the crystal. Take it out of the pouch and put it on the table. I've got something to show you."

Wesley headed down the hall toward the back bedroom. The old wooden floorboards of the house creaked with his every step, more so than usual, Billy thought. Thirty seconds later, his grandpa was back, carrying a deerskin pouch similar to the one Billy had brought.

After placing the bag on the kitchen table, he said, "Open it."

Billy set his coffee cup down and tugged on the bag's small opening created by the drawstring. Reaching in, Billy pulled out a crystal almost identical to the one already sitting on the table.

"Where'd this come from?" he asked, rotating the amazing gem over and over to examine it. "How come I've never seen it before?"

"This belonged to your Cherokee great-great-grandfather Moytoy the Rainmaker. He was part of the Keetoowahs with Redbird Smith. They were traditional full-bloods who wanted to separate from the rest of the tribe in the late eighteen hundreds."

Billy continued studying the six-sided mineral. The top two-thirds were clear, while the bottom third was milky white.

"This one came from a cave in Eastern Cherokee territory where our people used to practice writing the syllabary in secret," Wesley said. "It came with one of our ancestors on the Trail of Tears."

"Why didn't you mention you had this crystal while we were in the crystal cave?" Billy asked.

"Well, I'm old, and my mind doesn't always remember things like there's a very old crystal in the back of a closet in the room I haven't visited much since my wife died."

"Oh," Billy replied.

"What I'm thinking is that someday soon we'll take a trip over there to visit that cave—I think it's in Alabama. And I want to visit an Eastern Cherokee medicine man I met at a tribal culture conference a few years ago." He put his crystal back in its pouch and said, "So I'll put this one away for now. We'll use yours today to help someone connect with a loved one who has recently died."

"I'm not ready for that yet," Billy responded.

Wesley pulled up a chair across the table and sat down. "You've been gifted with more abilities and powers than any medicine person I've ever known," he said. "And the sooner you begin using those gifts to help people, the better. Better for you, better for them."

Billy didn't respond, but he put his crystal back in its pouch and pushed it farther away on the table.

"Mrs. Acorn arrived at six this morning, troubled by her son's recent unexpected death," Wesley continued. "She needs your help trying to reach his spirit on the other side."

Billy shot up out of his chair. "I can't help anyone else until I get my own questions about the afterlife answered. Are the Cherokee beliefs accurate or not?"

"All right," Billy's grandfather said as he, too, rose from his chair.

He moved to the kitchen cupboard and retrieved a coffee cup. Pouring himself a shot of caffeine, he gathered his thoughts.

"I've been thinking about that ever since you brought it up last night," he said, sitting back down at the table. "You need to ask your grandma that question. She experienced the whole process of dying and crossing over firsthand." He pushed the crystal closer to his grandson. "And you can use your crystal to help focus your effort to reach her. I think if you hold it in your hands, sing one of the stomp dance songs you know, and think about Awinita, you may be able to get through to her. Now, I'm going to go see my next patient."

The old man walked toward the front of the house. Billy had forgotten that he meant to ask his grandpa if he'd ever heard of a Cherokee healer named . . . what was it? Chattahoochee or Tuskalooska? He couldn't remember.

The teen looked at the crystal sitting on the table. Most of his previous interactions with his grandmother's spirit had taken place when she initiated the contact, often when he was about to go to sleep or the Sun Priest's helpers had begun their vibrational chanting. But could he do it on his own?

"I guess it's time to find out, Buckhorn," he said to no one in particular.

He thought it might work best if he was lying down, so he headed for Grandpa's bedroom and crawled on the bed. The old bedsprings squeaked and complained as he got comfortable.

He placed the crystal, flat side down, on his chest with the clear point of the gem aimed toward the ceiling. Emptying his mind of all thoughts, he brought an image of his grandmother into focus. He began humming one of the songs used during the stomp dance, hoping the vibrational pattern would spread across his body.

Try as he might, nothing seemed to happen. Billy remembered the message his grandfather had received during the spruce dance, that Awinita wouldn't be available for him to visit as often.

"Now what am I supposed to do?" Billy asked, sitting up in bed.

He put the quartz gem back in its bag and pulled the drawstring closed. He placed the bag back on the kitchen table and headed toward the front porch. He might as well make himself useful, he thought.

He was surprised to find a teary-eyed middle-aged Native woman waiting for him in the living room. Her energy field, which was quite visible to Billy, was weak and tinged in blue. Tissue in hand, she rose as he approached.

"I'm Mattie Acorn," she said, drying the corner of one eye with the tissue. "Wesley said you may not be able to help me today, so I can come back another time."

When Billy got close enough, he reached out to shake her extended hand. As soon as he touched her, the teen felt a shift in his own energy. Beginning at the top of his head, a vibration passed throughout his body. He stood frozen, still holding her hand, as a scene unfolded before him.

Mrs. Acorn tried to withdraw her hand, but Billy wouldn't let go.

"Wait," he said. "I'm seeing something. I think I need to keep holding your hand to see more of it unfold."

Without releasing each other's hands, the pair sat down on the sofa. With his focus set on some vision that was invisible to Mrs. Acorn, Billy sat quietly for a moment.

"I'm sorry to ask this, but did your son take his own life? Did he hang himself in your attic?"

In shock, the woman instinctively jerked her hand out of Billy's.

"What, did someone call you and make that accusation?" she asked angrily. "We are devout Catholics and don't believe in suicide! It's a sin!"

"No, no one called me," Billy protested. "I didn't know what you were here for until my grandpa told me a few minutes ago."

"I've never been so insulted in all my life!" the woman said firmly and stomped out of Wesley's living room.

Having heard a raised female voice from out on the porch, Wesley stepped through his front door just as the angry woman stormed out of his house.

"Your grandson is a complete fraud!" Mrs. Acorn shouted, making sure everyone in the immediate area could hear her. "Nothing comes out of his mouth but lies!"

Wesley, Billy, and everyone else nearby stood frozen in place as the woman marched off the porch and toward her car parked on the street.

Billy was greatly disturbed by the whole incident, because in addition to seeing that Mrs. Acorn's son had died by suicide, he also saw that the young man was trapped in a sphere in a gray zone just like the one he'd been trapped in.

Maybe that's what the whole gray fog experience was about, he thought. *So I'd know what her son is experiencing.*

"Any luck in summoning Awinita?" Wesley asked, hoping to distract his grandson from what just happened.

"I don't think any of this is going to work," Billy said angrily. "Communicating with the dead may not be for me after all. Not if everyone's going to react like that."

"You have to give it some time to—"

Wesley stopped talking when Billy put up a stop motion with both his hands. "Sorry, Grandpa," Billy said, "I'm done for today."

The boy walked briskly away as Wesley and everyone else on the front porch watched.

After getting in his truck and starting the engine, Billy beat his hands on the steering wheel a few times in frustration and anger. Not knowing where to go, what to do, or who to talk to, he sat in the driver's seat and ran his hand through his hair.

That was when his cell phone rang. He recognized the number. It was Lisa Lookout.

"Hello," Billy said. "You picked a good time to call."

"I had a vibe," she replied. "Is something bothering you?"

"Only everything. Are you back in Tahlequah?"

"Be there late tomorrow. I'll come see you then, if that's still okay."

"The sooner the better," Billy replied, and then regretted it. *You're sounding a little desperate, Buckhorn.* "I just mean—"

"I know what you mean," Lisa said. "Looking forward to it." After a brief pause, she asked, "Are you okay for now?"

Billy blew out a long breath of frustrated air. "Yeah, I'm okay. See you tomorrow."

He ended the call with a pleasant feeling from head to toe and a smile on his face.

That evening at the dinner table, he got up the courage to tell his parents about Lisa. "Tomorrow evening at some point I'll have a visitor," Billy said between bites. "A new friend—a girl."

"A Cherokee girl?" his mother asked hopefully.

"She's Osage, staying in the dorm at Sequoyah High School."

"How did you meet her?" Billy's father asked.

"She showed up here the day before winter solstice saying she wanted to talk to me. She left her phone number. I finally called her back the other day, and she said she'd come for a visit tomorrow. Just to chat."

"I assume we'll get to meet her since she's coming here," Mrs. Buckhorn said.

"I assume," Billy replied, a little annoyed with what seemed like his mother's avid interest in his love life.

The Sorcerer's Apprentice

On the second day of the new year, Chigger awoke with a new sense of purpose. Today he would begin his apprenticeship with a Cherokee medicine woman and start his journey to become a new persona named Checotah.

After breakfast, he lied and told his mother that he'd be out with Billy all day so she wouldn't worry about him. The teen wasn't ready to tell his parents about his new . . . hobby.

He knew he should be honest with them. Hadn't they just given him his own pickup truck for Christmas, along with a cell phone? His parents had witnessed firsthand the power of Cherokee medicine when Billy, Wesley, and several healers had freed their son from whatever spell he'd been imprisoned in by the dark crystal. Afterward they felt he deserved to have his own vehicle and some additional freedom to come and go as he pleased.

Chigger had witnessed how Billy and Wesley had worked together over the years, though he'd never sought help from the elder medicine man before the Horned Serpent affair. His parents never really believed in the old Cherokee ways until he was freed from the spell, but they hadn't been churchgoers either. The couple hadn't experienced much good fortune in their lives but hadn't turned to any spiritual tradition for help or comfort as so many people do. They just handled whatever came their way the best they could.

Both physically and figuratively, the teen's life was headed in a new direction as he drove his twenty-year-old brown Dodge Ram north on State Highway 10 from his mobile home. It had been quite a while since he'd driven up this way, because most of his time was spent in Tahlequah or Park Hill to the south. School and Billy were both in that direction.

No sign on the side of the highway announced the location of Buzzard Bend. Chigger did, however, receive a prompting in his mind to keep going north. He passed a couple of wood-frame houses, a general store, and a river float business for the nearby Illinois River. These structures occupied the four corners where Steely Hollow Road intersected the narrow highway.

The teen stopped his truck at that intersection, but it didn't seem like the right place to turn. He moved on. As he was approaching a sharp bend in the road about a mile farther north, he got a feeling he should turn left at the next driveway. He paused before turning, because the winding, narrow gravel road seemed to go nowhere as it pierced the dark, densely wooded property.

This seems just like the kind of place a conjurer would live.

Because his father had run a plant nursery when the boy was younger, Chigger recognized many of the species of trees he saw as he drove deeper into those woods—oaks, sycamores, black walnut, and elm. But the matted, pale green Spanish moss hanging from many of them gave this forest a kind of spooky feeling.

It was a little odd, too, to see so many of the long stringy strands hanging from trees in this area, because there were none visible along the highway. But the plant grew so thickly here it made all the trees look like old men with wispy beards.

In another few minutes, a clearing in the woods opened up, revealing an old two-story gray wood house covered with climbing vines. Across from the main house stood an older, smaller log cabin. Smoke rose from the cabin's chimney. The teen parked between the two structures.

Chigger wondered what Carmelita Tuckaleechee looked like in the daylight. He'd only seen her through night vision goggles, which rendered everything a sickly shade of green. The tattoo that cut diagonally across her face had been a little unsettling but somehow appropriate.

As he stepped out of his truck, the old woman came out of the cabin. In her left hand was a small tobacco pipe that she puffed on from time to time as she hobbled toward him. Her right hand was supported by a carved wooden cane that tapped the ground with each of her steps. A small leather pouch hung at her side, suspended by a strap that straddled one shoulder.

"Glad you found the place, boy," she said. "Come inside and have a look around."

She turned and hobbled back inside. Chigger hesitantly followed her, suddenly questioning his decision to be the old woman's apprentice.

"Oh, that's normal," she called to him from inside. "Every new apprentice feels that way at first. You'll get over it."

Chigger chuckled nervously at her ability to read his mind, but he stepped inside the one-room cabin anyway. The back wall was covered with shelves from floor to ceiling, and the shelves were filled with jars of dried-up things that Chigger assumed were medicinal plants.

A woodstove occupied one corner of the room; a stand-alone sink stood in another. An aging rolltop desk stood in the corner closest to the front door. Two well-worn overstuffed chairs inhabited the center of the room, separated by a round table that supported two teacups.

"Take a seat," Carmelita said, putting her pipe down on the table. "Make yourself comfortable."

The teen sat in one of the padded chairs. It was covered with a faded purple-and-black floral design. The old woman picked up a cast-iron teapot from the stove and sat it on the table near the teacups.

"I've made some medicinal tea for you," she said as she poured a greenish liquid from the teapot into the cup closest to Chigger. "This will open up your mind so you can more easily learn and remember what I'll be teaching you."

"Thanks," Chigger said, not sure he liked the looks of the concoction.

"The taste of these medicines takes a little getting used to, but they're harmless."

"No problem," the boy said. "It doesn't look that bad."

He took a tentative first sip and immediately had to control his gag reflex. The look on his face, however, betrayed his true reaction to the drink.

Carmelita sat in the other chair, pulled a little flask out of the pouch at her side, and poured a splash of the contents into her own cup. Holding up her cup, she said, "Drink up!"

Chigger gulped down the rest of his tea just to be done with it. Wiping his mouth with the back of his hand, he faked a smile and said, "Not that bad."

After gulping down the contents of her own cup, Carmelita reached into her pouch and pulled out a small bag of some herb. Picking up her pipe from the table, she stuffed a pinch of the dried leaves into the pipe bowl.

"Being my apprentice means that you will follow my instructions without question," the old woman said. "You may not understand what's going on at first, but you'll gradually catch on."

Chigger just nodded as Carmelita struck a match and ignited the contents of the pipe.

As the first puff of smoke billowed up, she handed the pipe to her apprentice. "Take a few puffs. It'll relax you."

The boy looked at the pipe and the stream of smoke.

"No hesitation," the conjurer insisted.

Chigger took in a lungful of the vapor and coughed.

"That's it," Carmelita said with a smile. "Keep going."

As the teen inhaled the smoke, Carmelita began an incantation in the Cherokee language, which Chigger didn't understand. As he finished up the last bit of fumes from the pipe, the woman pulled a small amethyst crystal out of her pouch.

His eyes shot wide open in fear, because the stone's purple color reminded Chigger of the dark crystal from the Horned Serpent's tail.

Seeing his reaction, Carmelita said, "Have no fear, young man. This is not at all like that cursed stone you held last year. In fact, you don't even need to touch it. Only look at it. Gaze deep into its core."

The teen was a little curious about how Carmelita knew about the dark crystal. He was sure she'd mentioned it when they first met in the woods the other night. *Maybe the medicine people all talk to each other,* he thought. That would explain it.

The tea he drank and the smoke he inhaled began to have their intended effects on Chigger. The room seemed to breathe in and out as he did. His vision became blurred, and his mind grew foggy. He tried to concentrate on the amethyst as Carmelita held it between her thumb and fingers, rotating it with a small circular motion.

In another few seconds, the boy slumped back in his chair.

"Perfect," the conjurer said.

After putting the pipe, teacup, and amethyst away, the old woman snapped her fingers in Chigger's face, making sure he was unconscious.

"Now for the hypnotism formula," she said, hobbling over to the rolltop desk. She located the document she was searching for in the bottom drawer. Returning to her chair with the yellowed parchment, she began reading aloud from the Cherokee characters written there.

Once that was completed, the old woman leaned closer to her so-called apprentice and whispered a special set of instructions in his ear. Her final command was that he would not consciously remember any of the secret message after he awoke but would faithfully execute the directives he'd been given.

After a few minutes, she clapped her hands loudly, waking the boy. He looked around, not really sure where he was or what just happened. But there was a nagging thought in the back of his mind that he had a task to accomplish. Just what it was, he couldn't put his finger on.

"That's enough for today," Carmelita said. "You did very well, I must say." She helped Chigger stand up and began ushering him toward the door. "I'll see you back here in a couple of days, and we'll pick up where we left off."

The teen drove home half in a daze, not really clear in his mind about where he'd just been or what had happened.

The following morning, Billy woke up in a bright mood, anticipating his visit from Lisa. What he hadn't anticipated was a surprise visit from Chigger—or rather Checotah, if that's what he was calling himself—after breakfast.

"After the way you talked to me the other night, I really didn't expect to see you anytime soon," Billy said as he opened the door. "Ever since we recaptured the Uktena, you haven't seemed like your usual self."

"Ah, well, that's why I'm here," Billy's friend replied. "I want to apologize. I was really in a weird place the last time I talked to you."

"That's good to hear, Checotah," Billy said.

Chigger chuckled. "Of course, just between you and me, I'm still Chigger. I'm not ready to start using my medicine name yet."

"Oh, okay, I get it."

"Can I come in?" Chigger asked, compelled to carry out a specific task but not sure why. "I kind of need to use your bathroom."

Billy opened the door wide to let his friend in and said, "I can't hang out today. I'm helping Grandpa over at his place for a few days until school starts again."

"Sure thing," Chigger replied. "I'll be quick."

The visitor headed for the bathroom closest to Billy's bedroom and closed the door behind him. Once inside, he began a quick search of the place, looking for a hairbrush. Finding it in a cabinet drawer, he removed a small plastic bag from his pants pocket. He plucked several dark hairs from the brush and stuffed them in the bag. Finally, he crammed the bag back in his pocket.

With a flush of the toilet, he exited the bathroom and headed for the front door. Before leaving, he turned back to Billy.

"I may stop by to visit you at Wesley's house later," he said. "That is, if you're not too busy."

"Well, that's different," Billy said, a little surprised. "I don't think you've been to Grandpa's house more than once or twice the whole time we've known each other."

"Hey, you know I just miss spending time with my buddies in the Paranormal Patrol," Chigger replied with a stiff smile. "Okay, see you later."

Billy escorted his friend out the front door, then watched him get in his pickup and drive away. *Odd behavior,* he thought and then put it out of his mind. Jumping into his own truck, he headed for Grandpa's house, having decided to give the whole medicine man thing another try.

The first thing Billy did when he got to Wesley's place was apologize to his elder. "This is all a little overwhelming," he said.

"I'm afraid I'll make a mistake or make someone's condition worse instead of making it better. It's a heavy load."

"I agree," Wesley replied. "It *is* a heavy load. But you can only do what you can do—nothing more and nothing less."

That wasn't what Billy expected his grandfather to say. He thought he'd get a lecture about being all you can be or thinking only positive thoughts. Not this kind of "it is what it is" approach.

"Trust is the key," Wesley added. "Trust in yourself. Trust in spirit. Trust in tradition."

After hearing that, Billy immediately relaxed. He hadn't even realized how tense he'd been, probably ever since he'd seen the trapped spirit of his uncle Frank. Or maybe even since the dark priest had tried to take over his own body in the crystal cave.

He took a couple of deep breaths and blew out the stale air he'd been carrying in his body.

Suddenly, he felt lighter.

"That's a relief," he said out loud as Wesley's house phone rang.

The elder answered it on the third ring and listened intently for a few minutes. After hanging up, he told Billy, "We need to make a house call."

People waiting for treatment on Wesley's front porch knew they'd have to wait a little longer when they were told about the house call.

"Earl Corntassle has a swollen, infected leg," Wesley told Billy as they pulled away from the house in the elder's truck. "He's out east on Highway 62 behind the Briggs Baptist Church."

When they arrived at the Corntassle house, Wesley said, "Billy, I want you to size up the situation. See if you can find out what's causing the problem."

"Sure," the teen answered, not sure at all he could do that.

After introductions to several family members waiting in the front room, the healing team stepped into Earl's bedroom. The old man was lying in bed next to an open window with one very swollen red leg propped up on pillows. An unpleasant odor filled Billy's nostrils as they approached the old man. The smell probably came from the infection itself. The man's wife, Betty, was busy wiping sweat from her husband's forehead.

"Earl is an army veteran," Wesley explained quietly to Billy. "He's got a war injury that's been hurting him off and on ever since he got out of the service. He's also hard of hearing."

The pair moved closer to the ailing Cherokee.

"Hey, Earl, I want you to meet my grandson, Billy," Wesley said in a loud voice. "He's been helping me out lately."

Billy extended his hand, which the man politely shook once.

"Betty, what's going on this time?" Wesley asked.

"Yesterday a fever came on him fast," she said. "It got up to a hundred and four, and he nearly passed out from the pain in his leg. I ran him over to the hospital, and they gave him a bunch of antibiotics. But he ain't no better."

"Okay, give us a few minutes to see what's going on with him," Wesley said. "We'll call you when we're ready for you to come back in."

"I'll fix you two some iced tea in the kitchen," she said.

With a very distressed look on her face, the woman left the room.

"Now see if you can get a read on the cause of Earl's problem," Wesley told Billy.

The teen put his hands out toward the man and moved them up and down his body at a distance of about two feet. In addition to being able to see Earl's distressed energy field, he could feel it as well. He detected a foreign substance that had been inserted into the man's leg behind the knee.

"A black object of some kind seems to be lodged on the back side of his knee," Billy reported. "It's damaging his whole system, physical, mental, and spiritual."

"Very good, Grandson. That's the same reading I got."

"But how did it get in there?"

"Witchcraft," Wesley replied. "Someone performed some bad intrusion medicine on Earl. We've got to act fast to expel the sorcery."

After telling Earl and Betty they'd return that evening with a remedy, the two healers got back in Wesley's truck with two iced teas to go. While Wesley drove, Billy looked through the handwritten syllabary pages of the Cherokee medicine book for entries that might be related to Earl's case.

"Look for information about datura, or jimsonweed, remedies," Wesley instructed. "Treatment for this kind of supernatural intrusion will require this medicinal plant, and I know where a plentiful supply of it grows wild farther east."

Billy thumbed through the pages until he found the entry and read the formula out loud, which included the incantation to be used while a strong solution made from boiling parts of the datura plant was applied to the affected leg.

Meanwhile, Chigger had received a mental prodding that told him now would be a good time to visit Wesley's house. Still operating under the subconscious hypnotic spell cast by Carmelita Tuckaleechee, the boy's objective was to somehow gather the elder's saliva and deliver it to the medicine woman.

Unbeknownst to Chigger, the old woman was planning to perform the "end of life" ceremony against Wesley, partly because she was jealous of his success as a healer but mostly because it fit in with a grand scheme of the Night Seers of the Owl Clan. None of her Cherokee neighbors knew she was a member of this ancient cult.

The "end of life" formula says you must first collect the victim's spit and then perform a complex sequence of steps while repeating an incantation that will lead to your target's demise.

When Chigger arrived at Wesley's house, he found that Billy's truck was there, and the old man's truck was gone. There were too many people waiting in front, and the teen knew he couldn't just walk up to the porch and open the front door. He parked out of sight and sneaked around to the back of the white frame house.

He easily entered through the unlocked back door and began searching for objects that might hold Wesley's spit, such as a handkerchief, napkin, or used tissue. In a wastebasket beside the bed, he found some used tissues, which the teen placed in the plastic bag he'd brought. In the bathroom was a hairbrush that held a few white and gray hairs from the man's head. Chigger put those in the bag too, in case they might be useful. The kitchen trash container held a few used paper napkins holding nothing but food particles, so he didn't bother to grab those.

I'll have to come back another time, the teen thought and exited through the back door.

Out on Highway 62, Wesley located the patch of datura he'd seen before just off the road. He and Billy collected the leaves, roots, and seeds from several of the plants and placed them in a burlap bag Wesley always kept in his truck.

"I have to warn you, Billy, about how dangerous this plant is," the elder said. "Many teens have been hospitalized after eating parts of the plant."

"Why would kids eat this?"

"It contains a known hallucinogenic ingredient that young people hear about and experiment with to get high. But it is very poisonous if used the wrong way or in the wrong amount."

Billy tucked that information away for possible future use.

Returning to the Corntassle's house, Wesley told Betty to boil all the ingredients until the water turned dark. While the plant parts cooked, the elder repeated the prescribed incantation over the patient. Once the boiled water was black, Earl's wife was to apply the liquid to his leg every hour until bedtime. The healer said he'd check with her the following morning to see how the patient was doing.

Back at Wesley's house, the pair continued working to doctor several patients, and Billy's ability to see the patients' energy fields helped enormously with diagnosing their illnesses. The process helped the teen feel more confident about his future as a healer.

But all day, try as he might to put her out of his mind, the thought of Lisa's impending visit kept popping up in Billy's brain. He found it both exasperating and exciting.

"This is ridiculous," he said to himself in late afternoon. "She probably has a boyfriend, or at least a line of potential boyfriends a mile long. Give it up, Buckhorn!"

At that moment his phone rang, and the ID read *Lisa*. He stepped out to Wesley's herb garden to take the call.

"Lisa, I was just thinking about you," he said and immediately regretted it. *Why do I keep doing that?* he thought.

That's nice to hear," she replied. "Would it be all right if we dropped by around seven o'clock this evening?"

"We? Who's we?"

"My dad, my grandfather, and me."

Billy paused a moment. "What's this about?"

"Possibly your future, my future, and the future of the world as we know it."

Billy was silent again.

"Crap," he finally said. "I was hoping for a quiet time with a nice Native girl who could help me forget about my future and the future of the world."

"We need to talk to you, your parents, and your grandfather," she said.

"Isn't it a little early in the relationship to talk about meeting the parents?"

"There's no time for normal formalities," Lisa replied. "These are prophetic times."

"That was a joke," Billy replied.

He went silent again. This relationship was over before it began.

"I'll tell my parents and grandfather to expect you around seven," he finally said and ended the call.

His disappointment was palpable.

At about the same time and compelled to complete a task his conscious mind couldn't comprehend, Chigger drove to Carmelita's cabin. He carried with him the hair cuttings he'd gathered from Billy's bathroom, along with the tissues and napkins he'd taken from Wesley's house. He moved as if in a waking dream.

"How's my young apprentice?" the conjurer asked as the teen entered. "Were you able to complete your assignments?"

"Assignments?" the confused boy asked.

"*Kaliwohi!*" Carmelita commanded. "Complete your task."

She snapped her fingers, and Chigger reached into his pocket and pulled out the two plastic bags, holding Billy's clippings in one hand and Wesley's discarded trash in the other. The old woman cackled with delight at the sight of Billy's hair but almost recoiled in disgust at the sight of the other.

"What am I supposed to do with a soiled cloth and a snotty tissue?" she roared with displeasure. "I told you to get his saliva, his spittle! You'll have to try again, you floundering fool!"

She threw the bag in Chigger's face, hitting him in one eye. The pain, though minor, jolted the boy out of his hypnotic trance. He blinked and looked around the room.

"How . . . what's going on?"

Realizing that her subject had come out from under the spell, Carmelita softened her voice.

"Ah, well, Checotah. I see you're ready for another lesson," she said in a syrupy-sweet tone. She cast her eyes around the room, looking for any handy prop. Seeing the cast-iron teapot on the metal stove, she moved toward it. "First, we'll have a nice cup of herbal tea to put you in the right frame of mind again."

Then the woman had a brilliant thought. *This will be a much better use of this boy's limited abilities.*

Step by step, the conjurer repeated the process she'd used during Chigger's first visit, to make his mind pliable and ready for hypnosis. He reached that condition rather easily, and she placed him under the spell once again. This time, her hypnotic instructions would send the boy on a valuable reconnaissance mission, spying on the Buckhorn household on her behalf.

"Now, run along and don't fail me this time," she admonished. "I've got work to do."

As the boy left her cabin, Carmelita picked up the plastic bag containing Billy's hair and sat down at her desk to search the pages of her dark medicine book for a particularly rare formula known as "Imprisonment in the House of Bones."

CHAPTER SIX

House of Bones

The Buckhorns had dinner at six and by seven were gathered in the living room, waiting. None of them knew what to expect, least of all Billy.

At a few minutes past seven, a tan van pulled up the gravel drive and stopped. On the side of the van was a printed round logo containing an image of a crossed trowel, pick, and arrowhead encircled by the words *Indigenous Archaeology Alliance*.

As the vehicle's three occupants made their way up the steps, Billy opened the front door and invited them inside. He could easily see the family resemblance in their faces, and he noticed that their energy fields bore strong, positive, and similar patterns as well. The eldest, Lisa's grandfather, had shoulder-length graying hair along with deep lines and wrinkles on a face that echoed the lines and wrinkles on his own grandfather's face. The elder wore a deerskin vest over a faded denim shirt and carried a canvas tote bag.

Lisa's father had jet-black hair tied in a single braid and wore a flannel shirt, cowboy boots, and jeans. His bronze skin and square jaw gave him a classic Plains Indian look, and the scar across his chin told you this man led an interesting life.

And then there was Lisa. She wore a leather bomber jacket, black jeans, and lace-up hiking boots. She was even better looking than Billy remembered, and he couldn't help but smile when they made eye contact, even though he resented not being able to see her alone.

Seeing that her son wasn't eager to begin introductions, Billy's mother took the lead. "I'm Rebecca," she said, extending her hand first to the Osage elder. "This is my husband, James, and his father, Wesley." After everyone else had finished shaking hands, she added, "Billy, of course, is my son."

She motioned toward the couch and chairs in the living room. "Please sit down. Can I get you anything?"

"It is I who have brought something," Cecil said. He reached into the tote bag and pulled out a bundle of items that he'd tied together. He approached Wesley with the bundle. "I've brought tobacco, sage, sweetgrass, and cedar for you, Wesley, since we've come to ask for your family's help with spiritual and cultural matters. It's a common practice for us Plains people to provide an offering when we ask for help with these matters."

He held out the items with a slightly bowed head.

"It is common practice for us Cherokees as well," Wesley replied, taking the gift. "Thank you. What could I, or we Buckhorns, help you with?"

Cecil began by explaining about the Intertribal Medicine Council and the need for a replacement member as Ethan and Lisa added details to the unfolding story. Then the three talked about the message from the ancestor spirits on the Full Green Corn Moon who said that the Time of Prophecy was about to be fulfilled. They finished their explanations with the additional spirit message delivered during the recent sweat lodge ceremony.

"It all comes down to these two points," Cecil said. "The members of the ITMC are inviting Wesley to fill the vacant seat on the council." Looking at Wesley, he added, "Bucky Wachacha of the Eastern Cherokees speaks very highly of you. Separately, and more importantly, Lisa thinks Billy is the one we're looking for, the one to fulfill our ancient prophecy. In other words—the one chosen by the Thunders."

The room was quiet for a moment before Cecil continued.

"To be certain about Billy's status, though, we need to hear the full story about recent events in his life. Lisa says the local newspaper accounts seemed to leave out a lot of details."

The room remained silent for another beat. One thing Billy had noticed while the Lookouts were telling their collective story was that every time his own name was mentioned, Lisa's energy field momentarily pulsated with extra energy. This gave the boy added courage.

Billy stood up and said, "Lisa, could I speak to you alone for a minute?"

The girl hesitated for a brief moment before standing up. "Okay."

"You all talk among yourselves," Billy said to the others. He headed for a far corner of the room, and Lisa followed.

"Before this goes any further, I need to know one thing," Billy whispered once they'd gotten far enough away from the others.

"What's that?"

"Do you have any interest in me personally, or am I just a part of your family's long-term prophecy plan?"

Lisa glanced over to the cluster of people across the large room and saw they were fully engrossed in their own conversation. Turning back to Billy, she reached up and placed the hand with the spider tattoo on the side of his neck with the web scar. Pulling herself toward him, she moved to kiss him. At first the surprised boy's posture stiffened at the unexpected action, but then he relaxed and allowed it to happen.

As their lips touched, the scar on his neck began to heat up and then tingle with a mild electric current. A color movie featuring the two of them began to run in his mind. That hadn't happened when he touched someone in months, but this girl's powerful positive energy must've reactivated this phenomenon, at least momentarily.

In the mini-movie, Billy rode behind Lisa on her motorcycle as they breezed down a winding road through the woods. But the combination of physical sensations and mental movie was overpowering to Billy. He broke away from the kiss and searched Lisa's eyes.

Who was this girl?

"I hope that answers your question," she said. "More later. First let's take care of family business."

She turned and headed back to the others, leaving Billy to gather himself before stumbling awkwardly after her. Slowly he regained his composure and took his seat in the living room.

Looking at all those seated around him, the boy said, "I don't know where to begin." After a pause, he continued with "The Sun Priest told me I had been chosen by the Thunder Beings to become some sort of spiritual go-between—a sort of modern version of him in this time period."

"The Sun Priest?" Cecil said. "Are you referring to our Sun Chief? How do you know of him?"

"Why, he's the one buried at Spiral Mounds along with the staff and falcon feather cape," Billy replied, confused by the question. "He used my body to speak the sacred words needed to recapture the Horned Serpent within the crystal cave right after his evil twin, the Snake Priest, tried to take possession of my body."

Cecil, Ethan, and Lisa sat stunned by this answer. They realized at the same time that Billy *must* be the real deal. Who else would know of the cape and staff buried with their ancestor a thousand years ago in that remote Spiral Mounds community? Who else would know that the Sun Chief and Snake Priest were really twin brothers and had clashed when they were alive?

"Historically, he is known to us as the Son of the Sun, or the Sun Chief, and ruler of the Mississippian Mound Builder community we called Solstice City," Ethan said. "According to our tribe's oral histories, his birth name was Shakuru." He hesitated a moment. "But the spirits failed to tell us of his connection to you or his communication with you."

Billy began to speak. "I—"

"The details of what happened to Billy have been a closely guarded secret to this point," Wesley interrupted. "I think we need a little time to ourselves to talk about the new information you've brought, to allow him to decide what he wants to do and what we think is best for him. We shouldn't—he shouldn't—rush into anything."

"That's not exactly what we expected to hear," Cecil replied as he stood up. "But it's only fair. Ethan and I are staying at the old Cherokee Inn near downtown Tahlequah. Lisa will be at her dorm at Sequoyah High School. Call us when you're ready to talk more. We thank you for your hospitality."

After the Lookouts left, the Buckhorns moved their discussions to the kitchen. The family munched on leftovers from the Cold Moon dinner while talking.

"So that's the Spider Woman your grandmother told me about," Wesley said to Billy.

"I suppose so."

Everyone waited to see what else Billy might add, but nothing was forthcoming.

"Honey, there are a few details about recent events we left out," the professor told his wife, breaking the silence. "Details we need to tell you about now before we can make any decisions as a family."

"Oh, really," Rebecca said. "Three generations of Buckhorn men have kept a few secrets from me? Shocking."

Taking turns, the three provided Rebecca with all the believable and unbelievable elements of the Raven Stalker episode, the Horned Serpent's escape and recapture, Billy's conversations with the Sun Priest, and his out-of-body travels.

As the strange story unfolded, Billy's mother was, in turns, shocked, horrified, and downright skeptical.

"We knew you wouldn't believe most of it," James said. "That's one of the reasons we didn't tell you all of it. Plus, we didn't want to worry you."

"It's a lot to absorb and process," Billy's mother said. "It goes way beyond my medical knowledge." She paused for thought, then continued. "But I think the Sun Priest's melding with Billy may help explain the recent unusual physical growth spurts. If what you're telling me is the truth, there could be long-term effects."

Rebecca looked at her son. "As your mother, Billy, I think you're much too young to be involved in any of this. But I learned long ago that you're gonna do what you're gonna do, no matter what I say, think, or do. Now all I ask is that you think long and hard about your next steps. I'll support you whatever comes next."

She stood. "I've got an early shift at the hospital in the morning, so I'm going to bed, though I doubt I'll be able to sleep."

Before leaving the kitchen, the woman hugged her son, kissed her husband on the cheek, and patted her father-in-law on the shoulder. *These men are a handful,* she thought. Her mind was a swirl of worries as she climbed the stairs to the bedroom.

Suddenly realizing how tired he was, Billy excused himself and started to head for his bedroom. He knew he'd be thinking about all this late into the night.

"Let's invite the Lookouts for breakfast at the Sunrise Café in the morning," Wesley suggested. "Maybe we'll have something to tell them after we eat."

"Maybe" was all Billy could muster. "I'm going to sleep on it. See you in the morning."

He left the room, knowing, once again, his future was being discussed. He tossed and turned in bed. He was so excited about the possibility of spending time with Lisa and so unexcited about the possibility of having a part in some prophetic future. That sounded as though it carried a heavy load with a lot of responsibilities.

What the Lookouts described involved having many people counting on him to do just the right things at just the right times. Sure, the Sun Priest had essentially told him the same thing, but in the heat of the efforts to recapture the beast, it all sounded exciting. But now?

"It's decision time, Buckhorn," he told himself. "What are you going to do?"

Just then, the boy heard an older woman's voice call his name. He didn't hear it with his ears. He heard it in his mind.

Maybe it's Grandma, he thought.

He finally got his mind to quiet down and focus by humming the song that sometimes allowed him to leave his body. At the end of the fourth time through the melody, the vibrational energy reached the peak that freed him from his physical self.

He heard the sound of separating Velcro that signaled the separation as he rolled out and up. That was when the teen remembered Awinita's cabin in the woods near the river he'd seen one time before. He still had a burning question to ask her, so maybe now he'd have a chance.

He pictured the cabin by the river, and within seconds he was hovering above it. But there was a slight problem. He saw two versions of the place, one sort of superimposed over the other.

Why are there two? he wondered.

He moved toward the closest one and soon was floating above it. The gurgling stream could be heard not too far away, but there seemed to be some sort of translucent barrier surrounding the log cabin itself.

"Grandma," he called as he began to float closer to the front of the house. "Grandma, are you here?"

No answer.

As he approached the structure, he came in contact with the apparent barrier for a moment, but with a little pressure, he was able to pass through it.

Seeing what looked like a piece of paper pinned to the front door of the place, Billy moved onto the porch, coming to a stop within reading distance of the note.

Searching for clues to solve an old mystery, the note read. *Come inside and wait. I shouldn't be gone long. Awinita Walela Buckhorn.*

Billy thought the way the note was signed was a little odd, because his grandmother seldom used her maiden name, as far as he could remember. The teen only knew about it as a result of the family history his father had prepared a few years ago. Walela, which meant "hummingbird," was Awinita's mother's name, and Grandma had used it as her maiden name from time to time.

Billy stepped inside the house. As soon as he did, the door closed behind him on its own. It sounded like a vacuum seal had sucked the door shut, similar to the sound the cave door made when the Horned Serpent was imprisoned back in his holding cell.

Billy pulled on the wooden door, then pushed on it, but nothing happened. It wouldn't budge. He looked around the interior of the cabin but found it bare. Why would his grandmother's cabin be bare, even in the spirit world?

Suddenly, the cabin's floor and walls began to shake. The boards rattled and rumbled as the shaking made Billy fall. But he didn't hit a wooden floor. Instead he fell on desert sand.

Looking up, he saw that he wasn't inside the cabin any longer. He was inside a cage made of bones—bones that looked like human bones, which had been strapped together to create the bars of his cage. Human skulls looked back at him from every corner of his prison. He was literally trapped in a skeleton house.

What the hell? he thought.

He shifted his gaze to the area beyond the bone cage and found that he was no longer in a wooded landscape near a river. Instead he was in the middle of a barren desert plain. Something in the far distance seemed to be moving, but he couldn't tell what it was.

Had the cabin in the woods been a mirage?

Standing up, he grabbed the nearest set of bone bars and shook them. Solid. He moved to a corner of the space and tried again to shake the bars, but everything was tight and immovable.

Then a rattling noise from the distance attracted his attention. What he saw shocked him to the core. What had been almost out of sight before had now become close enough to recognize and register within his mind.

Trudging along the barren sandscape were dozens of walking human skeletons, and they were all coming toward him! They looked a little like the zombies he'd seen in a horror movie. He began to panic but remembered what he'd been taught about spirit travel.

Picture where you want to be, and stretch to go there.

He tried it, concentrating on his body back in his bedroom with all his might. But something was holding him back. Some external force had a grip on his nonphysical self.

What the hell? he thought for a second time.

Meanwhile, back in the physical realm, Wesley and James had finished up their discussions in the Buckhorn kitchen. Wesley was about to head home when he sensed something was off. Intuition told him he should look in on Billy.

"I think I'll say goodnight to Billy on my way out," the elder told his son. Walking the short distance to Billy's bedroom, he looked in the darkened space. "Billy, I just wanted to say goodnight. Are you asleep?"

There was no response, but Wesley still had that nagging feeling. His grandson was lying motionless in bed, so the elder moved closer.

"Billy, wake up," he said, a little concerned. "Billy!" he called more loudly. Still nothing. "James, can you come in here?" he called very loudly.

Billy's dad stepped in, and Wesley gave him a quick rundown of the situation.

"Maybe he's just so tired he slipped into a really deep sleep," James offered. To test that theory, Wesley pinched his grandson hard on the arm.

"My intuition says there's something wrong here," the elder said. He thought for a moment. "Billy may have done some spirit traveling and can't get back."

James really didn't understand that concept but was now as concerned as Wesley. "I'll get Rebecca," he said and bolted out of the room.

In a few minutes he came back with Billy's mom. After hearing that her son might be in danger and somehow unable to get back home, she made a suggestion.

"Call the Lookouts. They're a medicine family and might be able to help us."

"Good idea," James said. "I got Ethan's cell phone number. I'll call."

A quick call to the Lookouts got a quick reply. Fifteen minutes later, Cecil and his son knocked on the Buckhorn door.

"Lisa's on her way from the dorm," Cecil said as he came in carrying a leather medicine bundle. "We need all hands on deck."

"I'll put on a pot of coffee," Rebecca said and headed for the kitchen.

Everyone else moved into Billy's bedroom, where Cecil opened his bag and removed several ceremonial items, including an eagle feather fan, an abalone shell, a lighter, and a bundle of dried medicinal plants.

As Cecil unpacked and set up, Wesley gave him a condensed version of Billy's recent experiences with spirit travel, spirit communication, and other details.

"All of Billy's high-level spirit work may have drawn the attention of medicine people with bad intentions," Cecil concluded. "Some are jealous of the powers, abilities, and success of those working to do good in their communities. As the head of the Intertribal Medicine Council, I have encountered this type of sorcery before."

Cecil finished his preparations, and Lisa showed up, ready to help any way she could.

"Wesley, we are on your traditional lands, ready to work with your family in this serious matter," the Osage medicine man said. "Do I have your permission to use my tribal medicine to help your grandson?"

"Yes, with my blessing."

Cecil assigned Rebecca, James, and Ethan the task of concentrating loving, positive energy on Billy's body as he lay helpless in bed. Their goal was to create a protective bubble barrier around him so that no intruder entity could enter.

"Wesley, I want you to call on any and every medicine helper or spirit guide you have to come to us from wherever they are," Cecil said. "We need them here now in spirit to add their energies to this rescue effort."

Wesley moved outside in order to have the access and quiet he needed for his task. Standing on the front porch, he began singing the stomp dance song used to call the spirits of loved ones to the dance at Live Oak stomp grounds. He was primarily calling on Little Wolf and Awinita simultaneously.

Inside Billy's bedroom, Cecil gave his granddaughter a special assignment. "Lisa, it's time for Spider Woman to use her gifts to rescue this boy's spirit."

The girl knew exactly what her grandfather wanted her to do. She made her way upstairs in the Buckhorn house to a room directly above Billy's bedroom. It appeared to be an office, and she guessed it was the college professor's study. Sitting on a rug in the middle of the room, she mentally prepared to carry out her assignment.

Inside Billy's bedroom, at the foot of the teen's bed, Cecil began his own work, that of bringing Billy's soul back from wherever it had gone. This procedure was rarely needed, but it was something other medicine men had performed for other people whose souls had strayed. It would require a spiritual search for the boy's location within the vast nonphysical universe, with no guarantee of positive results.

Little Wolf was the first to respond to Wesley's outreach efforts out in front of the house.

The little man stepped out from behind an evergreen in the Buckhorn front yard. "Whenever I get a signal from you, old man, I generally also check for a signal from Billy," Little Wolf said as he came up the front steps. "But this time I can't seem to get anything from him. What's going on?"

Wesley gave him the rundown of the situation and asked about Awinita's status.

"She's been spending time with Franklin and helping him decompress from his military mindset. There's a lot of spiritual baggage to unpack there."

"We need Awinita on this immediately," the elder explained. "She has the most reliable connection to Billy. His physical and spiritual well-being are both in jeopardy."

Meanwhile, up in the second-floor study, Lisa began the process her grandfather had taught her for spirit travel as Spider Woman, a process handed down through generations of her tribe's medicine makers. The technique called for her to imagine herself to be a tiny spider.

Because of the intimate moment she'd recently shared with Billy, Lisa was better able to home in on the boy's whereabouts than anyone else. In her spider mind's eye, she saw Billy curled up in a ball on the sand-covered floor of a skeleton house.

Typical, she thought, recognizing the structure and location as something a Native sorcerer would employ to ensnare someone's soul. Her grandfather had taught her to recognize the telltale signs of the work of evil-doing tribal witches.

First, the girl shrank her spirit body down to the size and shape of a spider. Next, she made her way to the dome roof of the Underworld desert site located in a realm known as the Valley of Stalking Skeletons. Finally, she began her descent from the dome roof on her spider thread into the House of Bones, where Billy lay.

And not a moment too soon from the look of things.

She came to rest on the sandy floor and then transformed herself back into the recognizable appearance of Lisa Lookout.

"I've never been more glad to see someone in my entire life," Billy exclaimed. "How are you here?"

"It's a long story," the girl said. "One we don't have time for right now." She nodded toward the outside of the bone cage that zombie skeletons had begun climbing. The rattling of their bones against the bone bars created a very unsettling sound.

"If they reach the top middle of this cage, we won't be able to get out."

"Okay, what do we do?" Billy asked.

"You need to shrink down in size so you can hop on my spider back and we can crawl back up this spirit energy thread I've created."

"That's a new one on me," the Cherokee teen replied. "Why can't I just picture myself back in my own body? I tried, but it didn't work."

"No time to explain now," Lisa said. "We gotta get a move on."

Billy pictured himself the size of a housefly, but the clattering noise of the climbing skeletons made it hard for him to concentrate. The image in his mind wouldn't hold steady long enough for him to achieve his goal.

"It's no use," he complained to Lisa. "I can't concentrate."

Lisa focused on an image of her own, and momentarily, a bubble formed around her and Billy. The round, foggy barricade blocked out both the sight of the bony climbers and the unnerving sound of their rattling noise.

Now Billy was able to concentrate and hold the image of himself the size of an insect, and soon he recognized the stretching sensation as it began. Instead of streaking off to another location as he'd done before, he quickly shrank to fly size. In the meantime, Lisa had transformed back into her Spider Woman self.

"Here we go," she said, and up they climbed on the thread, which retracted behind them as they ascended. In a few seconds, the pair had escaped the death trap and emerged in a space above it.

"Now you can return to your body," Lisa said. "We'll talk about this when you're safely back in the physical."

A few seconds later, the physical Billy opened his eyes as he lay in his own bed. "Man, that was weird," he said after inhaling a breath of fresh air.

"Thank God!" his mother said.

"I say thank Lisa and her family," Billy replied as he sat up. Then, looking at Cecil, he added, "I have questions."

Kiss of the Spider Woman

Wesley had suggested they get a late-night snack a the local Del Rancho greasy spoon located a five-minute drive from the Buckhorn place. Billy, who suddenly realized he was starving, was all for it. The group of seven found an unoccupied corner table that was a good distance from other customers.

Billy ordered their famous steak sandwich supreme, while everyone else got less ambitious meals. Between bites of the gigantic sandwich, he gave the Lookouts an honest summary of his supernatural experiences to date.

"Oh, Grandpa, I forgot to tell you that when I was deer hunting on New Year's Eve, the animal I was about to shoot spoke to me mentally," the teen added. "He called me 'young medicine man.' I didn't shoot him, though he had given me permission."

Lisa, who sat next to Billy, patted his arm and said, "Don't let it go to your head."

Billy smiled, revealing a variety of sandwich particles clinging to his teeth.

"Okay, so explain to me what I just experienced, trapped in a cage made of bones in the middle of a desert that was all really nonphysical," he said before taking another bite.

"The House of Bones is an Underworld location tied to the Afterworld beliefs of a few different tribes, and casting the spell based on those beliefs is a classic move of a Night Seer," Cecil said. "They've operated in the shadows and under the cover of darkness since at least the days of the Sun Chief's reign—in league with the Snake Cult. No one knows how long they've been around or who they are, but they're a bad bunch."

"I've been hearing about the Night Seers of the Owl Clan since the time my wife and I began our medicine practice," Wesley said. "But I sort of thought their supposed abilities and exploits were just exaggerated tales spread by frightened Native people."

"Lisa, why don't you tell the Buckhorns about one of the facts we've learned about the spirit world and the afterlife since we got involved with the Intertribal Medicine Council," Cecil suggested.

"Whether you're a Native traditionalist, Baptist, Buddhist, or Baha'i, your beliefs about the spirit world and the afterlife can affect your experience in that realm after death." She paused to let that sink in before continuing. "Strong beliefs held by entire communities over several generations create areas in nonphysical realms that reflect those beliefs. When you add a strong set of fears to those beliefs, you have a powerful creative force that results in self-fulfilling prophecies, in a way. Thoughts are things over there."

"What happened to you, Billy, is the result of Native sorcerers with bad intent taking a part of the existing beliefs of a tribe and using it for their own evil purposes," Ethan added.

The Buckhorns sat quietly absorbing this radical new information for a moment.

"I suppose you have experience or proof or some way to verify this?" James finally asked.

"Yes, and it will be part of Billy's training if he decides to fulfill his destiny," Cecil replied. "The Night Seers' attempt to trap Billy's spirit means he's already on their radar and they perceive him as a serious threat, which is even more proof that he is indeed the one chosen by the Thunders in the prophecy."

For a long few seconds, the only sound heard among the Buckhorns and Lookouts was the clanking of plates being bused at a nearby table.

Billy broke the silence. "I've come to a conclusion," he said. "After everything I've been through, plus just now being soul-trapped by the worst group of medicine makers in Indian country, why would I consciously choose to become the main target for this bunch of evil-minded, soul-sucking shape-shifters? It sounds like a total suicide mission to me, and I don't want any part of it."

Everyone at the table immediately froze mid-bite, mid-drink, mid-whatever they were doing. Cecil looked to Billy's parents, who sat next to each other across the table. Each of them wordlessly examined the other's heart by searching to see what was revealed in their eyes. Then, together, they cast their gaze on their son, who sat across from them blissfully devouring the rest of his steak sandwich supreme.

With encouragement from Rebecca, James spoke for them both.

"We've long suspected that Billy would follow in his grandfather's footsteps on the medicine path," he said. "It troubled us a little, because we've seen what difficulties that journey brought to Wesley and Awinita, and no parent wants to see their child suffer needlessly."

He paused momentarily to gather his thoughts. "As Billy said, he's already suffered plenty: electrocuted by lightning, stalked and attacked by a dangerous shape-changing thing, and killed by bats. Brought back from the dead. But this new medicine path, this big, wide track your family is describing, is . . . well, it's not a path but more like a four-lane expressway—a highway to who knows what!"

James let out a big breath of air. His fatigue was obvious. "Sorry," he said. "My brain's tired."

At this point, everyone at the table was equally tired and emotionally drained. "Frankly, I'm very disappointed, but not surprised," Cecil said. "Your family has been through a lot, and what we're asking is a lot."

He stood, ready to exit the restaurant.

"We thank you for this meal and your kind hospitality," he continued. "We've taken up enough of your time."

He signaled to his son and granddaughter that it was time to leave. Lisa patted Billy on the arm, smiled, and rose to follow her grandfather, who had headed for the door.

Billy was in the middle of chewing his last bite of food and was taken off guard by the abrupt departure of his new almost-girlfriend. Grabbing a napkin, he wiped sandwich sauce from his face and attempted to follow the Lookouts.

James grasped his son's wrist and said, "Let 'em go. They probably need to have a private family meeting."

Billy wrested his arm from his father's grasp and angrily replied, "Well, I need to have a private meeting with my possible new girlfriend!"

Meanwhile, just outside the restaurant, Cecil told Lisa, "Work on him, Spider Woman. I think he'll come around."

That said, he and Ethan headed for their motel, leaving Lisa lingering near the Del Rancho entrance.

Within a few moments, Billy burst through the door, thinking he'd have to chase the Osage girl down the street. "Oh, Lisa, I'm glad I caught you!"

"Can you take me to my dorm?" she asked. "I need to get some sleep. My dad can take me to pick up my motorcycle from your house in the morning."

"Yeah, sure. My truck's parked out back."

As they drove south on Highway 62 toward Sequoyah High School, Billy was able to ask the questions he'd been wanting to ask.

"Okay, how do you know how to change your spirit self into a spider and drop down into a nonphysical landscape?"

"What, no questions about my favorite color, my horoscope sign, or my best-loved song?" she said with a sarcastic tone.

"You and I both know we're not that kind of people," he replied. "Our starting point is way beyond any of those topics."

"You're right. My bad." She sighed a big sigh. "Being Spider Woman is something passed down through generations of women in my Osage family. What you witnessed is really my only spiritual skill, born out of the necessity to keep our medicine makers safe."

"Where did the whole Spider Woman idea come from? You know I'm a tribal legend geek."

"One of our Osage creation stories says that Spider Woman left the Upperworld and descended through a hole in the sky dome until she reached the waters below. There she wove a web that became the earth's surface."

"Cool," Billy said and then told her the Cherokee story of how spider brought fire to humans.

"Also cool," she said.

"So, you've had to do that Spider Woman trick before? Free somebody from bone prison?"

"Only a couple of times up on the Osage Rez in northern Oklahoma. You were right about becoming a target when you're an effective medicine maker. That kind of danger comes with the territory."

Not wanting to pursue that line of conversation any further, Billy shifted to a cautiously worded prompting about their relationship as the pair passed the Cherokee Nation tribal headquarters. "So, I was wondering if we might talk about going on a date."

"What did you have in mind?" the girl asked.

"Well, I thought I might take you to Lake Tenkiller so you could see where I got struck by lightning," he said with a smile. "Or maybe go to the plant nursery where the Raven Stalker tried to murder me and my former girlfriend."

"How romantic," Lisa replied.

Just south of the tribal headquarters, Billy turned his truck left into the wide expanse of area called One Fire Field, a popular location for tribal events. He brought the vehicle to a stop in the midst of a grove of trees at the edge of the big vacant field.

After he killed the engine, Lisa asked, "Is this where you and your former girlfriend used to come and park?"

"No, actually, this is where my friend Chigger and I come every year for the cornstalk bow-and-arrow shoot during Cherokee holiday, for which I happened to win first place last year."

"Who or what is a Chigger?" Lisa asked, ignoring his brief brag.

"Oh, I forgot—you don't know about him. He's basically been my best friend since we were little kids. But lately, he's been acting kind of weird. And he's definitely the jealous type."

Lisa scooted closer to Billy on the truck's bench seat. "I can be too," she said in a low, soft voice. "So there'll be no more mention of your former girlfriend."

As she'd done at Billy's house earlier that night, Lisa reached up and cradled his neck in her hand, pulling him closer to her. Offering no resistance, the boy leaned in to receive her kiss, which turned out to be brief, shallow, and tentative.

Momentarily, a moving image flashed in his mind. In it, Lisa was dancing at a powwow in the women's style known as fancy shawl. What was unusual about the scene was that she was surrounded by butterflies that seemed to be mimicking her moves.

Lisa pulled back from the kiss and said, "I have to say I'm disappointed you've decided not to embrace your destiny and accept your role." She looked out the truck window at the darkened stand of trees around them. "But I understand."

Looking back at Billy, she gazed into his eyes. Taking a risk, she opened her heart and mind, allowing him to see deeply into her soul. There were worlds he wanted to explore in her eyes.

Then a switch seemed to flip in his mind. Maybe he'd been too hasty in his decision to reject the Lookouts' view of his role in the bigger picture, he thought. Maybe he and Lisa were part of a package deal. Maybe he was the one chosen by the Thunders.

As if she knew what he was thinking, Lisa pulled Billy back to her and caressed his lips in a slow, passionate soul kiss. The kissing continued, but thankfully, the butterfly movie didn't.

Later that night, alone in his bedroom as he was falling asleep, Billy felt like he was on top of the world.

The following morning, he was slow to get out of bed. As he lingered, his thoughts returned again and again to images from the front seat of his pickup truck and the amazing moments of intimacy he'd shared with Lisa, his new favorite person on earth.

I'll do anything to keep her in my life, he thought.

Just then a knock came on his bedroom door, followed by his mother's voice ringing out. "Billy, are you awake?"

"Yeah, Ma, fully awake."

The door opened a crack, and his mother's face peered in. "Enjoy your last few days of winter break. I'm headed to work."

"Uh, wait," he said. "Even though I made that big announcement last night, I'll probably still at least follow through with being Grandpa's medicine apprentice."

"Okay," she said. "Is that all?"

"If I do, I'm serious about not going back to school," he replied. "It'll be the GED for me. They give the test at the tribe's education office."

She opened the door wider and leaned against the doorframe. She was wearing her sharply pressed nurse's uniform. "Your father and I are still talking about that. It's not final, but we're sort of coming to the conclusion that it could *only* work if you spent half of your time with Wesley learning his doctoring methods while at the same time getting some real medical training, like an EMT. But we're not there yet."

This was an amazing bit of news. Billy sat up in bed. "What do you need from me to help you get there?" he asked with a hopeful look.

"Good question. I'll keep you posted." She began closing the door but paused long enough to say, "Don't stay in bed all day."

There was really no danger of that. Just after Billy's mom left the house, his cell phone rang. It was Chigger.

"I'm surprised to hear from you," Billy said. "I thought you were too busy for me these days."

"Ah, you know not to pay attention to what I say. I don't. One day I'm into one thing and the next day I'm into something else. What's new with you?"

"You probably won't be happy to hear that I have a new girlfriend."

Momentarily, there was silence on the other end of the line, followed by a knock on Billy's front door.

"Chigger, there's someone at the door," Billy said into the phone. "I'll call you back."

Billy ended the call and was surprised again. When he opened the door, Chigger was standing there.

"Good for you, dude," he said as he moved past Billy into the house. "Maybe I can meet her. I'm sure we'll become good friends. What's her name?"

Billy knew something was up with his friend. He'd never called him "dude" in all the years they'd known each other. And his prediction of future friendship with his girlfriend was totally out of character. On top of all that, Chigger's energy field looked even more fragmented than before.

"Lisa," Billy said. "Her name is Lisa Lookout. She lives in the Sequoyah dorms."

TMI, Billy immediately thought. *Too much information. Better hold off until I figure out what's going on here.*

"Whatcha doing, Chig? What brings you by this morning?"

"School starts back in another couple of days, so I thought we could hang out before we get busy with classes and homework and stuff."

"Sure. Why not?" Billy said. "But I'm supposed to go help Grandpa this morning and then have lunch with Lisa." After a short pause, the teen added, "Why don't you meet us for lunch?"

"I thought you'd never ask!"

Billy told his friend to meet them at the Taco Bueno south of Tahlequah at around half past noon. Lisa would be arriving on her motorcycle then.

The cell phone in Billy's hand rang, and he answered.

"Billy, I need your help right now!" Wesley said. "I've got a patient here who's been shot, and he refuses to go to the hospital."

"Okay, Grandpa, what do you need me to do?" Billy turned to his buddy. "Got to go."

Chigger had gotten what he needed, which was information about Billy's girlfriend and an opportunity to meet her, so he was ready to report to his medicine mentor.

"See you for lunch," Chigger said as he headed for the door.

With the phone still to his ear, Billy headed for his bedroom to change clothes while listening to instructions from his grandfather.

"I need hickory bark," Wesley said. "And lots of it."

"I know where there's a stand of hickory trees out on old Highway 62," Billy said. "I'll cut some and get to you as quick as I can."

Two minutes later, Billy was in his truck headed as fast as possible for the spot he had in mind. Arriving there in record time, he used the hunting knife he kept behind the seat of his truck to collect the pieces of bark Wesley had requested. Then the teen lead-footed it to his grandfather's house.

Rushing inside, Billy found the elder Jonas Jumper laid out on the dining room table, his worried middle-aged son, Junior, at his side. Wesley was applying pressure to a piece of gauze that had been wrapped around the elder Jumper's foot.

"What happened?" Billy asked as he handed the bundle of hickory bark to Wesley.

"Ah, the old man accidentally shot himself in the foot," the younger Jumper said with an impatient tone. "The bullet went clean through, but he shouldn't even be handling a gun."

"Go to the hall closet and bring back one of the used crutches in there," Wesley told Billy, and the teen exited the room.

Meanwhile, Wesley peeled off the inner layer of bark from one of the pieces Billy had given him and put a chunk in his own mouth. He began to chew. Within a minute or so, a thick paste had formed in his mouth. Temporarily lifting the gauze from the wound, Wesley spit the concoction from his mouth onto the two wound sites, one on the top of the foot and the other on the bottom. Then he replaced the gauze and wrapped it tightly with first aid tape.

The final step was to utter an incantation, the healing formula for gunshot wounds in the Cherokee language, four times in the four directions.

When he finished, Wesley said in a stern voice, "I'll tell you again what I told you when you came in the door. Go to the hospital and have the wound treated. If you don't, you could end up with a serious infection."

He repeated the warning in Cherokee to make sure the old man understood him.

As Junior helped his father up from the table, he replied, "Like I said, doc, he's never set foot in a hospital, and he refuses to do it now."

Billy returned from the hallway with a well-worn crutch, which he handed to the elder Jumper.

With the crutch supporting most of his weight, the old man pointed to Wesley and said in broken English, "Best doctor in whole Cherokee Nation."

Smiling, Wesley handed the rest of the hickory bark to the younger Jumper, telling him, "Chew a little of the inner bark a couple of times a day, put it on the wound, and then rewrap it."

"Will do."

Billy and his grandfather watched as the Jumper pair left the house.

When Chigger left Billy's house earlier that morning, he made a beeline for Carmelita Tuckaleechee's place, excited to report his first bit of reconnaissance news. His conscious mind wasn't sure what the rush was, but something in the back of his mind insisted it was urgent to do so. The boy had no choice but to obey.

"So, the boy wonder has a new girlfriend," the old woman said. "And she lives where?"

"In the dorms at Sequoyah High School," her apprentice replied.

"Good work, young Checotah," Tuckaleechee responded, her mind calculating the factors involved in devising and executing her next steps.

Retreating to the desk in the corner of her cabin, the conjurer consulted her collection of spells and formulas in search of a particular one she knew she had.

"I really must organize these pages better," the old woman muttered under her breath as she searched. "Oh, I'll look for it later . . ."

She returned to Chigger. "Now, I'm wondering if you're up to the task ahead," she said. "I shouldn't risk being seen out in the open, but the next step requires my supervision. We've got to dig some holes and bury some herbs in very precise locations."

"Whatever you need," Chigger said with pride. "I'm your man."

CHAPTER EIGHT

The Buckhorn Boy and the Lookout Girl

It seemed that each of the Lookouts had their own agenda to pursue with the Buckhorns. Lisa and Billy, of course, were beginning to enjoy what could become a long-term serious relationship. Cecil was determined to get Wesley to join the Intertribal Medicine Council and become one of the Keepers of the Sky Stone. Ethan, the archaeologist, wanted James's help in obtaining the Sun Chief's staff and cape on behalf of the Osage tribe and the Lookout family.

To further encourage Wesley's participation in the council, Cecil had offered to visit Billy's grandpa at midday so he could see the Cherokee medicine man in action.

Ethan had asked James to set up a meeting with the university's archaeologist, Augustus Stevens, and the three of them met for lunch at noon at a café on campus. The school's spring semester hadn't begun yet, but Stevens was working in his office, preparing for a special research project that would keep him out of the classroom for several months.

"I'm expanding my research to examine other possible mound locations along the southern Arkansas and Mississippi Rivers," Stevens explained to Ethan after they took seats at a corner table in the mostly empty eatery.

"Peter Langford at Spiral Mounds said you took possession of the staff and cape that belonged to my family's ancestor who is buried there," Ethan said. "As a Native American archaeologist directly linked to those burial items, I'd like to respectfully request to take possession of them."

"I completely agree with your right to claim those items," Augustus replied, "but I sent them out of state to a radiocarbon lab to have them tested and dated. As you know, the process can take weeks."

"We don't have weeks!" Ethan replied with alarm. "You don't know what's at stake here!"

Realizing his loud outburst had been noticed by people at tables on the opposite end of the café, the archaeologist lowered his voice. He looked at James.

"How much does he know about the supernatural aspects of the buried objects and Billy's potential role in the unfolding ancient prophecy?" Ethan asked.

"I'm well aware of Billy's supernatural abilities," Augustus answered for himself. "I witnessed the entire event when the Sun Priest's spirit inhabited Billy's body to recapture the Horned Serpent in the crystal cave."

Ethan looked at his two lunchtime companions in surprise.

"We've both made the transition from disbelieving academic materialists to full-blown subscribers to the deeper truths behind many Native American mythic cultural stories," James said. "And we're aware that we can't talk about any of it to anyone else."

Ethan considered this revelation for a few moments before continuing. "You really don't have to waste time and money on dating the staff and cape," he said. "They're a thousand years old. We know when Shakuru died and was buried."

"Do you have documentation that proves it?" Augustus asked.

"It's information passed down through generations of our family by means of oral histories, oral traditions," Ethan replied. "It's direct knowledge."

"Speaking professionally, you know that's not good enough," Stevens said. "Only scientific testing and reporting is acceptable in our field."

"But speaking believer to believer, there's more at stake here than mere archaeological standards," Ethan countered. "Creatures spoken of in countless Native American cultural stories may be walking the earth and terrorizing people once again within the next few months, and you are one of the few people in the whole wide world who saw one!"

As the significance of the Osage archaeologist's words sank into Stevens's mind, his eyes grew large. He looked at James. "You mean there might be more Uktenas out there?"

"That's why the Lookouts have come to Tahlequah," James said. "To recruit Billy to help them in some kind of standoff between good and evil, a sort of Native American Armageddon."

"Oh my god," Augustus said. "I had no idea." After a short pause, he asked, "How do the staff and cape figure into this scenario?"

"It's the staff, mostly," Ethan said. "The gem on the head of the staff is like a key that fits into a cosmic mechanism that sets ancient processes into motion. But it helps if the one using the key is wearing the falcon cape."

Ethan could tell by the blank stares on the faces of both James and Augustus that neither man had the faintest idea of what he just said.

“All right then,” Ethan said. “I’m going to trust you with another piece of the puzzle.”

Reaching into his back pocket, he pulled out a folded piece of paper, unfolded it, and laid it on the table. The central images on the page were two drawings of the Sky Stone. The top image showed the round object as it looked when all its parts had been assembled. Below that was an exploded view that demonstrated how the five pieces fit together.

“This sacred object we call the Sky Stone was created about a thousand years ago by a highly specialized spiritual craftsman at Solstice City—that’s what you now call Cahokia,” Ethan explained. “The craftsman worked for the Sun Chief.”

He handed the paper to Augustus for closer examination.

“Most of it is constructed from ordinary limestone,” he continued, “but the section at the center was formed from a meteorite that fell to earth the same day the Sun Chief and his twin brother were born, the same day the supernova of 1054 appeared in the sky, which was observed and noted by sky watchers in cultures all over the world.”

“That’s the origin of the Crab Nebula, the cloud of debris in space that is left over from the explosion, isn’t it?” Augustus proposed.

“Exactly right,” Ethan confirmed. “Our people interpreted its appearance as a significant spiritual sign from the Upperworld that conferred divine status on the twins. That was further validated by the descent of Sky Stones—meteors—the same day.”

“Where is this object now?” James asked. “In safekeeping somewhere, I would assume.”

“Actually, the five pieces that make up the Sky Stone are kept in five separate places,” Ethan said. “But back to how the gem on the staff relates to all this.”

Ethan paused to make sure his audience was keeping up. “The five-piece Sky Stone is the cosmic mechanism I mentioned before,” he said. "The gem fits into the center piece and activates . . . let's just say it will allow Billy to summon help that will aid in his crusade. Without that key, the world as we know it may be doomed."

The wheels in the mind of the university archaeologist began spinning. He realized there was more at stake than just the outcome of a lab test. He somehow needed to get the staff and cape back from the lab he'd shipped them to. But how?

"If I request the return of the items, this university and the lab will consider it highly irregular," Stevens said. "In fact, that sort of action will be looked upon by the whole academic archaeology community as unprofessional and improper."

"I know exactly what you mean," Ethan replied. "Archaeologists are often an egotistical bunch of bastards who think they have the right to exhume the remains of Native Americans and dissect them in the lab—no offense. That's why I appreciate your refreshing attitude. So, what can we do?"

The three men in that little university café decided to put their heads together to devise a plan.

As this lunchtime conversation was taking place on the university campus, Billy and Chigger waited in a booth at the Taco Bueno restaurant south of town. Lisa was running late, and Chigger, for some reason, was becoming anxious.

"I thought you said she'd be here at twelve thirty," he complained. "Is she really coming, or were you just shining me on?"

This is really odd behavior, Billy thought. "Relax, Chigger. She'll be here. What's the rush?"

Chigger didn't really know why he was in a hurry to get this over with or why he was anxious about it. But for some inexplicable reason, he needed to take a picture of Billy and Lisa together and then leave. But he did realize he needed to stop pressing Billy about it.

"No rush," Chigger replied, attempting to cover his anxiety. He took a sip of his iced tea. "I guess she'll get here when she gets here."

Changing the subject, he talked a few minutes about the used pickup truck and cell phone his parents had unexpectedly given him for Christmas.

"Cell phones are great to have," Billy replied, "but there are so many dead zones around here where you can't get a signal. Our satellite phone works much better. Too bad the marshals didn't loan us two of them."

Just then, Lisa came through the door.

"Sorry I'm late, guys," she said, giving Billy a peck on the cheek. "I'm on the dorm improvement committee and our meeting ran long."

"Lisa, this is my friend Chigger I told you about."

"Glad to meet you," she said as she sat down next to Billy.

"Same here," Chigger replied and immediately took out his phone. Turning on the camera, he pointed it at the couple.

"Smile for the camera," he said. "I want to get a picture of the happy couple!"

Billy and Lisa moved closer together and smiled, though Billy was still troubled by his friend's odd behavior. His friend clicked off a couple of shots.

Before anyone could say anything else, Chigger looked at the clock on his phone and said, "Oh, look at the time. I've gotta get going!"

He slid off the booth seat and stood to go.

"I thought you said there wasn't a rush," Billy commented.

"I totally forgot that I'm supposed to go to Carmelita's for an apprentice session. You two have fun."

Chigger was gone in a flash, leaving Billy with many questions. Lisa could see the puzzlement on her boyfriend's face.

"Chig's been acting unusual lately," the boy said, answering Lisa's unasked question. "I don't know what's going on with him."

Meanwhile, Cecil and Wesley were comparing tribal medicine practices at Wesley's house when the phone rang. Wesley picked up the call after the third ring. It was his old Eastern Cherokee friend Bucky Wachacha, on the line from North Carolina, who also happened to be on the Intertribal Medicine Council.

"*Osiyo*, Bucky," Wesley said. "How are things among the Eastern Cherokees?"

"Strange," the old Indian answered. "We could use some help over here."

He proceeded to explain the Tlanuwa sighting, the abducted dog, and the disappearance of other small creatures from the area over the past few days.

"One other thing," Bucky said. "I'd like to meet your grandson. Cecil Lookout's family says he might be the One."

"Cecil just happens to be visiting me right now," Wesley replied, convinced that the phone call's timing was no accident. "My grandson and his granddaughter are becoming very close."

"A match made in the Upperworld, I would think," Bucky concluded.

Wesley was silent for a moment as he thought of a way to encourage Billy to travel with him to visit the Eastern Cherokee medicine man. Then he remembered something.

"Is that cave in Alabama with the Cherokee syllabary writing on the walls still open to the public?" he asked.

"You mean Manitou Cave?" Bucky asked.

"That's the one," Wesley confirmed.

"Yes, and more popular than ever since our tribe's archaeologist made a YouTube video there. 'Talking Stones,' he calls it."

"Good," Wesley replied. "I've been trying to figure out a time Billy and I could come see it. I guess now's the time. I'll let you know when we can come over."

After ending the call, Wesley called his grandson to tell the boy about the cave and a possible trip to visit their distant cousins in the original Cherokee Nation. And that evening, he joined Billy at the Buckhorn home to make the case for allowing the teen to miss the opening days of the school semester, and possibly skipping school altogether.

Wesley had suggested that Billy remain silent while the elder did the talking.

"This will be a valuable lesson in the history and culture of our people," the elder argued to James and Rebecca. "And he could begin studying for his GED exam while we're on the road."

"You're really serious about this GED thing, aren't you, old man?" James said. "Rebecca and I haven't had time to discuss it fully."

Wesley paused to collect his thoughts. "I believe if you make him go back to the classroom, you'll be denying him his destiny," he said with an emphatic tone. "If half of what the Lookouts told us is true, then Billy is *the* key factor in all our futures."

"Does that mean you're going to accept Cecil's invitation to join the Intertribal Medicine Council?" James asked his father.

"Yes, it does."

Billy was surprised to hear this.

James pulled a folded piece of paper out of his back pocket and handed it to his father. "Take a look at this," he said.

Wesley unfolded the paper and saw the Sky Stone image that Ethan had shown James and Augustus at lunch.

"Ethan explained that the man you'd be replacing on the Medicine Council died mysteriously and his piece of the Sky Stone has gone missing," James reported matter-of-factly. "They suspect foul play."

He let that fact sink into the minds of his listeners.

"That's the level of danger you'd be stepping into," he continued. "And Billy would be stepping into that same level of danger, or greater, if he accepts the role the Lookouts talked about."

"I've finally come to believe this is what I was born to do," Billy said abruptly and to everyone's surprise.

The teen stood and leaned against the kitchen counter.

"All my life," he continued, "whether you knew it or not, all of you have been preparing me for this moment. Bullseye, Grandma, Grandpa, Mom, Dad—even Uncle John in his own way—have been pointing me in this direction, pushing me to use my life to make a difference."

"But you said—" Billy's mother protested.

"I know what I said before. I didn't really understand what all this was leading to or how important it was. Now I think . . . I'm accepting this as my destiny, and I'm going to commit to carrying it out, wherever it leads, whatever it means."

All were quiet for a few moments.

"I'm going with Grandpa to see the cave," the teen said with authority, "and when we get back, I'm going into full-time medicine training with Grandpa and Cecil."

"Stubborn and rebellious," Billy's mother said, looking at her husband. "See how your son is?"

"You *will* eventually have to take the GED exam," James said. "Do it for me, please."

"And me," Rebecca added.

Billy nodded as Grandpa stood.

"I promise I will," Billy told his parents.

"I think we should leave day after tomorrow," Wesley said. "That gives us time to pack and let people know we won't be around here for a few days."

"How long will it take to get there?" Billy asked.

"The six-hundred-mile drive should take about twelve hours. We can go in my truck and take turns driving."

That was that.

Later that night, Billy made a video call to Lisa to give her the news about the cave trip and his decision to ditch school for full-time medicine training.

"Wow, that was sudden," she said. "You didn't say a word about the cave trip or your decision at lunch today."

"You're right. It does seem sudden. I think I already knew what I was going to do, but it took Grandpa announcing out loud tonight that he's going to join the Medicine Council for me to voice it, to commit to it, too."

"Did I—"

"Yes, you definitely played a part in that decision," Billy said. "I think you knew what you were doing."

Lisa's sheepish smile told Billy all he needed to know.

"Will I see you tomorrow?" Lisa asked, already missing Billy.

"Of course. Just tell me where and when."

"Tomorrow's my first day back to class, so I'll text you when I figure out my schedule." She paused, then added, "I think you and I are going to have a very meaningful and unusual relationship, Billy Buckhorn."

"I totally agree, Lisa Lookout," he replied. "I like the way our names sound together, Billy Buckhorn and Lisa Lookout. The world had better *look out*, because here we come!"

They laughed freely as they thoroughly enjoyed each other's company, even if it was only on the phone during a goodnight conversation.

After leaving the Taco Bueno earlier in the day, Chigger headed straight to a nearby QuickPrint location in downtown Tahlequah, where he, as instructed, was able to print out four copies of the photo he'd taken of Billy and Lisa. Then he took the printouts to his mentor's cabin at Buzzard Bend.

"Excellent work, my young apprentice," Carmelita said with a smile as she absent-mindedly stroked Chigger's back as if he were a pet cat.

Then the conjurer looked at her rolltop desk across the room and hurried—appearing to her apprentice to smoothly glide without taking a step—to it. As though in some altered state, she seemed to command physical objects to do her bidding, thrusting open the desk's curved top with the touch of a finger, effortlessly removing her aged medicine book from a drawer, rifling through the pages without actually touching them in search of the right spell . . . until the correct page suddenly revealed itself, causing the book to fall open on that page.

Using her ancient forefinger as a guide, Carmelita quickly scanned the lines of handwritten text on the yellowed pages.

"Here it is," she uttered under her breath.

"To Cause Conflict and Confusion" were the Cherokee words written on the page.

She picked up the book and carried it to the table near Chigger.

"The Buckhorns and the Lookouts cannot be allowed to join forces," the old woman said in a raspy whisper, not to Chigger so much but seemingly to other unseen listeners. "We all know they must not be allowed to build an alliance. The boy's escape from the skeleton house proved that."

Finishing that discourse, she looked at her apprentice. "We have an important job to do at midnight tonight. Can I count on you?"

"I guess so," Chigger said with hesitation in his voice. "I'll have to sneak out of the house." Building up courage, he added, "But I don't seem to be learning anything about Cherokee medicine making. When does that begin?"

Annoyed, Carmelita realized her apprentice was coming out from under the spell again. Fortunately, she'd already prepared a stronger concoction to extend the desired effect. Reaching her hand into a bowl filled with a dark purple powder, she grasped a bit of the stuff in her palm.

"I first had to test you to make sure you were totally trustworthy," the old woman said, moving closer to her protégé.

Leaning toward the boy's left ear, she acted as though she was about to whisper something there. Instead, she blew a puff of the powder into that ear.

"What was that?" Chigger asked, surprised by the move. He brushed some of the powder away.

"Medicine for your mind," the conjurer replied. "This will help to unclutter your thinking so you can more easily tune in to my thoughts."

"Okay," Chigger said. "Now what?"

Carmelita projected a thought into the boy's mind: "Now I'm sure of your commitment to the medicinal arts, so tonight is the night your true instruction commences."

"Tonight's the night," Chigger said with a smile. "I heard that in my mind!"

"Tonight's the night," she repeated aloud with a gleam in her eye.

Chigger had no trouble sneaking out of his family's mobile home before midnight, and because he'd parked his pickup away from the trailer, he had no trouble driving away without waking his mom and dad.

One part of his mind realized it wasn't normal for him to slip out of his house in the middle of the night, but an overriding subconscious command demanded that he do so. During the last few days, he'd performed several tasks while in the same condition. This night was no different.

Sequoyah High School was located south of Tahlequah, less than a mile from the Cherokee Nation tribal headquarters. This Native American school with under five hundred students consisted of several buildings, including the dormitory.

Chigger turned into the entrance of the high school campus and drove to the back of the property near the football field so his truck wouldn't be seen from the main road. As planned, Carmelita was waiting for him, though Chigger didn't see any car nearby she might have used to get there. She carried four small leather pouches, two clutched tightly in each hand.

"Did you bring a compass?" she asked, forgoing any friendly greeting.

"Yeah," Chigger replied, "and the small spade you wanted from my dad's tool shed."

"Good, good, good," the old woman said. "Now let's get to work before anyone comes along to interrupt."

Standing near the dorm building, the conjurer instructed her apprentice to locate due east on the compass. The pair walked a few yards in that direction and stopped.

"Dig a small hole here," the conjurer commanded.

"What for?"

The boy heard her response in his mind: "Just do it."

The teen dutifully dug the hole and, at about a foot deep, Carmelita told him to stop. Then she dropped one of the pouches into the hole.

"Now shovel the dirt back in."

Chigger, though having no idea what this was all about, did as he was told.

The duo repeated this procedure at the other three compass points several yards away from the dormitory building.

"What's in the pouches?" Chigger asked after filling in the last hole.

"Never you mind, sonny," the witch said.

"You told me I'd really start learning some Cherokee medicine tonight," the boy said forcefully.

Exasperated, Carmelita blew out a breath of air. "When you're right, you're right," she admitted. "Okay, here goes. You know those photos you printed of the Buckhorn boy and the Lookout girl?"

"Yeah."

"I ripped those down the middle, separating the two, and then I performed the 'conflict and confusion' formula over the girl's half. After that I prepared the dried herbal blend that accompanies that spell and placed the torn pictures and herbs into the pouches. Burying the pouches in the four directions around the place where the girl sleeps will achieve the desired effect—eventually, not right away."

"Conflict and confusion? But why?"

"For one thing—and you should appreciate this—these steps will cause this couple to break up. The other thing is part of a bigger plan that I'll soon be able to share with you."

Chigger's disappointment was apparent on his face.

"But I *can* tell you that you, young man, will be part of a history that people will be talking about for generations to come."

"That sounds important," he replied, changing his disappointment to pride.

He again heard a message from Carmelita in his mind: "Now let's get out of here before we're discovered."

Chigger had a thought of his own. *I guess I can really read people's minds! Way cool!*

Carmelita chose not to share her next thought with the boy. *Your simple little mind is so easily fooled. This is going to work out great.*

CHAPTER NINE

The Conjurer's Complaint

Back at her cabin later, Carmelita Tuckaleechee used a step-stool to reach a top shelf and take down the scrapbook she'd kept for more than a hundred years. Reminiscing about her younger life was one of the few pleasures she'd allowed herself in recent times. But it had been a while since she had perused the tattered, brittle pages that reminded her of the glory days.

The conjurer hadn't lived 147 years without some help. As a Cherokee witch of the Night Seer variety, she'd hastened the demise of more than one seriously ill victim in all that time.

That was how it worked, that was how you got to cheat death, or at least outrun him for a while.

Born in 1874, the woman had seen a lot of history in her time. Of course, she'd gone by a different name in the early days: Kituwah Redbird. Later, and for much of her life, she'd been called Svnoyi Waya, Night Wolf. Carmelita Tuckaleechee was a very recent name change, and one she quite liked. The name had such a staccato rhythm to it.

She had been only eighteen when Cherokee outlaw Ned Christie was murdered by US Marshals in 1892 for a crime he didn't commit. It was big news at the time. Christie had been a proud member of the Keetoowah Society, made up of traditional Cherokees who fought for traditional culture and tribal sovereignty against the encroachment of white citizens on Indian lands. He became a folk hero among the Cherokee, both because of what he lived for and what he died for.

That was when the young woman realized the white man's laws were prejudiced against Indians, and she took the name Kituwah Redbird, after the famous leader of the traditionalists, Redbird Smith. She also decided white people couldn't be trusted, and neither could the white man's medicine. She began learning medicine ways from a famous Keetoowah Society medicine maker named Waholi (Eagle) Catawnee.

It wasn't until years later that her feud with the Buckhorns began, during the lifetime of Moytoy Buckhorn, the Rainmaker. Known for his ability to control the weather, Moytoy was adept in other areas of Cherokee medicine, including the power to block the conjurations of dark medicinal practitioners. He'd successfully reversed a few of Night Wolf's best spells.

Then there was Bullseye Buckhorn, not a particularly gifted medicine man but bothersome to Night Wolf just the same. He was best known as the "Stickball Doctor" because stickball teams he ritually blessed often won their games. Losing to Bullseye damaged the reputation of any medicine person who dared oppose him.

And now, to add insult to injury, Bullseye's son Wesley Buckhorn possessed Benjamin Blacksnake's medicine manual! This rarest of volumes contained the only known written remnants of the ancient and highly secret Owl Clan incantations. The problem was that these spells, when recited backward, could not only reverse the effects of their magic but put an end to the Night Seers altogether. No living medicine person had that knowledge, but

Billy Buckhorn's expanding powers might one day allow him to discover the powers of the old language.

That was why Wesley and his grandson needed to be dealt with as soon as possible. And that was one of the reasons Carmelita was so interested in Chigger. This teen, she thought, was actually a twofer. First, he provided direct access to the Buckhorns, and second, he had the potential of bringing new, young blood to the Owls—that is if he proved smart enough to learn the medicine.

Most of the current crop of Night Seers were probably as old as Carmelita, but as old as they were, they wouldn't live forever. So they needed to attract some younger members. True, the boy really wasn't too bright, but if Carmelita was patient, the teenager might be able to deliver her long-sought-after target, Wesley Buckhorn.

For ten years, Night Wolf had been carrying a very big secret. The witch had been successful in poisoning Wesley Buckhorn's meddlesome wife, Awinita, with a deadly plant that left no trace of its presence. That do-gooder had blocked Night Wolf's medicine magic too many times, so she had to be dispensed with.

Carmelita turned a few of the aging pages in the scrapbook until she came to one of her favorites. It showed her in her Night Wolf days, with the love of her life, Benjamin Blacksnake. They had lived happily together in the Eastern Cherokee Nation for several years. He had been her mentor, teacher, friend, and partner in the Owl Clan. That was until the locals rose up against him, dragged him out of his home, set him on fire, and burned him alive.

Carmelita's thoughts were interrupted by the gong of the alarm on her lunar calendar wall clock, a timepiece that tracked the phases of the moon. The chime reminded her that the moon had just entered its new-moon phase, the darkest stage of the satellite's monthly cycle.

Time to contact Benji, she thought. *I hope I can get through to him this time.*

To make contact with the ghost of Benjamin Blacksnake, all the woman had to do was open the large lead safe that stood in the closet at the back of the cabin and retrieve the black Aztec obsidian mirror she'd owned for more than a hundred years.

After using her well-memorized combination to open the safe, 3-9-13-15, Carmelita pulled on the door's brass handle. Seldom used, the portal to her personal vault resisted being opened but finally gave way.

Resting on the middle shelf was an ornately carved wooden box with a metal clasp. The old woman took the box and carefully carried it to the table in the middle of the cabin. Before sitting down, she unhooked the clasp and opened the lid, revealing a round object about twelve inches in diameter covered with a black felt cloth.

The box also held a small, folded metal easel, which Carmelita removed and unfolded. Then, after peeling away the black cloth, she admired the round, highly polished disk of black obsidian that had been created long ago by Aztec magical priests south of the border.

Each of the thirteen members of the Owl Clan possessed just such an object, though many of those were manufactured more recently. Carmelita's had once belonged to her long-dead beau Blacksnake, and he'd used it for the same purposes she was about to.

In the 1300s, the Aztecs of Mexico had used these polished obsidian mirrors to contact the spirits of the dead, and members of the Owl Clan used it for that purpose too. But the Night Seers had also adapted the object for an additional purpose, that of contacting other members of the clan who were all very much still alive.

But first things first. She'd reach out to Benji's ghost, which had been confined to the Shadow Zone, a layer in the Afterworld closely associated with entities like himself. All who resided there had been trapped by their own negative vibrational energy and the envy they harbored for those still in the flesh.

To magically transform the disk from mirror to spirit communicator, its owner merely had to recite the spirit vision incantation while applying a specially processed oil concocted from bilberry leaves and rattlesnake venom. This incantation had to be vocalized in the old Nahuatl language of the Aztecs, not an easy tongue to master.

Carmelita followed the steps necessary to activate the mirror. Then she closed her eyes and visualized Benjamin in her mind, not the shriveled-up old man others thought of but the young, vivacious man she'd known in her younger days. But alas, just as before, all she could see in the mirror was a faint, grainy, distorted image of the medicine man.

She blamed the youngest Buckhorn for her soulmate's current condition.

"Blasted Billy Buckhorn!" she screamed into the dark night. "You will pay for this!" Carmelita was all too painfully aware of the Raven Stalker incident last fall when the troublesome teen had foiled Benji's efforts to fully reincarnate in the form of the Ravenwood gym teacher. Sucking the soul from that Cherokee girl would've been the final glorious step of the process, and then Carmelita and her beloved could have been together once again in the flesh.

But a Buckhorn had interfered yet again, projecting Benji even deeper into the lower vibrational zone. What psychic barriers had been put between him and her? How was she ever going to see Benji again in this lifetime?

Carmelita was now so distraught she abandoned her plan to contact the head of the Night Seers in Montana, Thomas Two Bears. She was in no mood to interact with the Northern Cheyenne conjurer, because she'd have to tell him of her failure at imprisoning Billy Buckhorn in the House of Bones.

The hag gently rewrapped the black mirror in the velvet cloth and closed it up in the box. She was tired, and her very old bones ached. She would drink the blue-green liquid that helped her sleep. Maybe she would be lucky enough to dream of Benji this night.

CHAPTER TEN

Portals to the Underworld

The following morning, Billy began preparing for his trip to Manitou Cave with Wesley. He threw some clothes in a suitcase and hoped they'd still fit him the following day when they explored the cave. He made sure to include a flashlight and fresh set of batteries. And finally, he coiled up the cord to his cell phone charger and stuffed it in a side pouch, because he had to stay connected to Lisa at all times.

Billy's mom and dad had already left for work, so the teen was surprised to hear someone calling his name from the front of the house. He was further surprised to find Wesley and Cecil standing in the living room waiting for him. Billy recognized the aging leather medicine satchel his grandfather held at his side. The elder Lookout carried his own similar carrying case, the same one he'd brought to help rescue Billy from the skeleton house.

"Your grandfather told me of your decision to skip school and take up the medicine path full time," Cecil said. "I'm here to perform a small ceremony for you and your grandpa to welcome the both of you to the fold of the Intertribal Medicine Council. We'll do a proper full-scale ceremony later in the presence of the entire council."

"All right," Billy replied, ready to participate. "What do I need to do?"

"Just stand next to Wesley while I smudge you."

The Osage elder removed his eagle feather fan from the satchel, along with an abalone shell, a short sprig of prairie sage, and a lighter. After lighting the tip of the sage, he placed it in the shell and fanned it. As the sweet-smelling smoke rose from the shell, he moved closer to Billy and Wesley. He began singing a song in his language and then wafted the smoke over both of them, top to bottom, front and back.

Having participated in smudging ceremonies before, Billy used his hands to gather some of the billowing smoke to his heart area and head. Wesley did the same. Cecil patted both of them in several places with the eagle fan as if to compress some of the smoke into their bodies.

Billy was quite surprised to visibly perceive the purifying effects of the sage's smoke on his grandfather. It was as if the energy field of the smoke was purging little bits of negative debris from Wesley's energy field. Billy had learned that the smoke from sage had the ability to cleanse a person, a room, or a whole house. He was now able to witness that in action.

When he'd finished the ceremony, Cecil ended his song and said "A-ho" loudly, which Wesley and Billy repeated.

"I love burning sage," Billy commented. "It smells and feels clean." He took in a deep breath.

"We'll induct Wesley into the Medicine Council first," Cecil said. "Then, as I said, we'll perform a complete ceremony and sweat lodge for Billy with all thirteen members of the council and begin his training."

"When will that happen?" Billy asked.

"Middle of January," Cecil replied. "That gives everybody time to wrap up anything else they're doing before we plunge headlong into our shared prophetic future. There won't be time for much of anything else once we start."

Cecil began putting the eagle fan and other ceremonial items back in his carrying case. Billy hadn't really thought about what his future would look like, but Cecil just painted a very vivid picture of an all-engulfing experience.

"Won't be time for much of anything else," Billy mused out loud as the concept sank in.

"I hope you two have a good trip to the east," the elder added. "Ethan will join you at the cave because there's a new development there. But he'll tell you all about it when you arrive."

Billy was still trying to wrap his mind around Cecil's view of his future as the elder shook his hand and left.

"I've got patients to tend to," Wesley told Billy. "What about you?"

"Today's my last day to spend time with Lisa for a few days, so I'm going to connect with her at some point." He checked his phone for messages. "She was supposed to let me know when she had some free time, but I haven't heard from her."

"Ah, the impatience of young love," Wesley said with a chuckle. "See you first thing in the morning. You need to be all packed and ready to go."

"I will be," the teen replied as he followed his grandpa out the front door.

Billy quickly drove the three short miles from his house to the Sequoyah High School campus. He, of course, hoped to track down Lisa, but he wasn't sure how to do that.

Entering the main building, Billy explained his mission to the receptionist sitting in the front office. The middle-aged Native woman was working at her computer.

"What's your relationship to the student?" she asked, barely looking up.

"I'm her boyfriend," he answered.

"I'm sorry—only blood relatives may contact students during class hours."

"But I'm going out of town tomorrow, and she said she'd let me know when and where we could meet up today."

The woman finally looked at Billy and seemed to recognize him. "Best I can do is pass a message along to her." She pulled out a pad of paper and pen from her desk drawer and handed them to Billy. "Fill out the 'to' and 'from' parts and then write your message."

Billy blew out a breath of air in frustration and hastily scribbled a message. He wrote, *Came to see you. Hope to connect today. Leaving with Grandpa early tomorrow.*

He handed the pad back to the receptionist.

"I'll be sure to put this in her mailbox in a little while."

Billy was not at all convinced she actually would follow through.

To kill some time, he headed to the Tahlequah Walmart to look for a book that would help him study for the GED exam. He bought the only one they sold, a paperback manual called *The GED for Dummies.*

We'll just see who's the dummy after I sleep on this book and ace the test, Billy thought as he left the store.

Back home, he busied himself by finishing his packing for the trip to the cave, charging his cell phone, and thumbing through the GED book. Finally, his phone rang. It was Lisa.

"I was beginning to worry," he said after hearing her voice. "Are you all right?"

"I've felt out of sorts all day—like I woke up on the wrong side of the bed or something. Then I got turned around on the way to my math class and couldn't seem to get oriented."

"That doesn't sound good," Billy replied. "Can I come see you? You know I leave in the morning."

"I think I'm just gonna lie low, go back to my room, and try to sleep it off."

"I'm going to miss you," Billy said in a mournful tone.

"Don't get all weepy on me now. I'll see you soon enough."

The call suddenly ended.

That's odd—first Chigger, and now Lisa. What is going on?

He tried to put it out of his mind and focus on the road ahead, the future as Cecil had painted it.

"No time for anything else," he said out loud.

Next morning, he said quick goodbyes to his parents, slurped down a cup of coffee, and gulped down a homemade breakfast burrito. When Wesley pulled up out front and honked the horn, the teen bolted out the door and climbed in the truck.

"Ready for a new adventure!" he said, burying his worries about Lisa.

Then, using a combination of the GPS maps on his phone and Wesley's well-worn printed atlas, Billy charted a course to Manitou Cave that allowed them to intersect the historic Cherokee Trail of Tears in several places in Arkansas, Tennessee, Mississippi, and Alabama.

Among other things that Wesley noted during the drive, he pointed out that the names of all the states they'd be traveling through were derived from Native American words. In fact, the elder was literally an overflowing font of information about the history of the forced removal of the Cherokee people in the 1830s and the creation of the Trail of Tears National Historic Trail in 1987. He said a part of the congressional funding to establish the trail also helped to begin preserving several landmarks and waypoints that played a part in the tragic journey.

Unlike most teenagers, Native or otherwise, Billy was actually interested in hearing everything his grandfather had to say about the history of his people. To him, it was way more interesting and meaningful than just reading about it in a book.

About halfway through their drive, the pair stopped in Memphis, Tennessee, to get a bite to eat and put gas in the truck. Studying the maps to see what was up ahead, Billy found historical markers at a few places along the trail where Cherokees died on the arduous journey.

"Can we stop at a couple of these markers?" he asked after taking his last bite. "I just want to see what those places feel like."

"Of course," Wesley answered. "I can fill your head with facts about our history, but sensing our past with your heart will make a deeper, longer-lasting impression on you."

There were several locations where the road they were driving on ran parallel to or crossed the actual path walked by thousands of Cherokee adults and children. At one such crossing point, Wesley parked the truck, and the two of them walked a stretch of the trail. A row of leafless trees flanked the trail on either side, and the barren winter branches gave the area a somber feel. The setting sun added to the already dark mood of the place.

Billy closed his eyes and concentrated as he walked to see if he could pick up any traces of the spirits of the people who'd passed that way almost two hundred years ago. He was startled when he began hearing the sound of footsteps shuffling through the fallen leaves that lay on the ground.

Opening his eyes, he was surprised to see the dark shadow figures of dozens of people of various sizes, shapes, and ages moving along the trail. Maybe his eyes were playing tricks on him in the growing evening darkness, but the sadness that accompanied the figures was unmistakable. Billy wanted to ask his grandpa about what he was experiencing but decided to wait until they were back in the truck to discuss it.

Then the teen came upon a gravestone that had been erected next to a large ancient tree with a large exposed root system. Reclining with his back against the tree was the ghost of a Cherokee man. Billy, of course, was growing accustomed to seeing spirits and ghosts and such.

He approached and tried to communicate with the man, who was unable to perceive anything outside his own sphere of grief.

The ghost, however, seemed to be communicating a mental message to Billy, almost as if he were part of a historical display that performed a memorized set of lines to tell his story.

Billy tapped into the ghost's mind and heard this message:

"The day came on us cold and hard, another in a seemingly endless stream of days. How many had there been since they'd forced us Cherokees from our homes? I cannot remember. How many more would there be until we arrived at our destination? No one would tell us. The blue-coated soldiers merely prodded us along. Bayonets drawn. Rifles at the ready. Day after day.

"As torturous fatigue racked my ravaged body, my restless mind raced back to revisit a question whose answer I already knew. What crime had we committed that deserved such punishment as this? To be removed from our homelands and driven like dogs elsewhere, to an unknown land they called Indian Territory?

"We'd tried our best to be like them. We dressed like them. We ate like them. We built our houses like them. We taught our children to speak their language. And all for naught. What crime had we committed? I'll tell you. We had the audacity to live, to persist, upon lands coveted by the white man. And so, our fate was sealed.

"My thoughts having drifted, my attention momentarily diverted, I tripped on a bare root exposed by the steps of thousands of Natives who'd passed on this trail before me. My useless, soggy moccasins no longer did their job, and pain shot up from my bloodied, swollen foot right to the center of my brain. A cry of exhausted agony escaped from my throat as I stumbled.

"In my attempt to remain upright, I took a few rapid, awkward steps, a movement the nearest infantryman misinterpreted.

The butt of his rifle found its mark on the side of my head and rendered me unconscious.

"How many hours have passed since that blow? I know not. I find myself alone now, propped up against this tree whose roots betrayed me. A fellow Cherokee must've taken the time, at peril to themselves, to arrange me thus. But they are long gone, as are the others of my kind. All that's left is a westward trail of dragging footprints left in the light snow that has fallen upon the wooded landscape.

"Night will overtake me soon, and with it an unsympathetic frost. Why would I even try to go on from here? To this tract of land, I now stake my claim. Home *and* grave it shall be, and none but my brethren shall know my name.

"In these, my final hours, I know that the soldier's bayonet would've served me better. With no fire to warm me, and only the memory of my deceased wife and children to comfort me, I will be frozen before sunrise. No matter, for soon I will join my family in the afterlife. As my soul journeys westward to the land of the dead, perhaps I will pass by the living line of Cherokees headed in the same direction.

"There being no word for goodbye in my native tongue, I will simply say what any Cherokee says when departing. *Donadagohvi*—'Till we meet again.'"

When the verbal message in Billy's head ended, he was at a loss to understand what he'd just experienced or what mechanism was at work that allowed him to hear this well-educated man's dying thoughts.

The teen stepped over to the stone grave marker and read aloud the words that had been etched into its surface. "Here lies an unknown Cherokee male who died on the Trail of Tears in 1838."

Back in the truck, Billy rode in silence for miles—he didn't know how many. Finally, after turning onto Route 35 east of Huntsville, Alabama, on the last leg of their journey, Wesley spoke.

"Billy, I know you don't realize this, but from what I've seen, you are becoming . . . no, you *are* the most intuitively sensitive person I've ever known. Most medicine people have been given one or two gifts they use to help people, to heal them, to set them on a good path, or to hear and understand what they're going through. But you . . . you have been given *all* the gifts, all the tools ever needed to heal, transform, and restore the minds, hearts, and bodies of hurting people."

"That's a little over the top, isn't it?"

"No, it isn't," the elder quickly replied. "But there's a very real danger you have to protect yourself from."

"I'm listening," Billy said.

"That kind of sensitivity means you may absorb the sadness, the illness, and the difficulties of the people you come in contact with," Wesley explained. "I haven't done a good enough job of teaching you how to guard against this happening, to guard against being sucked into the depression, the sickness, the worries of your patients."

"Okay, what do I need to do?"

"Well, the first thing is you can't make yourself completely open and vulnerable to other people's problems. I know it's a little confusing. You must be open enough to sense what their ailments are, but you can't be so open that the ailments come into your energy field and begin living there. They'll take you down with them."

Wesley pulled the truck over to the side of the road and told Billy to get out and stand beside it. Then he opened up the back of the camper shell and grabbed his leather medicine bag.

"I should've smudged you like Cecil did before we set foot on the Trail of Tears site and then again before we left it," the elder said. "My bad. The older I get, the worse my memory is."

He pulled out a plastic bag containing a bundle of herbs, a lighter, and a large seashell. The bundle featured lengths of dried sage, braided sweetgrass, and sprigs of cedar tied together with lightweight strings. As he set the lighter's flame to the bundle, he waited until the herbs caught fire.

"In addition to cleansing you, when combined, these sacred medicines can prevent the intrusion of negative energy and remove it as well," Wesley explained.

The elder repeated the smudging ceremony much the same as Cecil had performed it the previous day.

"Better?" Wesley asked when he'd finished.

"Better," Billy confirmed.

Billy felt lighter and less sad as they covered the last ten miles of their journey, which took them to the Mountain View Motel on the east side of Fort Payne, Alabama. After checking into their quaint and aging motel room, Wesley showed Billy a local map that depicted the nearby mountain and the cave they would visit tomorrow.

"I think you'll be interested in this," Wesley said, pointing to a spot on the map. "The name of this mountain we're sleeping next to is Lookout Mountain! What a coincidence!"

"It must be a sign," Billy said with a smile.

"A sign of what?"

"A sign that it's time for me to call the most important Lookout, Lisa."

"Ugh!" Wesley responded. "Please go outside if you're going to get all gushy with your girlfriend. I don't want to hear it."

The smile on his grandpa's face told Billy that he was teasing, but Billy did indeed step outside their motel room's door to make the call.

"Today has been a mental and emotional roller coaster for me, and I don't know what's going on," Lisa said on the phone. "So ignore me right now. I should have it sorted out by the time you get back. In the meantime, be safe."

She ended the call abruptly, but the teen was relieved that she sounded a little improved since yesterday. After plugging the phone in to recharge, he dug out his GED study book and laid it on his pillow.

"Hope this still works," he said as he rested his head on the not-so-comfortable substitute pillow. "Goodnight, Grandpa."

The elder was already fast asleep.

That night Billy dreamed about the Sun Priest or Sun Chief or whatever his name was. There hadn't been any sign of the spirit man since the Horned Serpent was recaptured in the cave. Billy, however, continued to have a sense that he and Shakuru were connected. But how?

In the dream, Billy walked along the spiraling path at Spiral Mounds that led to the mound in the back. He somehow had X-ray vision and could see through the dirt into the mound where the bones of the Sun Priest lay and had lain for a thousand years. What the teen hadn't paid any attention to before were the four other sets of human bones also buried in the same mound.

The boy looked up and saw the translucent spirit of the Sun Priest floating above the mound. Around him floated the four assistants who had originally helped Billy leave his physical body.

"I need to show you something," Shakuru said.

He pointed to a silver-looking thread that connected his energy body to the underground collection of his bones. Then he pointed to the four assistants, who had no such thread attaching their spirit bodies to their buried skeletons.

"As you can see, I am still tethered to my bones," Shakuru said.

"How did that happen?" the teen asked.

"The witches of my brother's Snake Cult cast a spell at my death that prevents me from moving very far from my bones," the Sun Priest said. "The Snake Cult and the Owl Clan were closely aligned in those days."

"What about your assistants?"

"The five of us were in the middle of an annual sacred ceremony that aids the souls of the departed as they make their way along the Path of Souls after death," the priest said. "My assistants—

spiritual warriors, really—bravely sacrificed themselves trying to defend against the assassins who attacked."

The spirit man answered the next question Billy was about to ask. "My loyal aides stayed at my side down through the ages even though they could've left at any time," he said. "I'll be eternally grateful. That's how they were able to guide you to Solstice City in your dream vision. They can travel anywhere."

Billy sent his feelings of admiration to the four assistants, who, in turn, communicated their willingness to be of service to Billy if ever called upon.

"Now for the reason you're here," Shakuru said. "I think you may be able to break the spell and free me from the tether."

"Me? How am I supposed to do that?"

"I don't know, but I've seen you in action. You can figure something out, I'm sure."

Unexpectedly, Billy's dream began to dissolve like it was being eaten away at the edges.

"Free me, Billy," the spirit man continued to say. "You'll need my help in the coming battle for Middleworld."

That was the last thing Billy heard before everything went black. He awoke, sat up in his motel room bed, and looked around. Had the Sun Priest really spoken to him? Wesley snored away in the other bed, and Billy didn't want to wake him. But how was the teen going to free the Sun Chief's spirit? He came to the conclusion that he'd have to talk to Cecil about that, and soon.

At about the same time Billy had his dream, a creature of ancient and unknown origin was making its way toward the tiny Native American community of Bogue Chitto located on the Mississippi Choctaw reservation in the eastern part of the state. The beast resembled drawings found in caves from the Great Lakes of Michigan down to caverns in Alabama and Mississippi. The images depicted it with the head and paws of a big cat, horns like a deer or buffalo, and scales with daggerlike spikes running along its back and tail.

Known to devour any human or animal it came in contact with, the creature was the terror of the ancient Mississippian Mound Builders. It was believed to be one of the lords of the Underworld and in perpetual conflict with the Thunderbird and other powers of the Upperworld.

Newly reawakened, this wild thing was answering the call of a Night Seer named Willy James of the Mississippi Choctaw Nation as it darted and dashed through the wooded countryside. The old man, one of the thirteen shape-shifting Owls, had grown tired of waiting for "the right time," as the leader of the Owl Clan had called it. Willy felt he had the right to conjure the creature anytime he damn well felt like it. What could Thomas Two Bears do about it anyway?

So what if the beast had been spotted by civilians outside the town of Tuscaloosa, Alabama, and reported on the TV news? That just heightened the fear factor in the public's mind, which was part of the point of reactivating the old Owl Clan and reanimating the dwellers of the Underworld.

"People who claim to have seen the strange creature give conflicting descriptions of it," the white news anchor reported on the TV that Willy James watched on his screened-in porch. "Those who've seen it from the front say it has a face like a mountain lion and horns like a bull steer. Others who saw it running away claim its back and tail carry lizard-like jagged spikes. My question is, What have these people been smoking or drinking to cause such vivid hallucinations? Has the government put something in our water? Or is there really a menace roaming our streets? Stay tuned to WBMG-TV for updates."

Willy cackled with delight to see modern-day white folks confused and scared by the ancient mysteries of Native America.

"You're gonna get what's coming to ya, and it's long overdue," he said, addressing imagined members of mainstream Anglo-American society through his TV.

He turned off the TV and headed to the back of his five-acre property, which sat along aptly named Owl Creek, to check on the readiness of the accommodations he'd prepared for the approaching beast. Oral traditions regarding the successful care, feeding, and confinement of the wild thing had been preserved and passed down for at least thirty generations, maybe longer.

At the Mountain View Motel the following morning, Billy woke up ravenous. As he sat up in bed, he rubbed his left ear and the side of his head, not sure why they hurt. Then he remembered the GED book he'd slept on.

Picking the paperback up from his pillow, he thumbed through it until he found the first set of sample exam questions. If he could answer one of them, he'd confirm that he could still study by sleeping on a book. He read one of the math questions.

"Jimmy can run at a pace of six miles per hour. Running at the same rate, how many miles can he run in ninety minutes?"

No answer popped into his mind, so he tried picturing the page that revealed the answers.

Still nothing.

Uh-oh, he thought. *It doesn't work anymore. It worked after the lightning strike last September. It's been a few months. Does that mean all my abilities will eventually fade?*

Seeing that Wesley was waking up, Billy said, "Looks like I'll have to study for the GED the old-fashioned way—reading the book while I'm wide awake. Yuck!"

The pair quickly dressed and ate a hearty breakfast at the nearest diner. Then they drove the three miles to the cave site.

"I forgot to mention that admittance to Manitou Cave is by appointment only," Wesley said as they neared their destination. "So we're meeting the site manager at the site. And I also forgot to mention that a few other folks in addition to Cecil's archaeologist son will be joining us this morning."

"It seems like 'I Forgot' has become your middle name on this trip," Billy commented a little sharply, then caught himself. That was no way for him to talk to his grandfather, even though he was now a little apprehensive about the whole trip. "Who are the other people? I thought this was supposed to be a private grandpa-grandson event."

"You'll see soon enough" was all the answer he got.

From the main road, Wesley turned onto a narrow lane named Cave Street. Three Native men and a white woman were huddled around a gated entrance in the side of the base of the mountain. Billy easily recognized Lisa's archaeologist father, Ethan, as one of the men.

As Wesley parked his truck, the woman was pointing to the metal bars that were meant to block the entrance to the cave's mouth. The bars appeared bent and mangled on one side. Wesley removed two flashlights from a side pocket of the driver's-side door. He handed one to his grandson.

As they approached the cave, the two Oklahoma Natives could tell that the group was very upset by what they were observing. A closer examination of the misshapen bars revealed that they had been twisted outward from the inside, like something in the cave had pried them apart and escaped.

"Mr. Lookout," Billy called as he neared the cave. "What's going on?"

Ethan looked back to see Billy and Wesley approaching. "Actually, it's Dr. Lookout, but please call me Ethan." He then gestured toward the younger man standing nearby and said, "This is Bear Samuels, the historic preservation officer and archaeologist for the Eastern Band of Cherokees."

Bear stepped forward and shook hands with Wesley and Billy.

Ethan introduced the other man. "This is Cherokee ranger Joseph Saunooke from the Great Smoky Mountains National Park."

He, too, shook hands with the new arrivals.

"Finally, this is Ms. Anne Renard, managing director of the Manitou Cave site."

She, likewise, shook hands with Billy and Wesley.

"Each of these people has a key part of the incredible story of what's going on here and elsewhere in the traditional homelands of the Cherokees," Ethan explained. "But what's more important right now is the discovery made a couple of days ago here at the mouth of the cave."

"Ethan, why are you here?" Billy asked. "Did Lisa send you to check up on me?" He smiled to let the man know it was a joke.

"No, she doesn't know I'm here," Ethan said. "I was on my way to Oklahoma Choctaw territory to investigate the death of one of our Medicine Council members when Bear notified me of the issue here at the cave."

"Ethan and I have worked together on a couple of projects over the years," Bear said. "He's been wanting to see this site for himself for a long time, because there are Mound Builder–related inscriptions in the deepest recesses of Manitou."

Billy walked over and examined the twisted metal closely. It was apparent that a very powerful someone or something had done the mangling. He reached out and touched one of the deformed bars and immediately got a mental image. He tried not to display a reaction to it.

What he saw he decided not to share just yet, because it didn't seem real, and he wasn't even sure what he was seeing. Wesley was the only one in the group that knew Billy well enough to realize the youth had seen something. It was only a small facial movement, but the elder had seen that reaction before.

"We'll have to have this security gate repaired, but in the meantime, I see no reason to cancel your planned visit to the cave interior," Ms. Renard said. With the help of Bear Samuels, she swung the damaged gate open. "Bear will serve as your guide this morning. I have to get back to my office to get someone out here to fix this."

Bear turned on the flashlight he was holding, and everyone else did the same.

"Wesley, I have to thank you for calling to set this little tour up for your grandson," Bear said before entering the cave. "If you hadn't, we might not have discovered this problem with the security gate for weeks. No one comes out here in the winter. It's still a mystery to me why someone would want to break into the cave."

"No one broke into the cave," Billy said. "Something broke *out* of the cave."

The group of men stopped dead in their tracks and looked at the teen.

"What makes you say that?" Joseph asked.

"When I touched the twisted metal, I saw an image in my mind of what caused it."

Ethan opened a binder he was carrying and began thumbing through the pages.

"How is that possible?" Bear asked.

Having found the page he was looking for, Ethan thrust the binder toward Billy. "Did it look anything like this?" he asked.

Billy took a look at the photo Ethan was indicating. It showed a drawing done on a cave wall with some kind of red paint. It depicted a strange four-legged, long-tailed animal with the face of a mountain lion, a pair of horns, webbed claws, and sawtooth spikes running along the length of its back and tail.

"That's it!" Billy exclaimed. "But what is it exactly?"

"Underwater Panther," Ethan replied. "A supposedly mythological beast that appears prominently in Mississippian Mound Builder cultural sites. Those people are the ancestors of the tribes we know today, including the Cherokees and the Osage. This cave, and others in the region, were used for ceremonies, because caves are portals to the Underworld."

"Where did this cave drawing come from?" Bear asked, indicating the image in the binder.

"Deep within the recesses of this very cave," Ethan replied.

"I've only visited portions of the cave within a few hundred feet of the opening, the ones bearing the Cherokee syllabary inscriptions," Bear said. "I've never seen this."

"This drawing, and others like it, come from the cave's dark zone," Ethan said. "The deepest parts where light never reaches. Billy, I have a lot of information and insights to share with you when you begin your training."

"Right now we'd better get a move on if we're going to see the Cherokee inscriptions," Bear advised.

Wesley and Ethan followed Bear as he led the way, but Joseph pulled Billy aside and told him about the Tlanuwa sightings near the Eastern Cherokee Nation. The teen immediately lost interest in seeing the Cherokee inscriptions in Manitou Cave. He wanted to get a glimpse of the giant bird with the metallic wings as soon as possible.

As Billy toured the cave with the others, his mind kept attempting to assemble the pieces of a puzzle that was just forming. Tying the discovery of the Horned Serpent last November in the crystal cave together with the evidence of the Underwater Panther he'd seen just now, along with Dr. Lookout's statement about portals to the Underworld, led him to a frightening new possibility.

Does that mean that every cave in North America harbors one or more of these supernatural Underworld creatures? Does it also mean that in the very near future an unknown number of these beasts might be stalking and terrorizing inhabitants of the continent?

Billy literally shuddered to think of it.

CHAPTER ELEVEN

The Foul Fowl

On the same day Billy and Wesley had begun driving toward Manitou Cave, Cecil headed southeast toward Tuskahoma, Oklahoma, the original capital of the western Choctaw Nation. The historic tribal council house, built in 1884, still stood at the northern edge of that tiny rural community.

His mission was to further investigate the death of Choctaw medicine man Elmore Proctor, one of the longest-serving members of the ITMC. As Ethan had reported to the council, Proctor died during the autumn. His piece of the Sky Stone had still not been found. That was a serious problem, given what apocalyptic events would soon unfold.

Hearing of the Osage elder's planned trip, Billy had immediately offered Cecil the use of his own truck, which the boy wouldn't need since he and Wesley were using Wesley's truck to drive to the cave.

Cecil knew there were three types of medicine people among the Choctaw, each with his or her own set of skills and knowledge.

Proctor was an *aleckchi*, a healer, similar to Wesley, who used medicinal plants and incantations to help heal patients. Cecil also knew that it was highly likely that a *hoshkona*, a Choctaw witch, had killed Elmore.

Not accustomed to using GPS apps to obtain directions, the elder relied on a precise set of instructions he'd gotten from Elmore's wife, Yimmi, over the phone. Around midday, Cecil made his final turn on to Ninepine Road and crossed over the Kiamichi River south of Tuskahoma. The Proctor home, an old frame house with a screened-in front porch, was a mere stone's throw from the river.

Elmore's granddaughter, Ellie, came to the door when Cecil knocked.

"I'm Cecil Lookout with the Intertribal Medicine Council," he said as the door opened. "I've come to visit with Yimmi. Is she home?"

"Yeah, she's expecting you," Ellie said as she invited the elder in. "She's in the front room next to the fireplace. Can I bring you some coffee?"

"Yes, thank you," Cecil said as he walked into the house, which smelled of fry bread grease and roasted corn.

He found Yimmi—a thin, frail dark-skinned woman—wrapped in a Pendleton blanket and seated close to a roaring fire. Old frame houses like this one, built before insulation was a regular part of home construction, made it hard to keep out the cold.

After some initial small talk and a few sips of coffee, Cecil got to the point of his visit. "My son Ethan came to visit you shortly after your husband died," Cecil said. "Do you remember?"

"Yeah, I remember. He said he came on behalf of your Medicine Council, but I didn't know him, so I wasn't gonna talk to him."

"I'm sorry it's taken me so long to come see you," Cecil said. "But I'm here now. Can we talk?"

"Yeah, I know you, and I know Elmore would want me to talk to you about medicine."

"Good. That's real good. Can you tell me about what was happening during Elmore's final days? I heard he got sick."

"Elmore was the healthiest man I knew," she replied. "Never sick a day in his life. He doctored his patients almost till the very end."

A couple of coughs interrupted her story.

"Can you tell me about his symptoms when he got sick?" Cecil asked.

Yimmi took a few swallows of coffee before answering. "It started with stomach cramps, and then the runs and the heaves hit him. He got headaches, got to feeling dizzy. It was somethin' terrible."

"Did he try doctoring himself or go see another doctor?"

"You know he could never doctor hisself. He said the medicine didn't work that way. I even called in a white doctor from town, but he couldn't do nothing."

"Anything else?" Cecil asked.

"Well, after a few days of all that, I swear he got to feeling better." She paused. "Then, boom! He took a turn for the worse. It's like his inside body parts quit working all at once. Two days later he was gone."

Cecil thought about all Yimmi had said and came to a conclusion. "It's all the classic signs of mushroom poisoning," he said. "Not just any old mushroom either. Death cap mushrooms have that name for a reason."

"We don't generally eat mushrooms, and he didn't eat any I'm aware of," the elderly woman observed. Then she had a realization. "Come to think of it, there was an old Indian woman staying at the Kiamichi RV Park just down the road who called Elmore and asked him to come doctor her."

"When was that?" Cecil asked.

"The day before he started puking. She was from out of town. What was that woman's name?" She tried to remember but couldn't.

"Anyhow, Elmore said she'd given him a few dollars and a couple of cups of coffee that tasted a little funny."

"She could've put a sprinkle of dried death cap mushroom in that coffee," Cecil said out loud as he realized what might have happened. "Well, I'm just as sorry as I can be for Elmore's passing. He was a good man and a good friend."

Yimmi remembered one more thing. "He gave me somethin' to pass along to you," she said. "I'll be just a minute."

The old woman got up and walked slowly to a back room, then returned a few minutes later.

"Near the end, he musta lost his mind, 'cause he wasn't making a lot of sense." She handed Cecil a piece of lined yellow paper, torn from a notepad. "He said I should give you this, but what he wrote here—it don't make no sense."

Cecil examined the paper. It contained four lines of writing, recorded with a shaky hand by a man who knew his days were numbered and believed the secret he held was vital to the world's future. Cecil read the words aloud. "Peace waits for those who know. Take counsel at the house to the north. Kneel at the foot of red warrior. Leave no stone unturned."

He thought about possible meanings. One thing jumped out at him as a clue. Cecil knew the historic Choctaw Council House was north of where he now sat.

"Yimmi, could I borrow this? I'll get it back to you. It could help me find Elmore's piece of the Sky Stone."

"I never heard about this Sky Stone until after Elmore got sick. My husband never said nothin' about it before then. But a couple of days after he passed, a young Native fella came here claiming to be Elmore's medicine apprentice. He said Elmore wanted him to take it and protect it."

"You mean someone was here asking about it back then?" Cecil said with worry in his voice. "Did you show this paper to that man?"

"No, of course not. Elmore said to only give it to you. Hell, my husband ain't had no apprentice for a long time," Yimmi said. "He'd been complaining for years that he can't find no young ones to teach. They ain't interested in the traditional ways." She paused as she remembered another detail. "Your son came a few days later, and he was asking about it too. At the time, I didn't know what it was all about or who to trust."

"Like I said, I'm so sorry I didn't get down to see you sooner," Cecil replied.

Cecil once more offered condolences to Yimmi on behalf of the Medicine Council before leaving her home, and then he headed north toward the historic Choctaw Council House. He'd seen it once before on a previous visit with Elmore but had never been inside, and if his hunch about Proctor's coded message was correct, his piece of the Sky Stone was buried on the grounds.

Five minutes later, he pulled into a parking lot on the north side of the red-brick building. Nearby, within walking distance, was an outdoor amphitheater, a Choctaw souvenir store, a cultural center, and a stickball field.

As he approached the front of the council house, which now served as a tribal museum, he saw a tall bronze statue of a Native man holding a bow and nocked arrow. The sculpture was surrounded by a circular brick wall.

Cecil walked along the paved sidewalk that encircled the wall and statue until he came to a bronze plaque on one side. Above the plaque were large bronze letters that read *Tuska Homma: Red Warrior*.

"Aha!" the elder exclaimed.

He reread the last two lines of Elmore's note. "Kneel at the foot of red warrior. Leave no stone unturned."

He noticed that the sculpted warrior was bracing himself in a half-kneeling position on a large stone with a slanted top. Cecil looked around to make sure no one was watching before he tried climbing up and over the brick wall. But the task proved too much for the eighty-year-old man.

"Time to call in backup," the elder said to himself.

Walking back to the truck he'd borrowed from Billy, he made a call to his son Ethan on his cell phone. The call went straight to voicemail, and Cecil knew his son was probably in an area with poor cell phone service. He left a message.

"Ethan, I know you're busy over in Alabama, but I found an important clue about a possible location of Elmore's piece of the Sky Stone. Call me when you can."

After leaving the message, the elder returned to the truck and picked up a well-worn map of Oklahoma he'd brought. He found Spiral Mounds Archaeological Site on the map and calculated that it was less than a two-hour drive to the northeast.

Couldn't hurt to pay a visit to the bones of my ancestor, he thought. *Thank goodness Billy discovered the whereabouts of those bones.*

He started the truck and headed for Route 271 and the Oklahoma historical site now known as the Spiral Mounds Ceremonial Complex.

Meanwhile, after they left the Manitou Cave site in Alabama, the four-hour drive to the town of Cherokee, North Carolina, took Billy and his grandpa directly through the heart of traditional Cherokee territory. The wooded, mountainous terrain was thick with tribal legends and lore, formed over the course of hundreds of years and shaped by mysterious encounters and experiences in the vast countryside.

Park ranger Joseph Saunooke had given the pair written directions to his uncle Bucky Wachacha's house on the reservation, a typical modest red-brick home built through a federal housing program for Indian reservations. Joseph met them at the front door of the house and invited them inside.

To Billy, Bucky seemed like an older version of his own grandfather but with fewer teeth. The wiry old man, wearing a red plaid shirt and overalls, sat in a well-worn overstuffed chair, watching, and laughing at, a black-and-white rerun of *I Love Lucy* on a big flat-screen television. His wide-mouthed laughter revealed more than a few gaps in his dental structure.

"Uncle Bucky, they're here," Joseph announced loudly. "The boy who came back from the dead and his grandfather."

Bucky immediately turned his attention to the pair as they approached him. Grabbing the remote control, the elder clicked off the TV.

"*Osiyo*, my Cherokee cousins," he said brightly. "I'm honored that you've come."

"We are the ones who are honored to be in your home," Wesley said as he shook his elder's hand. "This is Billy. He's the one you've been wanting to meet."

Bucky shook Billy's hand but didn't let go. "Cecil says you're the real deal," the elder said, looking into the teen's eyes and pausing. After a moment, he continued. "I can see it in your eyes. You're kinda young for the job, but I guess you're all we got."

Billy didn't know exactly what to make of that statement and kept quiet.

"I'm going to take them straight up to the Smokemont Campground," Joseph told Bucky. "Maybe they'll have a chance to see the Tlanuwa for themselves."

"The last few generations of our people said the prophecy was just a fanciful old Indian tale," Bucky said. "But I never gave up on it. And now I believe the time has come. We can't escape it, so we have to face it. Hope you're up to it, young man."

"Hope so too, sir," Billy replied.

After bidding the old man farewell, Joseph drove Billy and Wesley to the campgrounds, because the enormous bird was still hanging around the nearby Oconaluftee River.

"We never found that kid's dog, so we posted a warning that campers should leave their pets at home," the ranger said. "Some people didn't listen, and their pets went missing as well."

He led them along the hiking trail that ran along the river, the same trail where Corky had been abducted. Since they were hunting a wild animal, Billy switched his mind to hunting mode, just as he'd have done if he were hunting deer with a bow back home in the eastern Oklahoma woods.

A deer spoke to me just a few days ago, Billy thought. *Maybe this thing will too.*

As they moved quietly down the trail, the teen scanned his surroundings, sweeping his eyes from the river, up the mountainside, to the cliffs, and into the sky. It wasn't long until he spotted the cave Joseph had mentioned earlier.

"That's where the nest is?" Billy asked.

Before Joseph could answer, Billy saw the head of a very large bird peek out from the cave. Everyone froze in place.

Billy sent a thought in the form of a question to the bird: "What are you, and how are you here?"

The bird stuck his head farther out and looked down. Seeming to see Billy, the metallic fowl squawked several times. This is what Billy heard in his mind: "Obey Yonaguska. Wait for master's signal. Inhale the fear. Take control. Conjurers rise."

Billy was stunned by the message. Was it real or just his imagination? He told the others what he heard.

"The only conjurer named Yonaguska I know of died a few years back," Joseph said. "Amos Yonaguska. At least I thought he died. He was really old."

"Why don't you try communicating back?" Wesley suggested. "Maybe you can tap into the creature's connection to the conjurer."

"It's worth a try, I guess." Billy projected questions from his mind to the bird: "What signal do you wait for? What will you take control of?"

An immediate troubling reply came to Billy. "Wait for call of the Owls. Rule Middleworld."

Billy again reported the response to the group.

"This is serious," Joseph said. "We have to tell Bucky." Then he remembered that Wesley and Billy were now part of Bucky's inner circle, that they would be directly involved in whatever response there would be to the bird's dark message. "Wesley, what should we do?"

"Get prepared," Wesley said. "Billy—"

"I'm way ahead of you, Grandpa. Some kind of battle is coming, and we've got to do our part. Time to get back and begin my training."

Just then the Tlanuwa released an ear-piercing squawk and catapulted himself from the cave. Folding back his metallic wings, he swooped down toward Billy and the men. The two men scattered for cover in opposite directions, while Billy stood firm where he was.

Again projecting his thoughts, the teen spoke to the bird. "I forbid you to harm me or my companions. Take your talons and fly away down the river."

Surprisingly, the giant fowl changed direction midflight, spread his huge copper-colored wings, and turned upriver. His penny-hued claws glinted in the sunlight as they skimmed the water's surface.

Glancing back at Billy one last time, the bird sent this parting thought: "You and I meet again soon. Many friends will join me then."

Billy now had complete confirmation that big, bad things were yet to come.

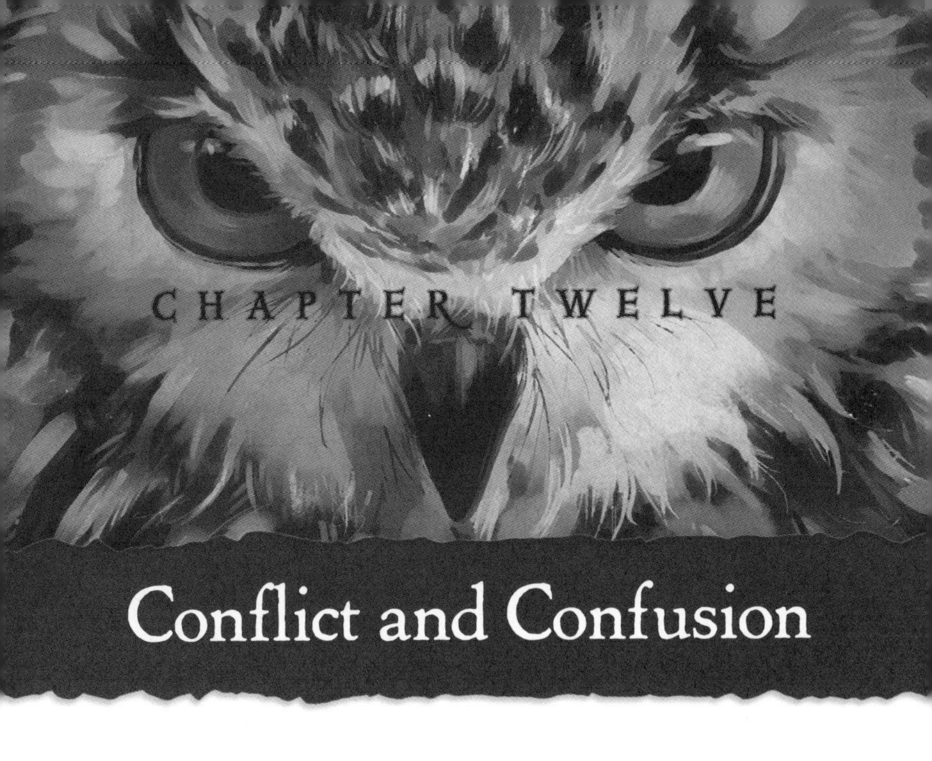

CHAPTER TWELVE

Conflict and Confusion

Lisa had awakened the past couple of mornings in an odd mental fog. Her dorm room at Sequoyah High School seemed unfamiliar, and she had trouble coming fully awake. True, she'd spent the last couple of nights worried about Billy, waking at odd hours with the sense that someone was watching him closely.

Once her boyfriend had been rescued from the House of Bones, he really hadn't given the experience much thought. But Lisa knew he had just declared his total dedication to the medicine path and was still not convinced the decision had made him a target. The truth was he was now on the radar of dark tribal medicine forces that would like to see him fail or, worse, succumb to darker impulses.

From her experience as the granddaughter of the head of the Intertribal Medicine Council, Lisa knew that some nearby purveyor of the dark arts had cast the skeleton spell on Billy. And quite possibly that same witch had Billy's girlfriend in their sights as well.

Maybe a ride will give me a chance to clear my head, the girl thought. *Skipping one day of classes won't hurt.*

Bundling herself up in warm clothing, Lisa grabbed her riding gloves and helmet before leaving her dorm room. Her motorcycle was parked just outside the girls' dorm, chained to a bike rack. Once she'd removed the protective tarp and unlocked the chain, she was ready to ride.

On a map, she'd seen a wildlife management area in the wooded mountains south and west of the campus but had never had time to check it out. That was where she was headed today.

It was only a twenty-minute ride down Highway 62 to reach the turnoff to the entrance to her destination, and the brisk January air would've cut through her clothing if it weren't for the full-body thermal undergarment she had on beneath it.

As she rode deeper into the wilderness, the cracked paved road became more of a narrow gravel trail. Tire tracks in the trail told her that many four-wheel ATVs had passed that way before her, but there were no other visitors to the wildlife area today. Twists and turns in the path followed the contours of the landscape through the shallow mountains, and the mixture of pine and oak in the forest made for an interesting combination of bare branches and evergreen needles among the trees.

Lisa began to feel generally better as her ride unfolded, as if a fog in her brain was lifting. When she reached the summit of a hill with a scenic overlook, she parked the bike. The morning sky had been sunny when she'd left the dorm, and she expected to look upon sun-kissed treetops across the wooded vista.

However, as she watched from her elevated vantage point, a sudden wind quickly brought dark, threatening clouds into view. A few seconds later, those clouds began to move in a slow swirling pattern.

Tornadoes don't form in January, she thought. *They usually come in the spring.*

A sudden blast of air hit her in the face, causing the girl to pull her coat's hood up over her head. A second, stronger blast whizzed by her, slapped her motorcycle, and knocked it over.

I'd better get off this hill. I'm a sitting duck.

Lifting the bike, Lisa jumped on and tried starting the engine. It cranked and cranked but wouldn't start.

That's just great. Scanning the area behind the hill, she spied a thick cluster of trees. *That area should provide some protection.*

Lisa muscled her motorcycle down the backside of the hill as hail unexpectedly began to pummel her.

What is this, the motorcycle ride from hell?

Fortunately, the wind and hail were coming from behind her and actually aided her efforts to push her bike down the hill and seek shelter from the storm. Within a few minutes she'd reached the trees, which initially blocked both wind and hail from reaching her.

Before pushing farther into the woods, she checked the sky. The swirl in the clouds was increasing its speed of rotation, and the whole swirling mass was moving closer to her location.

Crap!

Again, the girl tried to start the bike's engine, but it still wouldn't come to life. Pulling her cell phone out of her coat pocket, she checked the signal strength. Zero bars.

What next?

She didn't have to wait long for an answer to that question. In the distance, from deeper in the woods, came the sound of footsteps on fallen leaves. And it wasn't a single set of footfalls she heard. There were several, but no one was visible.

"Hello," she called. "Is anyone there?"

No answer.

But the direction the footsteps came from shifted. Instead of just coming from one direction, they now sounded as if they were coming from all around her. It wasn't long before she found out why.

The sound was coming not from humans making their way through the forest but from wolves. A pack of five of them, to be exact. As if they were well-practiced synchronized dancers, the pack revealed itself in unison, each member stepping from behind some tree, bush, or boulder. Their guttural growls, drooling mouths, and bared teeth signaled their intent to do her harm.

Panic engulfed Lisa as she began looking for an escape route. Close by, she discovered a bent oak tree that, at about three feet up its trunk, took a forty-five-degree turn.

Abandoning her motorcycle, she ran for the tree.

Jumping with all her strength, she grabbed a sturdy branch that allowed her to hoist herself off the ground and up onto the angled trunk. Climbing a few additional feet put her out of reach of the beasts below—she hoped.

The growls and snarls intensified as the wolves moved in and encircled the tree. The pack leader, the alpha, seemed to size up the situation rapidly, and with a quick signal from him, the rest of the pack began attempting to climb the tree. But the lower section of the tree was devoid of limbs to grab hold of, so all their efforts were futile.

The pack, however, was not deterred from its mission. Circling the base of the tree, all five animals began to howl.

Are they calling in reinforcements?

From time to time, one wolf would jump toward Lisa and growl. It was obvious they'd been sent to track and attack her. But who was behind this? The same evil conjurer that cast the House of Bones spell on Billy, no doubt.

The girl tried her cell phone again but got the same result: no bars.

With no other viable options, she tried climbing higher up the angled tree trunk to move farther away from the threat below and possibly into a better zone for cell phone reception. After climbing another minute or so, she pulled out her phone and checked for a signal again. A half of a bar showed up, and she was ecstatic.

Standing precariously on the slanting tree trunk and using a nearby branch to steady her, she placed a call to the only person she could think to call, Billy.

Several hundred miles to the east, Billy's phone rang. He and Wesley had already begun their drive back to Tahlequah. Looking at the phone's screen, the boy saw it was Lisa calling.

"Hello," he said. "Lisa?" He listened for a response but only heard crackling static. "Lisa, I can't hear you. Is everything okay?"

In the midst of the hissing interference, Billy could only make out the words "wildlife," "wolves," and "help." Then the call went dead.

"Lisa's in some kind of trouble," Billy told his grandfather, who was driving. "I think for some reason she's at the wildlife management area south of Tahlequah being threatened by wolves. What can I do?"

"Try calling your father to see if he can alert the police," Wesley suggested. "Or try calling your friend Travis at the Marshals Service to see if he can organize some sort of rescue."

"How would they even find her?" Billy answered, his mind filling rapidly with several possible negative outcomes. "She needs help now!"

Meanwhile, back in Oklahoma, a blast of air unexpectedly hit Lisa as she balanced precariously in the tree, causing her to lose her balance. As her body toppled from the branch, one flailing gloved hand found a branch to grab. Holding on for dear life, she managed to get both hands around the branch, but the rest of her body dangled not far from the ground.

One by one, each wolf tried to reach Lisa's feet as they dangled like tantalizing meat snacks waiting to be plucked from the branch. The girl kicked at them as they jumped, eventually landing a blow right on a snout. A whimper of pain from the injured animal caused the others to end their quest for the girl's feet and return to their circling routine.

Back in Wesley's truck, the elder had a thought.

"Grandson, you have so many spiritual gifts and abilities," he said. "Maybe one of them can help you now."

Billy thought hard about that idea. He was usually lying down in a relaxed state of mind when he floated out of his body or performed spirit travel. But he also realized that when he saw mini-movies about other people's lives, he was usually standing or walking.

"Okay, I'm going to try to see what's happening to Lisa in my mind," Billy said. "Just keep driving as fast as you can so we can physically get to her as soon as possible."

"No problem," Wesley replied as he put his foot on the gas.

Billy leaned back in his seat and calmed his mind. Then he mentally replayed the staticky phone call he'd just received. Finally, he pictured his girlfriend in the wilderness with a few wolves nearby. He concentrated mightily, trying to will his view to go to her location.

But nothing happened.

That was when he realized he was very tense—from his feet to his neck to his shoulders. Every part of his body was wound up and tight. He blew out a big breath and tried again. An image of him and Lisa kissing in the front seat of his truck came to mind, and he allowed himself to experience the wonderful feelings that accompanied that scene.

In the next moment, he found himself floating above his grandpa's moving truck. As the vehicle sped along Interstate 24 just south of Chattanooga, Tennessee, Billy's energy body sped along with it. He scanned the surrounding landscape just in time to see a roadside sign that read *Lookout Mountain Next Exit*.

How many Lookout Mountains are there? he wondered as he turned his attention to Lisa Lookout. That was the motivating impulse that propelled his nonphysical body westward.

He experienced the familiar stretching sensation, and within moments he was hovering above Lisa trapped in the leaning oak tree. She was in the process of pulling herself up to a branch, straining with the effort.

He moved closer and tried to get her attention, but she was focused entirely on the circling pack of wolves below her. The animals, likewise, were completely focused on her and hadn't noticed him yet.

Billy remembered that a deer, as well as the Tlanuwa, had spoken to him. He was pretty sure he could communicate with the wolf pack, or at least grab their attention.

He zoomed down to a point just above one of the wolves, and that was when he noticed an odd thing about its energy field. In the area above the animal's eyes, in the center of the forehead, there was a dark spot. As Billy concentrated more closely on the spot, he saw a faint, thin dark thread attached to it. Following the line of the thread, he saw that it was attached to the same spot on the forehead of another one of the wolves.

One final detail became apparent to Billy. The four other animals were all connected by a similar thread to this wolf, which must be the alpha animal of the pack. If the boy could manipulate that one, the others would follow.

He projected a thought into the animal's mind: "I'm right here within reach. Come and get me."

Then he taunted the pack further by flying around the tree trunk, holding out his spirit hand and passing through the physical faces of each of the wolves. The animals' well-known psychic sensitivity allowed them to feel his hand as a cold slap. They stopped circling and looked to see what caused it.

Billy lowered himself to ground level, waved his arms and legs, and yelled taunts at the animals. His movements were enough to make them lose interest in the girl in the tree. They slowly began creeping toward the apparition that taunted them.

That was when the teen noticed one more detail about the alpha wolf. There was a faint human energy body superimposed over the animal's own energy body. As Billy continued to lead the group away from the vicinity of Lisa, he focused more attention on the lead wolf. There was a blurry, faint human face superimposed on the wolf's face!

Just as that realization appeared in Billy's mind, the human element of the wolf shifted focus to Billy. It was similar to the experience the boy had when he'd dreamed of the Raven Stalker's presence within the body of the high school gym teacher last fall.

The alpha immediately turned away from the chase, and the rest of the pack followed. That was the moment Billy realized that both he and Lisa really were the targets of evil forces. He hovered near Lisa as she watched the animals flee deeper into the woods. She looked up and around her with searching eyes.

"Billy, are you here?" she asked out loud. She paused and waited, trying to sense any response at any level. "Was that you just now? Did you scare the wolves away?"

Billy didn't quite know how to respond in a way Lisa would perceive. Then he had a thought and decided to give it a try. Moving up close to her position in the tree, he put his spirit lips on her physical cheek and kissed her. The girl experienced a chill as shivers spread from her cheek to her head to her toes.

Not sure what that was about, Lisa decided it was time to climb down from the tree. Once she was on the ground, she tried to start her motorcycle one more time. Surprisingly, it cranked over and easily sprang to life. She jumped on and headed back toward the hilltop where the nightmare experience had begun. Strangely, the wind, dark clouds, and threatening skies were completely gone.

Remembering that she'd awakened in such a state of mental fog and confusion that morning, she decided it wouldn't be safe for her to sleep in the dorm for a while. But where could she stay? Then she had a thought.

Maybe the Buckhorn family could help me out. She aimed her motorcycle for Billy's house.

When he was sure Lisa was in the clear, Billy stretched and returned to his physical body, which was sitting in the passenger seat of Wesley's truck in Tennessee as they drove home. Once the teen was firmly back, he told his grandfather about his experience.

"Strange changes are afoot," Grandpa said, repeating the warning issued by Awinita last fall.

CHAPTER THIRTEEN

The Gathering

Thomas Two Bears left his home on the Northern Cheyenne reservation in Montana in time to arrive at the gathering site at precisely 3:33 a.m., the traditional time for a meeting of the Night Seers. His destination: the flat oval-shaped top of the geologically unique Devil's Tower located in the northeast corner of the state of Wyoming. Known as Bear Lodge in Native American circles, this culturally significant and hard-to-reach meeting place was his favorite spot for Owl gatherings.

Two Bears had been the leader of the Owl Clan for almost fifty years, and as a result, he knew he'd arrive before anyone else. Unlike his predecessor, whom Thomas had relieved of his position with great finality, Two Bears valued punctuality.

On the other hand, members of the Owl Clan, an unruly bunch, resented having to be at any specific place at any specific time. But Thomas, they found, had an annoying way of making himself heard and obeyed. He'd mastered the art of being in thirteen different places at once so he could harass the twelve other members of the secretive group at the same time, even though they lived in far-flung corners of North America.

As Two Bears transformed from his owl configuration back to his human form, he mentally reviewed the membership list of his wayward followers.

There was Daniel Arkekeeta, a Kiowa from western Oklahoma. Jacki Birdsong of the Agua Caliente tribe in Southern California. Elouise Firekeeper, an Iroquois Indian from the state of New York. Willy James, who was a known troublemaker from the eastern Choctaw reservation in Alabama. Natalie Nokomis, a Chippewa from Minnesota. Geraldine Osceola was a Seminole who lived in the Florida Panhandle. Jackson Peacemaker of Massachusetts was a member of the Wampanoag tribe. Kway Soowahly was from the Coast Salish of Seattle.

Lawrence Tokala came from the Lakota of North Dakota. From Arizona was the Navajo medicine maker Kla To-yah. Many people thought the Eastern Cherokee conjurer Amos Yonaguska had died, but he was still very much alive in North Carolina. And finally, there was Night Wolf. Scratch that—Carmelita Tuckaleechee was the name she used now.

As he finished his review, the Night Seers began arriving and altering their outward physical appearance. Shape-shifting, after all, was one of the powers required for membership in the Owl Clan.

"Every last one of you is late!" he called to them. "Whatever it was you were doing back home that you thought was so important pales in comparison to what we're accomplishing in the coming months. So, when I call an emergency meeting, you'd better drop everything and get here pronto!"

A general grumbling tumbled from their mouths as they complained under their breaths about their leader, his rules, and his reprimand.

"Zip it or you'll join the others down at the bottom of this tower who dared defy me," Two Bears roared. "A pile of their broken bones is all that's left of them."

Resembling a gigantic tree stump with vertical striations—which, according to Native legends, were caused by the claws of a giant bear—the nine-hundred-foot-tall tower was famously featured in Steven Spielberg's movie *Close Encounters of the Third Kind.*

After the undisciplined troublemakers settled down, Two Bears continued.

"I hate to do this, but your constant tardiness and absence from our meetings are forcing my hand. If everyone isn't on time next meeting, I'll call roll just like they do in school. Anyone absent or late will be severely punished!"

That drew even louder grumbling and complaining from the group until the head Night Seer began psychically demonstrating his considerable power. He reached out toward the assembled crowd of conjurers with a furrowed hand and then proceeded to crush an invisible object within it.

Each and every conjurer in the bunch felt the grasp of that hand around their necks. The more tightly he squeezed, the less oxygen they received. Their whining and pleading ceased only when the sorcerer finally relinquished his hold.

Again, silence settled over the gathering.

"Why are we here, Two Bears?" an impatient voice yelled from the back of the group.

"Okay. You want to get right to it. More than a couple of you have jumped the gun and acted early, which jeopardizes the effectiveness of our plan," he said. "Yonaguska, where are you?"

Amos Yonaguska stepped out from behind another Night Seer, who he'd been standing behind. He pushed back a tuft of long white hair with a withered left hand. His other hand rested on an ornately carved wooden cane.

"You know you weren't scheduled to activate the Tlanuwa yet," Two Bears admonished. "No one is supposed to act until after the spring equinox in March."

"And you know I don't like waiting," the old man replied. "None of us do. What's the point of scheduling all our activities, anyway?"

"You'd know the answer to that question if you'd shown up for our last meeting!" Two Bears replied angrily. "The time foretold by the Snake Priest is almost upon us. That's when the veil between our world and the Underworld will be the thinnest, weakest, and easiest to pass through. That's particularly useful for dwellers of the Shadow Zone, because they'll be able to manifest here in the physical."

Two Bears scanned the group.

"And Willy James, from Mississippi, I see you back there," he said. "I just learned that you released the Underwater Panther a couple of days ago from its cave. Why did you do that?"

"I was just practicing for the main event," James replied. "It's been ages since I conjured anything meaningful, much less one of the ancient beings. I forgot how hard they are to control."

"Listen, people," Two Bears said. "These premature actions may tip our hand to give Cecil and his friends a preview of what we've got planned. The timetable is set. We can't veer off course now. We've waited too long. You two need to clean up your messes."

He paused, looking for another member of the clan.

"Night Wolf, from eastern Oklahoma, is here to give us a firsthand report on the Intertribal Medicine Council and their search for the so-called Chosen One, the Red Messiah," Two Bears said.

The old, tattooed woman moved toward the front of the crowd and stood next to Two Bears.

"I go by the name Carmelita Tuckaleechee now," she said with a smile. "I kinda like the way it sounds."

The Night Seers, none of whom were impressed, remained silent.

"Okay, straight to the point," she continued. "His name's Billy Buckhorn, a sixteen-year-old descendant of Cherokee medicine man Moytoy. And the boy's grandfather, Wesley Buckhorn, will be replacing Elmore Proctor on the Medicine Council."

"How's a sixteen-year-old going to be a threat to us?"

"The Buckhorns have been a problem for us for generations, and their latest offspring, young Billy, is following in his family's medicine tradition, but with capabilities far beyond normal."

An interrupting question came from another woman in the group. "Is he the one who prevented Benjamin Blacksnake from succeeding in his ill-advised attempt to reincarnate in human form last year?"

"Benji—I mean, Benjamin—had every right to try a flesh transition," Carmelita replied. "Who wouldn't want to experience life in a physical body again? Especially if you're trapped in the Shadow Zone like he is. He and I belong together again here in Middleworld!"

"Let's get back on topic, shall we?" Two Bears said loudly. "We don't have all night!"

"All right, all right," Tuckaleechee responded.

She recomposed herself.

"I'm going to need help with this one, especially since the boy is in the process of joining forces with the Osage Lookout family and the rest of those intertribal medicine fools. I cast the House of Bones spell on him, but the Lookouts freed him."

This brought a round of chatter from the group.

"Since then, I cast the 'conflict and confusion' spell on the girl called Spider Woman and sent my wolf pack to trap her, but so far all my efforts have been frustrated by the young Buckhorn."

"I got a doozy of a spell passed down from our Aztec forebears you could try," said Florida Seminole conjurer Geraldine Osceola.

"You two get together after this meeting, or use your Aztec mirrors to connect, because we still have one last important issue to address," Two Bears said.

Carmelita returned to her place with the others.

"Our planned weather events," Two Bears continued. "As you know, the spring equinox falls on March twentieth, when the hours of daylight and darkness are equal. That's the beginning of the period when our powers become enhanced, and that's when our abilities to create earth incidents and weather events start to ramp up. No one—"

"You're going too far this time, Thomas!" Kla To-yah, the Navajo Skinwalker, interrupted. "You can't tell us when, where, or how to cast our spells. Sure, we joined the Owl Clan to boost our abilities and expand our knowledge, but you trying to control what we do and when is too much!"

All the Owls echoed the Navajo's complaint with shouts of "That's right" and "It's too much."

Two Bears closed his eyes and concentrated amid the noise. Rotating his hands in a spherical pattern as if he was forming a large ball, he began uttering a mantra in his Cheyenne language. Simultaneously, a spherical pattern of pressure formed around the gathering of Owls on top of the tower.

Two Bears then began shrinking the size of the imaginary ball, and the Owls were compressed into an ever-tightening space. Caught off guard, none of the conjurers had time to transform and fly away. All were caught in the supernatural trap and felt the increasing constraint that forced them into a tiny space, unable to escape.

"Have you forgotten why we are doing this?" Two Bears roared. "Have you forgotten that the white man destroyed our Native peoples, our homes, our communities, and our cultures? Have you forgotten how they reduced us to cowering victims, unable to fend for ourselves?"

He allowed his words to sink in, to resonate within their minds.

"Now, shall we take a vote?" Two Bears bellowed. "All those in favor of following the timetable I've set out, say aye."

"Aye!" the crowd responded, fearful of what their leader might do if they said otherwise.

"All those against?"

No one uttered a sound.

"The ayes have it, then."

Two Bears separated his hands, and the pressure surrounding the Owls subsided. The Cheyenne sorcerer had won. His followers would obey him, at least for now.

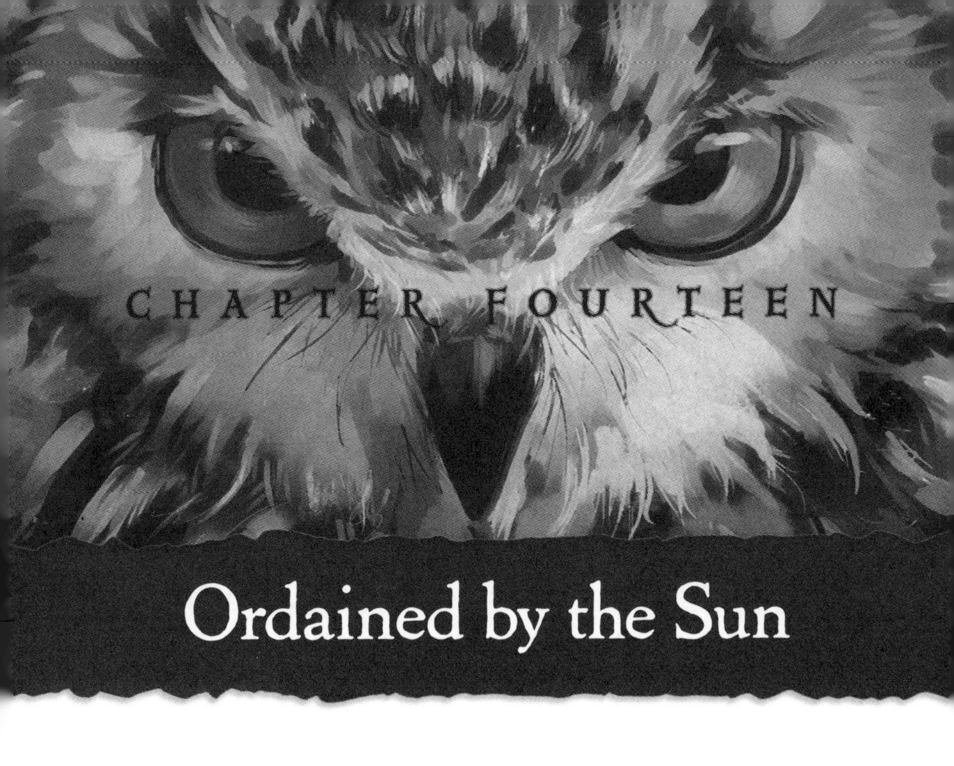

CHAPTER FOURTEEN

Ordained by the Sun

When Billy returned from his trip to Eastern Cherokee territory with Wesley, he was pleased to learn that his girlfriend was now staying in the family's spare bedroom.

"I'm afraid my decision to take part in the prophecy has put you in danger," he told Lisa when they had a chance to be alone. "That's the last thing I want, but I'm glad you're staying here with us."

"There's someone here in Cherokee country who doesn't want you and me to be together, or doesn't want our families to join forces," she said. "My instincts say it's the medicine person Chigger has gotten mixed up with."

"Chigger would never—"

Billy checked himself before finishing that statement. He remembered his friend's ordeal with the purple crystal and his reaction to the last girlfriend Billy had.

"Let me rephrase that. My oldest and bestest friend, the Chigger I knew before the Uktena incident, would never do anything to harm me or my family. But now I'm not so sure."

Billy pondered that thought for a moment.

"Well, I'm not hanging around here waiting for another supernatural attack," Lisa said with finality. "I'm going with you for the medicine initiation ceremony."

"That's the best news ever!" Billy said with a great deal of excitement.

The Osage Nation's one-and-a-half-million-acre Oklahoma reservation sat just south of the Kansas state line. The tribe had reluctantly accepted this property in exchange for lands they were forced to give up in the 1800s, as the federal government made room for white, land-hungry settlers. The centrally located town of Pawhuska served as the capital of the tribal nation, and its modern, sleek office buildings served the current needs of the Osage people.

About three miles east of Pawhuska on a high point of land stood a stone memorial to one of the tribe's most beloved chiefs, Fred Lookout, a distant relative of Cecil, Ethan, and Lisa.

As he stood near that memorial, Billy took in the wide natural view. Down the hill to the southwest flowed the twists and turns of tiny Bird Creek. Barely visible several miles to the east sat the medium-sized town of Bartlesville, at the outer edge of the reservation. A few scattered farmhouses dotted the otherwise sparsely populated Oklahoma landscape.

All the Lookouts and all the Buckhorns had arranged their schedules so they could participate in Billy's ordination ceremony, which was about to take place. Also known as the initiation dance, the ritual would be the beginning of his "reign" as the long-awaited Chosen One, the Son of the Sun for these prophetic times.

But there would be several steps and multiple locations involved in the process, and this location was but the first. Billy had arrived early to allow himself time to reflect on the extraordinary events that had led to this monumental moment and contemplate the challenges that lay ahead. Would he be worthy of the new role? Would he be able to summon the strength needed to defeat Underworld forces? What did that even mean?

He checked the clock on his phone. It read 11:45 a.m. The others would be arriving at noon. The 120-mile drive from Tahlequah to Pawhuska only took about two hours, and Billy had driven by himself in order to be alone with his thoughts.

I wish Chigger was here to witness this like in the good old days. I miss him.

But that friendship had mysteriously ended rather abruptly, signaling a final end to childhood. Lisa's simultaneous appearance in Billy's life signaled the beginning of the age of maturity and responsibility. The fun times were over, but the teen hoped there were still plenty of good times ahead.

The distant rumble of a caravan of cars traveling over the gravel road interrupted Billy's reverie. Leading the parade was Lisa on her motorcycle, now with an attached sidecar filled with camping gear. Immediately behind her followed her father in his archaeology van and her grandfather in a rather rare 1948 Ford "woodie" station wagon with one busted headlight.

Behind them came the Buckhorns, Wesley in his red-and-white Ford pickup and Billy's mother and father in the family Jeep. Wesley honked his truck horn when he spotted his grandson standing just outside the low fence that surrounded the twelve-foot-tall memorial.

Three other members of the Lookout family who lived in Pawhuska also arrived, invited by Cecil. These were Ethan's brother Chester and his wife, Sarah, along with Lisa's older brother, Michael. To Billy, the family resemblances and their similarly patterned energy fields were quite noticeable.

After everyone parked, got introduced, and gathered around Billy, Cecil explained why they were there.

"We've come to pay homage to my uncle Fred, who served as principal chief of the tribe for a total of twenty-eight years," Cecil said. "More importantly, he helped preserve our family by protecting our relatives during the 1920s, when sixty of our fellow tribal members were murdered for their oil rights. The actions he took in his life demonstrate the impact each of us can have if we take a stand to improve and protect the lives of those around us. It's important to remember the sacrifices made by our ancestors as we ready ourselves to face the battles ahead."

When Cecil finished speaking, Chester stepped forward in the circle. He'd brought a hand drum with him that he used to accompany himself in an Osage honor song. After the song began, all the members of the Lookout family joined in singing.

Their voices echoed across the landscape that surrounded them. Billy, standing next to Chester and Cecil, began moving his feet up and down in rhythm with the drumbeat. Without leaving the spot where he stood, the boy made a full 360-degree rotation, dancing in place.

His unfocused vision seemed to capture faint images of Native spirit dancers who were scattered over the nearby land. Each faced the beating drum and danced where they stood.

"Call on us, for we are ready to help you," they seemed to say to Billy. Was that his imagination playing tricks on him?

Cecil, who had been watching the boy, leaned over and whispered in Billy's ear, "I really brought you here because this is a place of visions. What you may see is real. Have no doubts. Trust yourself."

Billy stopped questioning the scene that unfolded before him.

The message continued: "We've been watching and waiting for you to appear, and now you are here. Though we live among the stars, we stand ready to join you on the plains of Middleworld as you fight for the people and Mother Earth."

As Billy completed his 360-degree circle, Chester's song ended.

"It is done," the man said and nodded to Billy. He reached out his hand, Billy shook it, and the brief ceremony ended.

"We have two other stops to make before we conduct the final Son of the Sun ceremony," Cecil told Billy. "But remember what you saw here, for it may help you in the near future."

The elder stepped away from Billy and called to the others, "Next stop: Sugarloaf Mound, St. Louis."

Pulling Lisa aside, Billy said, "Won't you be in trouble with the school for missing your classes?"

"The whole world will be in trouble if we don't defeat the gathering dark forces," she replied before giving him a kiss on the cheek. "Supporting you is the most important thing for me to do now. My father gave the school a note of permission to take an extended absence. Maybe your mom and dad could do that for you."

With that, she put on her helmet and got on her motorcycle, leaving Billy with what seemed like a great idea.

The caravan of cars, trucks, vans, and one motorcycle made its way to Cecil's house as the sun was setting. Cody, who'd stayed behind, had timed the heating of the stones so they'd be ready for the sweat lodge at about this time. Only Cecil and Billy would be participating in this particular sweat, and that was why Cecil's younger sister had prepared food and drink for everyone else, who'd be waiting inside the house.

The elder and the teen quickly changed clothes, grabbed towels, and presented themselves at the door to the sweat lodge. Cody signaled that he was ready, and Cecil spoke to Billy.

"This will be your introduction to the ancestor spirits who work with the Medicine Council and provide spiritual protection. The night before your initiation, we'll perform a separate sweat with all the council members to welcome your grandfather into the circle."

Then the ceremony began. As before, the ancestor spirits entered the lodge during the fourth round. After entering the lodge, the thirteen sparks of light circled the interior four times and then took up positions around the central pit of heated stones.

The many voices whispering as one said, "Time is short, and the need is great, young warrior. Only a resident of the Middleworld who can reach into the past and also unite with dwellers of the Upperworld will once again subdue denizens of the Underworld. As you rise to meet the challenge ahead, we will assist you with all the power we can muster."

Then the many voices whispering as one spoke in a language Billy recognized, the sacred language used by the Sun Chief to recapture the Horned Serpent in the lower cave. This time he understood the meaning of the words.

"May Waconda, the Great Mystery, empower and protect you from this day forth!"

Then the thirteen sparks began circling the interior of the lodge, but before exiting through the roof, each passed directly through Billy's physical body, discharging light-filled energy into him. The passing of each spark through the boy's flesh was accompanied by a distinct and resounding crackle as his bones, muscle, brain, and skin were infused with high-frequency energy.

It was almost more than his physical body could stand. As Cecil watched, Billy's body began to glow. He'd never seen anything like it. He'd never heard of anything like it happening to anyone else in the history of the Intertribal Medicine Council.

Billy slumped over sideways as he passed out from the overwhelming energy.

"Cody, come in here quick!" the elder shouted to his grandson. "We need to pull Billy out of the lodge!"

Cody sprang into action, flipping the flap door open and entering the lodge. He, too, saw that Billy's body was literally glowing.

"Help me get him out!" the elder shouted, seeing that Cody was frozen in place. The pair pulled and tugged to get the boy out of the lodge and onto a blanket.

Lisa, who was inside Cecil's kitchen serving food to guests, heard the commotion and raced out the back door of the house.

There lay her unconscious, glowing boyfriend. Cecil quickly explained what had happened as members of Billy's family arrived on the scene.

Not able to think of anything else to do, Lisa grabbed the ladle from the water bucket and threw a ladleful of water on Billy's face. The boy jerked and opened his eyes, to everyone's relief. Billy's glow quickly subsided.

"What . . . what happened?"

"You passed out in the lodge after the spirits left," Cecil replied. "What did you experience?"

"I was standing in a circle surrounded by thirteen buffalo who were speaking to me," Billy said. "We were out on the prairie somewhere. Then one by one, they charged toward me and passed through me. Their energy was so powerful it overwhelmed me and lifted me off the ground."

He looked down at his body, touching various parts as if it felt odd to the touch. "For a few seconds, I *was* a buffalo—with horns and hooves and fur."

"Excellent, young man," Cecil said. "The buffalo symbolizes victory over struggles and challenges as well as new beginnings. They infused you with these qualities and empowered you to succeed."

Billy was a little wobbly as he stood, so Lisa and her grandfather helped the teen walk to the house for food and water.

"Next stop—Cahokia," Cecil told Billy as they stepped inside. "Sunrise tomorrow. Better get a good night's sleep right after we get a bite to eat."

Billy slept a hard, dreamless sleep that night in a tent in Cecil's backyard. He awoke the next morning to the sound of sirens. They weren't the kind one might hear from an ambulance or fire truck that quickly passed by, creating a Doppler effect. These were steady, stationary danger signals emitted from public sirens attached to the tops of tall poles scattered around the city.

He unzipped the flap on his tent and peered out. Wesley, who'd slept on Cecil's living room couch, stepped out of the back of the house and looked skyward.

"What's going on, Grandpa?" Billy asked as he tumbled out of the tent.

"Tornado alert," the elder said. "TV news says it's a big one to the southwest of us."

Billy stood next to Wesley and squinted his sleepy eyes at the cloud-filled atmosphere. "I thought tornadoes came in the spring, like in April or May."

"That was in the good old days before climate change," Wesley said. "Now weather everywhere seems to be out of whack."

"Shouldn't we go to a shelter or a bunker or something?" Billy asked.

"Cecil has a storm shelter basement under the house. We'll head down if the twister gets close."

The pair continued gazing upward for another moment as the sirens continued to wail. "Come inside and grab a bite of the wonderful breakfast Cecil's sister made. We can see what's happening with the tornado on TV."

With a breakfast burrito in one hand and a cup of coffee in the other, Billy sat down in a worn, overstuffed chair near Cecil's TV. A local weatherman was describing the action.

"There's never been anything like it," the middle-aged man was saying as he stood in front of a weather map of Oklahoma.

An almost straight red line ran on the map from the town of Pawhuska on the Osage reservation in Oklahoma to the center of Osage County in the state of Missouri.

"First of all, there were no weather models forecasting possible tornadoes at this time in this region," the man continued. "This thing just came out of nowhere! Second, this is January, not

April, so any tornado of any category is a rare event. But add to that the sheer size of this twister and the distance it stayed on the ground . . . Well, it's downright unbelievable! A category four on the ground for three hundred miles! The devastating Kentucky twister in 2020 touched down for one hundred and sixty miles, killed dozens of people, and did billions of dollars' worth of damage. I can't even imagine what death and destruction this one is going to leave behind."

As the man finished his report, the local sirens died down, leaving a deafening silence.

Cecil and Wesley both noticed a few unusual details about this weather event, which they discussed in hushed tones in a corner of the living room.

"What are you talking—or should I say whispering—about over there?" Billy asked after finishing his burrito.

"A common concern we both share," Wesley replied. "But it's too early to tell anyone else about it until more information comes to light."

Billy decided not to probe any further as he headed to the bathroom to get ready for the next step in his initiation process.

Back in Anadarko, Oklahoma, someone else was keenly interested in the weather news.

"I still got it!" Kiowa Night Seer Daniel Arkekeeta exclaimed loudly after seeing the tornado news coverage. "Thomas Two Bears can't control me like I can control the weather!"

Arkekeeta crossed the living room of his dilapidated frame house and picked up an aging photo from a sagging bookshelf. Pictured in the grainy black-and-white image taken in 1870 was a young Daniel Arkekeeta standing next to the Kiowa chief known as Kicking Bird.

"My friend, the time is finally at hand," Arkekeeta said. "I've worked my whole life to avenge your death at the hands of the white man. Poisoning you in prison was a cowardly act."

The old Indian studied the photo another few moments, remembering younger days on the Kiowa reservation.

"I can't believe it's been more than one hundred and fifty years since we took this photo together," he said, still talking to the long-deceased Kiowa chief. "I'm sorry it's taken so long."

Arkekeeta returned to his TV to watch more of the results of his weather handiwork. "More of the same is coming at you, Cecil Lookout," the Kiowa man said. "You and your teenage savior will be no match for the combined power of the Owls and the Snakes!"

The Cahokia Mounds State Historic Site was located only about fifteen miles to the northeast from Cecil's house. Billy rode to the site with Lisa's father in his van, and the archaeologist explained a few facts about the sacred location as they traveled.

"It doesn't look like much now, but a thousand years ago the site was home to the Children of the Sun. That's what we, the people that became the Osage, called ourselves. Our political and spiritual leader was known as the Son of the Sun or the Sun Chief, but you know that already. He was considered the human manifestation of Waconda, the Great Mystery who created the universe."

The pair arrived at the historical site and parked in the visitors' parking lot.

"Our cultural and religious influence once stretched to Florida, the Carolinas, and northern Ohio," Ethan told Billy as they exited the van. "Thousands of Indigenous peoples across the Americas looked to us for sustenance, spiritual guidance, and protection. That was until the Snake Priest's followers assassinated our Sun Chief and his inner circle down at Spiral Mounds. Until we met you, no one in our realm ever knew what happened to his spirit."

"He showed me a vision of what this place was like a thousand years ago," Billy said. "It was spectacular! But he couldn't leave the Spiral Mounds area because of the curse."

"That still blows my mind!" Ethan replied. "You've actually seen and spoken with him, and we had no clue why he'd gone missing or how to contact him in the Afterworld."

As the pair walked from the site's parking lot toward a flat-top hill known as Monk's Mound, Ethan talked a little about the current park's history and a little about the archaeology at the site. They made their way to Monk's Mound and climbed the stairway that led to the mound's flat top. Ethan said the base of the earthen structure was larger than the largest pyramid in Egypt.

When they reached the top, Ethan pulled a large book from the satchel he carried. The title on the five-hundred-page volume read *The Illustrated Encyclopedia of Native American Indian Mounds and Earthworks*. He handed the oversized book to Billy, opening it to an introductory page containing a bookmark.

"I want you to know it's not just me bragging about the scope of Mississippian Mound Builder culture at its apex," the man said. "Read what it says at the bottom of this page."

Billy saw a paragraph Ethan had highlighted with a yellow marker. He read the passage out loud.

"I am fairly certain that over one million mounds once existed in North America, designed and built by the ancestors of today's Native Americans. In truth, the large majority of America's mounds have been completely destroyed by farming, construction, looting, and total excavation."

As Billy thought about the facts presented on the page, Ethan flipped the book open to another page he'd bookmarked. It was a section specifically about the Cahokia site. Billy again read aloud.

"Cahokia was the largest and most powerful of the Mississippian-era chiefdoms, and the city was probably home to about twenty thousand people at its peak about AD 1100–1200."

"Can you imagine that many Indians living within a few miles of this spot?"

Billy tried to imagine it as he gazed out at the local landscape that included a few grass-covered hills, an interpretive center, and beyond that a sprawling industrial city. After a few minutes, Lisa's dad indicated it was time to go, and they headed back to the parking lot.

"As you've heard, Shakuru and his twin brother, Monkata, were born on the same day. What you may not know is the supernova of AD 1054 appeared on that day, a heavenly event seen and written about in cultures around the world. And, if that wasn't spectacular enough, a small meteor plummeted to earth that day, hitting the center of the town plaza—the original source of the Sky Stone's core."

As they reached Ethan's van in the parking lot, he said, "End of today's lesson." Then his friendly demeanor changed.

"One day real soon, I need to have a heart-to-heart talk with you about your intentions toward my daughter," the archaeologist said.

"Okay," Billy said with an uneasy smile and a quiver in his voice.

Lisa's dad let that thought hang in the air for a moment for effect. "But it can wait until after the initiation dance," Ethan finally said. Billy relaxed—a little.

The following day, a caravan of cars, trucks, and vans headed west on Interstate 64 out of St. Louis. Their destination: a secluded location on private property in Warren County. More famous than Manitou Cave in Alabama, Picture Cave of Missouri contained the most-studied thousand-year-old ceremonial art in the nation. And nearby that cave sat an ancient ceremonial ground used by the priests and leaders of the Children of the Sun.

Billy rode in Ethan's van with Cecil, Wesley, and a week's worth of camping supplies. The drive only took about an hour, but it was slow going over rough terrain for the final few miles. During the trip, Cecil previewed the upcoming medicine ceremony for Billy so he'd know what to expect.

"Each of the thirteen members of the Intertribal Medicine Council has contributed an element of your initiation ceremony to represent the medicine powers of thirteen tribal nations," he explained. "Initially, we planned on having you symbolically experience death and resurrection, but you've already experienced that in real life, so that's not necessary. What you will experience combines baptism, vision quest, stomp dance, ghost dance, and sun dance."

As the van drew closer to the site, Billy saw an active village of busy Native people hard at work. A dedicated group of volunteers had already been staying at the site to set up for Billy's initiation ceremony. A small tent city was already in place at the edge of a central clearing.

Just as the teen stepped out of the van, a tall, freshly cut tree that had been lying on the ground dramatically rose from the level, grassy field. A group of men used ropes to stand it upright and steady it in place as the base of the tree was thrust into a deep hole in the ground.

A large bird's nest rested in the forked top branches, and multicolored ribbons hung from other branches. About halfway up the tree's main trunk, a red strap with four loops was attached. Two sets of ropes hung from each hook.

"That represents the sacred tree of life," Cecil said. "The Thunderbird's nest on top represents the Upperworld. The roots of the tree reach down to the Underworld. The ropes hanging from the middle of the tree are where we inhabitants of the Middleworld connect and unite with it all."

The three walked toward the center pole, and a small army of workers began constructing a brush arbor that encircled the pole at a radius of about forty feet from it.

"You and I and two other men will dance for four days attached to and hanging from that center pole," Cecil continued. "For many people, this ceremony is their introduction to soul travel, but you . . . you've already mastered that skill. I'm sure you'll experience things far beyond the realm of beginners."

They unloaded the van and set up camp alongside the others in the tent city. Their neighbors in the camp included the twelve other members of the Intertribal Medicine Council, all of whom would be dancing in support of Billy—including Wesley.

"Wesley, tonight in the sweat lodge you will be welcomed to the council so that tomorrow you can participate in the initiation ceremony for the Chosen One," Cecil said.

"It will be my honor," Wesley replied. "I only hope I will be able to adequately fill the shoes of Elmore Proctor."

Billy didn't participate in the Medicine Council's sweat lodge to welcome Wesley into the council because his important future role lay outside the regular operation of the ITMC. Billy, instead, spent some quiet time with Lisa, which he knew would be the last time he'd have time to focus on her for the next four days.

"Yesterday at Cahokia your father surprised me when he said we needed to have a talk real soon about what my intentions were toward you," Billy said as they lay beside each other in Billy's tent.

"Classic Dad—always looking out for me," Lisa replied. "So, what are your intentions?"

"I intend to spend as much time with you as possible," the boy said, putting his arm around her waist. "I also intend on kissing you as much as possible," he added just before going in for a kiss.

She allowed a brief kiss but ended it quickly. "What else?"

When he didn't answer right away, she pushed him back a short distance and looked into his eyes.

"I'm serious. What else?"

Billy sat up, a worried expression now on his face. "I intend to survive whatever terrible ordeal is coming, which I've agreed to jump into without even knowing exactly what it is I am committing to."

Lisa sat up as well. "Well, I intend to face the ordeal with you, however I can," she said, now resting her head on his shoulder.

"Like I said before, the only thing I think you've done by being with me is to make yourself a target." He moved away from her, turned, and looked her in the eyes. "Maybe this is the perfect opportunity for you to step away until whatever's coming is over," he said, continuing his gaze. "Maybe it's best for you to get on back to Tahlequah so at least one of us comes out alive and sane."

Turning away, he stepped out of the tent and walked away. Billy's change in mood had come so quickly Lisa didn't know what hit her. She followed after him.

"Billy, wait!" she called after him.

He kept walking, hands in his jeans pockets.

"What's going on with you? I'm no helpless girl. Have you forgotten who rescued you from the House of Bones?"

He stopped and turned back to her.

"No, I haven't forgotten," he replied. "But I've never really been responsible for anyone else but me before. If I go through with this initiation, I'm taking on the responsibility for the whole world. Everyone on the planet will be relying on me to save them! It's too much pressure!"

With a panicked look on his face, he ran a hand through his hair, then pulled on the ends in the classic Billy Buckhorn stress maneuver.

"You're sounding rather pathetic right now," Lisa countered. "Poor me, poor me. I'm not good enough. The weight of the entire world is on my shoulders, and of course I'm going to probably fail."

"That about sums it up."

"Don't tell me that you believe for one minute that the ancestor spirits, the Intertribal Medicine Council, the Thunder Beings, and the rest of the Upperworld thought you could handle any of this on your own?" Lisa said angrily. "Naive or egotistical—I don't know which it is."

"What are you saying?"

Her tone softened as she stepped closer to him. "That there's a whole team of much more experienced people, forces, and allies at your side. And that includes me. I'm in it, no matter the outcome."

Billy relaxed his body and hugged his girlfriend. "I don't deserve you," he admitted.

"You'll get no argument from me," Lisa replied as she moved his lips to hers.

At precisely six the next morning, Billy heard the flap on his tent being unzipped.

Before he knew what was happening, two Native men thrust themselves into the tent and grabbed him. They dragged him out of the tent and stuck a black cloth bag over his head. The teen had gone to sleep fully dressed, as he often did when camping. Billy struggled against his captors until he heard Cecil's voice.

"First you must be reborn from the womb of Mother Earth," he said. "That is where we are going now."

Billy was shuffled off with the bag over his head. The two men held him up as they trekked over the uneven ground. A few minutes of walking brought them to the bluffs the teen had seen as they arrived at the camp yesterday. He could tell by the way the sounds of their voices and footfalls echoed back to his ears from the wall of stone.

"Some call this place History Cave because of the thousand-year-old drawings inside," Cecil said. "But we know it as the Womb of First Woman, the place of birth for the human race."

Billy was led into the mouth of the cave, and he experienced a momentary flash of fear as the memory of bats pelting his body jumped into his mind. He swallowed hard and kept moving as a heavy sulfurous smell filled his nostrils and the sound of dripping water filled his ears. The air inside was very warm and humid, just the opposite of the cave he and Chigger had explored last Thanksgiving.

Two strong sets of hands on his shoulders kept the boy moving into the vast cavity along uneven ground. Their footsteps echoed off stone walls, and the sound of moving water intensified. Cecil said something in his tribal language, and the two men stopped moving.

Suddenly, the bag was ripped off the boy's head as two high-powered flashlights were turned on and aimed at a nearby cave wall. The boy blinked a few times as his eyes adjusted to the brightly lit painted panorama that came into view.

"Here is recorded the epic tale of the creation of humankind, as well as the deeds of the Hero Twins, who freed us from the terrors of the giants and slayed the monsters that preyed on human flesh," Cecil explained. "Oral traditions passed the stories to our medicine men priests long ago, and they depicted those events here. Our tribe's medicine men are traditionally called Men of the Great Mystery."

Billy was amazed at the detailed drawings of both Upperworld and Underworld supernatural characters spread out over a hundred-foot space of the flat cave wall.

"You will hear the whole story as part of your initiation ceremony," Cecil added.

Then Billy was ushered a little deeper into the cave, where another smaller set of drawings could be seen. Two warrior figures occupied the center of the mural.

"When Shakuru and his twin brother, Monkata, were born on the same day the bright sign in the sky appeared along with the falling Sky Stone, everyone believed the pair was the reincarnation of the Hero Twins," Cecil said. "Monkata even exhibited the gift of prophecy. But as the boys grew and Monkata increasingly displayed dark behaviors and interests, the people's attitudes toward him changed."

The group moved closer to the cave drawings, and Billy saw a series of drawings of the twins. The one on the left consistently looked strong and radiant. But the figure on the right looked increasingly misshapen and dark. The figure immediately reminded Billy of the misshapen entity that had tried to take over his body in the cave of the Horned Serpent.

"By the time the boys had become young men, the community could no longer tolerate the actions and attitudes of Monkata, and he was banished from the village. Soon afterward, he formed the Snake Cult, took the title Snake Priest, and immersed himself in the dark medicine."

Cecil aimed his flashlight at the final image of the panorama, which portrayed the figure on the right, Monkata, as a completely deformed figure.

"His descent into the culture of the Underworld was so deep that it began to deform not only his body but also his spirit," Cecil concluded.

"Why are you showing me all this?" Billy asked.

"So you'll have a complete picture of what we're up against, what forces will be brought to the battle, and what forces are on our side."

A gust of hot damp air unexpectedly hit Billy in the face. The strong draft seemed to come from within the fathomless cavern.

"That's our cue," Cecil said. "The first step of the ceremony is about to begin."

The black bag was immediately replaced on Billy's head as he was escorted down a narrow path that led deeper into the cave. As they walked, Cecil spoke.

"People from several tribes have visited this sacred space for generations for healing and rebirthing ceremonies," he said.

The smell of sulfur was strong now, and the air was much warmer. For a second time, the bag was suddenly pulled off Billy. This time, what lay before him was a turquoise pool of milky water covered by a layer of steam—a natural hot tub. The body of liquid glowed as if lit from within.

"What makes this water glow?" Billy asked.

"The phosphorescence is caused by rare minerals present throughout the cave. The walls of this pool are filled with them. As I mentioned, the healing waters of this ancient spring have attracted Indigenous people for hundreds, if not thousands, of years."

Cecil pointed with his lips to a boulder behind Billy.

"Please take your clothes off and put them over there. You must be wearing nothing but your birthday suit for this."

Billy was surprised by these instructions, but because he trusted Cecil, he did as the elder asked. Then Cecil led the teen into the warm pool of water, leaving one of the Native escorts behind. The other one accompanied the elder and the teen into the waist-deep pool.

"Today you begin the process of being reborn. You begin the transition away from being a mere Cherokee boy from eastern Oklahoma. In four days, you will emerge as a new being, a spiritual warrior with a new identity and purpose."

Like an old-time gospel preacher baptizing a new convert, the escort supported Billy's back as he leaned the boy backward and dipped his head in the mineral water four times.

"I purify you in the healing waters of our ancestors so that your mind, body, and spirit will be strengthened for the struggle ahead," Cecil said as the baptism proceeded. "In the name of the sacred four: Waconda the Great Mystery, Morningstar, the Sun, and the Son of the Sun. A-ho! It is done."

When they were finished, the three stepped out of the water, where Billy was handed a towel and a pair of fringed pants made of soft deerskin.

"This is what you'll wear for the next four days," Cecil said as Billy was led out of the cave.

The four walked to the dance arena where the sacred tree stood. Dozens of people were seated in the circular arbor that surrounded the central dance area. Billy's parents, along with Lisa and her father, sat next to each other. The thirteen members of the ITMC, including Wesley, took up half of the seating.

A traditional drum group with four male singers occupied the northern area of the arbor.

In the eastern segment, Billy saw several faces he recognized. They were dancers from his home stomp dance grounds dressed in Cherokee dance regalia. The head man dancer briefly nodded his greeting to Billy.

"I didn't know there would be so many people watching," Billy said.

"These are not spectators," Cecil observed. "Each one has a part to perform in the ceremony, even your mother and father."

Cecil led Billy and his two Native escorts into the center, where they stood next to the sacred tree. The old medicine man removed his shirt, revealing for the first time multiple scars in the area covering his pectoral muscles, and an intricate tattoo covering his chest and belly. Billy studied it for a long minute.

The central image of the tattoo was surrounded by a circle. Within the circle stood a pole that displayed the double helix of human DNA. Right in the center of the pole was a small circle with the four-directional cross. At the top of the pole sat a majestic bird with wings spread wide.

At the bottom of the pole, seeming to support it, were two Horned Serpents like Billy had seen in the cave near Spiral Mounds.

"In my tribe, all the spiritual leaders, known as Men of the Great Mystery, wear this tattoo," Cecil said. "It represents the cosmos as we see it, with the Thunderbird at the top. He's resting on the sacred tree of life, the central axis that connects the Upperworld, Middleworld, and Underworld."

Billy continued to examine the details of the finely embedded image. Cecil pointed to different parts of the tattoo as he talked.

"The image also represents the three aspects of us human beings. At the top is our higher self. In the middle is our conscious self, the part we identify with most. At the bottom we find our lower nature as well as our subconscious self. A successful life on earth requires a balance of all three parts."

Cecil nodded toward the drummers seated in the arbor. The head singer beat the drum once. And then it began, a ceremony like no other, to honor and elevate a mere mortal who would rise to almost immortal stature, at least in the eyes of those gathered there.

The drum group began with a northern-style song as a line of Plains Indian dancers moved into the arena in a clockwise direction. As they circled the area, the line formed a spinning, dancing spiral around the sacred tree. Their feet stirred up a cloud of dust that continued to hover just above the ground.

Stomp dancers entered next, adding their rhythmic rain effect. But they moved in the traditional Cherokee counterclockwise direction, careful to move in between the line of Plains dancers going in the opposite direction.

Other participants, those seated in the arbor, joined the dancers, each taking up a place in whichever line reflected the direction they were accustomed to. Even James and Rebecca Buckhorn joined in, demonstrating their full commitment to their son's spiritual path.

Cecil, Billy, and the other two Native men in the center stood in place and moved their feet to the beat of the drum. The ceremonial song and dance continued for another ten minutes or so. The pounding and singing intensified as singers, drummers, and dancers moved ever more deeply into their own hearts and minds.

Earth and sky seemed to absorb and amplify the sights and sounds that circled around and reverberated from the nearby cliffs until a synchronized final syllable and beat halted the entire panorama, and a resounding note echoed through the valley.

Holding an obsidian knife in his right hand and two short wooden skewers in his left, Cecil approached Billy in the silence. All eyes in the dance arena were focused on the pair.

"Do you, Billy Buckhorn, of your own free will, accept the role of the Chosen One with all the responsibilities that go with it, which we are about to confer upon you?" he said loudly enough for all to hear.

Billy took a moment to search the gathered crowd with his eyes. Finding his father and mother, he looked at them questioningly. They both nodded their ascent. Then the boy swept the audience until he found Lisa. With a hand on her heart, the girl mouthed her assent as well.

"Yes . . . yes, I do."

Immediately, a line of elderly Native men entered the arena and formed a circle around the central sacred tree where Billy and Cecil stood. Once they'd found their places, Cecil signaled them, and they began singing a different song.

Billy immediately recognized the melody as the one the Sun Chief and his four helpers had hummed every time he'd left his physical body. It was similar to one of the songs used at the Live Oak stomp grounds.

"To symbolize your willingness to sacrifice yourself in order to save humanity, I will pierce your flesh and tie you to the sacred tree, where you will remain for the next three days. When the ceremony is complete, the scars from these wounds will remind you in the years to come of the commitment you made today."

When the elder came close with the stone blade and skewers, Billy immediately regretted agreeing to take on this role. This was going to really hurt! Cecil saw the apprehensive look on the boy's face.

"You won't actually feel this too severely because you will have already begun your spirit travel before I make the cuts," Cecil assured him.

At a signal from the elder, the singing circle of men closed in on the pair, singing their song more loudly than before. Four of the men stepped even closer to Billy and reached their arms out until they touched him from the four directions.

The familiar vibrations engulfed the boy's physical body, and within a few seconds, his spirit body sprang to freedom as his physical body collapsed on the ground. The two Native escorts picked up his unconscious body and placed it on a nearby blanket.

Kneeling beside him, Cecil proceeded to perform a common procedure in sun dance rituals all across America as he cut two sets of slits in Billy's upper body in the pectoral muscles. As blood began to spill out of the wounds, the elder thrust one of the skewers into each of the through-and-through lesions. There was no apparent reaction from Billy.

Then, with support from the two escorts, Billy's body was raised off the ground and turned to face the sacred tree. Cecil tied two sets of ropes that hung from the tree's trunk to the ends of the skewers as Billy's feet were set on the ground. The two escorts, still supporting the weight of the boy's body, leaned the boy backward until the ropes tied to the skewers were taut. With his feet still on the ground, Billy now hung at an angle from the tree.

One of Cecil's helpers brought him a bucket filled with a liquid herbal concoction that was used to wash some of the blood off Billy's chest. Cecil turned to those watching from the arbor.

"If any of you would like to join the ceremony in support of Billy, please come forward now. Find a place in the circle to face the tree and dance for as long as you can. Send your positive energy and prayerful thoughts to this brave young man."

Lisa immediately rose from her seat and headed into the circle. Standing as close to Billy as she was allowed, she turned her gaze to the Thunderbird's nest in the top of the tree and began dancing in place. Familiar with the ancient rhythmic chant being sung, she joined in.

CHAPTER FIFTEEN

Billy's Journey

Billy's release from his physical body felt like he'd bounced on a trampoline and then shot skyward. He landed in the nest at the top of the sacred tree. Looking down, he watched as Cecil cut into his chest with the glassy black blade. He felt some minor pain in the corresponding area of his energy body, but it seemed like it was happening far away.

He began drifting higher as the rest of the dance arena came into view. So many people had come to participate in the ceremony! As Cecil and the two escorts manipulated his physical body, Billy searched the arbor to see if he could spot Lisa. But the leafy branches spread over the top of the circular structure made it hard to find her.

Moments later, people began leaving their seats and stepping into the circle around the sacred tree. That was when he spotted his girlfriend moving toward his physical body. She took up a position nearby and began dancing. His parents came into the dance circle as well, and that was the last thing he saw before being rapidly drawn away.

Zooming, stretching, hurtling—these were the sensations Billy felt next as his spirit body sped toward some unknown destination. He had the feeling he was somehow passing through layers. The first couple of layers seemed thick and dense, but the upper layers . . . Was he moving upward? He wasn't sure. But the upper layers felt lighter, less dense.

Suddenly, his motion ended as he burst onto a scene, a landscape, a space—how to define it? He had landed somewhere he'd never been before. Of that, he was sure. But where? He was in a large dome-shaped room that contained familiar objects and designs. The curved ceiling was clear, and millions of stars were brilliantly visible.

Seven brush arbors stood in a circle along the outer edge of the space, like those at Live Oak stomp grounds. On the floor was a counterclockwise spiral pattern, echoing the spiraling dance pattern created by stomp dancers and the paths at Spiral Mounds. In the center of the space, rather than a fire, was the sacred tree, like the one in the dance arena he'd just left. Only this one was more like a living pole that seemed to extend from under the earth up into the Upperworld.

"I see you have questions," a voice said, coming from out of visual range. "It's only natural that you would."

Billy looked around the space, searching for the source of the voice. A soft light began to shine down on him from above the dome's ceiling, and the boy looked up in time to see a ball of light descending toward him. The object's brightness grew as it drew nearer, causing him to shield his spiritual eyes.

"Sorry," the voice said. "I'll turn down the brightness level."

In a few seconds, the ball of light became a glowing man about twelve feet tall. He wore pieces of regalia like those in drawings Billy had seen in the big Mound Builder book Ethan had given him at Cahokia.

"Is that better?" the man asked.

"Much," Billy answered.

"What is this place, and who am I. Those are the first things you want to know, right?"

"Totally."

"This is your new home in the nonphysical realm—a base of operations, so to speak. You can launch your explorations from here and plan your strategies."

"Huh?" Billy blurted out.

"And I am what you are becoming," the man continued. "The process began when you saw the ladder with the thirteen steps at Live Oak at the end of last summer."

"Uh . . . okay," Billy replied. "Who are you exactly?"

"Indigenous people of North America know me as Morningstar. Some legends say I helped the Hero Twins rid the Middleworld of giants and monsters so humans could live there. Other legends say I defeated the monsters that used to live in the Upperworld and cast them down to the Underworld."

"Okay, which is it?"

"Neither and both," the man said. "Those are the legends of humans trying to make sense of the past hardships of physical life and only partially remembering what really happened."

He paused, allowing Billy to process that answer.

"More about that later," the man continued. "For now, let's say I'm available to you as a teacher, guide, and chaperone—someone you can come to when things get tough. And they will get tough."

"Don't you already know everything that's going to happen? Aren't you all-seeing? Why don't you just use your Upperworld powers to prevent whatever it is that's about to happen?"

"I *have* experienced several human lives in several different eras, but transitioning from the physical back to this realm doesn't automatically make you a know-it-all."

"But my grandma Awinita seems to know an awful lot," Billy said. "What about that?"

"Your grandmother is exceptional," Morningstar said. "She's the exception to the rule. She's been playing an important part of the plan that you're also involved in. More will be revealed soon."

Billy took time to formulate his next question.

"On your way here, it felt like you passed through some sort of layers," Morningstar said, anticipating the boy's words. "You want to know about that."

"Lucky guess," Billy said, attempting a little joke.

"Belief zones of the Afterworld," the glowing man said, ignoring the joke.

"Whoosh," Billy said, making the gesture of something flying over his head.

"People's own beliefs about the Afterworld affect where they end up, at least temporarily. The stronger the belief, the longer the stay. Works the same with fears. It's complicated and yet simple at the same time."

Billy remained silent for a while.

"And then there's the Shadow Zone," Morningstar added. "That's a whole other phenomenon we have to deal with."

"Doesn't sound good," Billy said.

"Maybe this will help clear things up," the spirit man said. "The Upperworld, Middleworld, and Underworld are cosmically connected."

"Right," Billy said. "I get that idea."

"The Afterworld overlaps a little with those three," Morningstar continued.

"Nope, that didn't help clear anything up. Are you sure I'm the right man—uh, teen—for the job?"

"You will be once your training begins. You've had experiences and been given powers that put you ahead of anyone else on the planet. We'll be seeing a lot of each other for a while."

Billy noticed what looked like two roiling clouds above and behind Morningstar. Flashes of lightning were visible within them.

"Ah, here they are," Morningstar said. "The brothers have come to share something of themselves with you."

"Brothers?" Billy said.

"The twin Thunders, the Thunder Beings, the ones who chose you."

"Another myth comes to life," Billy said as a feeling of amazement filled him. "Won't Grandpa be pleased."

The two cloud balls remained at some distance from Billy's domed space, and he got the idea it was for his own good.

"That's as close as they can safely come," Morningstar said. "Now don't move from the place you're now standing, even if it seems like you should."

Billy wondered what that meant just as a ball of lightning shot from each of the thundering clouds. The white flashes of light merged into one as they flew toward him. He stood his ground as the energy washed over and through him.

For a moment he felt like pure electrical energy, and the memory of being struck by a lightning bolt while fishing at Lake Tenkiller came to his mind. This time he didn't pass out, but if he had skin right now, and there were hairs on that skin, they would be standing on end!

"Now you are truly the child of the Thunders," Morningstar said as the two thunderclouds began to recede. "And they've given you a spiritual energy reserve that you'll be able to call on in desperate times."

Suddenly, Billy began feeling an urgent need from the physical plane, coming from his body back at the dance arena. He tried to ignore it.

"When I get back to Middleworld, what should I do first?"

"One important task is to release Shakuru from the dark force holding him bound to his bones. Shadow Zone dwellers have been able to tie him down and conceal his whereabouts for quite a long time."

The physical signal suddenly came in strong, and the energy of Billy's nonphysical body began to flicker and fade.

"Time to go," Morningstar said, reading the situation. "To be continued."

"How do I find this place again?" Billy thought to ask before leaving. "Seems like trying to find a needle in a cosmic haystack."

Duplicating an action Billy had seen the Sun Chief perform, Morningstar propelled a small energy ball toward the teen. It quickly washed over him and left something new behind.

"I've programmed this location into your energy field, like how you'd use a GPS signal to get directions on your phone," the spirit man said. "This place is part of Level Four, just above the highest Afterworld level. You'll have no trouble finding your way back here."

And that was the end of the encounter.

Billy's path back to the physical took him through the layers again, and he was able to get only brief snapshots of settings and circumstances as he whizzed by. He slammed back into his body like an airplane hitting the runway a little too hard. He was immediately met with excruciating pain from the cuts in his chest.

"Ow!" he yelled as his body awakened. Realizing that his shout had startled nearby dancers, he followed it with "Oops."

But the mind-blowing memory of the out-of-body experience he'd just had made him remember the bigger picture he'd been shown. Feeling the rhythm of the song sung by others around him, he leaned backward against the pull of the ropes tied to the sacred tree. He searched nearby faces until he found Lisa in the throng of dancers and smiled.

Intuitively he knew what had to be done within the ceremony: pull against the ropes until the skewers that had been threaded through his flesh broke free and he fell backward.

Billy tried mightily to remain conscious as he danced. He actually wanted to be present and feel the pain of the experience. Somehow he knew he'd need to remember this moment and that pain in the challenging days ahead.

But however much he tried, the effect of the song and its mesmerizing melody could not be denied. His nonphysical body once again separated from the physical. This time, however, instead of drifting upward, he fell backward, seemingly into the earth.

He felt the sensation of passing through layers once again, but these were dense, oppressive layers that were physically and psychologically suffocating. And dark, so dark. The phrase "seeing through a glass darkly" came to Billy's mind, but he didn't know its source.

Billy's descent came to an end within a shadow-filled area, and Morningstar's words about the Shadow Zone along with "beliefs about the Afterworld" immediately popped into his mind.

Compared to the wide-open spaces of the upper layers, this area was a murky mess. And it was very different from the gray fog Billy had experienced once before. There were entities mucking around down here. And *mucking* seemed like the right description, because when he tried to move, it felt like he was moving through molasses.

But an idea inserted itself into Billy's mind. Even though he "fell" out of his body and dropped down into the earth, this area wasn't really underground. That was more of a symbolic idea. There was nothing of the nonphysical realm to be found underground. The Underworld wasn't really beneath the earth's surface, just like the old ideas of Hades and Hell weren't literally underground. Those were just metaphors for afterlife concepts.

It dawned on Billy that these last few ideas didn't come from within him. He didn't regularly use terms like *metaphors*, *Hades*, or *Hell*. Who was feeding him this information?

Then, in his mind, he heard, "Morningstar, at your service."

Must be another lesson, Billy thought as another question formed in his mind.

"How did those souls get down there, you ask?" Morningstar posited.

"Exactly," Billy thought.

"Using metaphors again, the souls of people who've primarily helped and served and benefited others on earth become light and tend to float upward at death," the spirit replied. "The souls of people who've primarily taken advantage of or hurt others in their physical lives become heavy with negativity, and they fall downward. It's pretty simple, really—metaphorically speaking, of course."

Billy detected a hint of humor in Morningstar's response but had no time to think any more about it, because he suddenly rejoined his physical body just at the moment that the wooden skewers broke free from his chest. The ripping pain was excruciating, and he screamed louder than he'd ever screamed before as his body fell back and hit the hard physical ground.

Everything in the arena came to a complete halt. The singers stopped mid-note, and the dancers ceased moving mid-step. All was quiet.

At that very moment, a lightning bolt cut through the cloudless sky, striking the sacred tree in the middle of the dance arena. The accompanying loud crack forced everyone in that valley to cover their ears. No one dared to move or speak.

The tree had split and splintered into several pieces, releasing a blast of fire and smoke along with the pungent smell of burnt wood. Grabbing a nearby bucket, Ethan doused the burning tree with water. When the smoke cleared, Billy saw the darkened core of the tree trunk still standing in the hole where the sacred tree once stood. The outer layers of the tree were splayed out on the ground around the core in the four directions.

Cecil approached the smoldering wooden shaft and touched it lightly to see if it was hot to the touch. Finding it only slightly warm, the elder lifted it from the hole and tapped the end of it on the ground. Soot and burnt wood splinters fell off.

The grain of the five-foot-long piece of wood formed an unexpected spiraling pattern, making it almost look like a finely carved walking stick. Holding the wooden shaft with both hands, Cecil looked to the sky and said loudly, "*Oweena*"—"thank you" in the Osage language.

Cecil, still carrying the lightning wood, and Wesley came to help Billy stand up. The boy's body was bloody, dusty, and tired. He looked like he'd just come from the battlefield. Cecil spoke to Billy but in a voice loud enough for the gathered crowd to hear.

"You entered this ceremonial arena as Cherokee teen Billy Buckhorn. Chosen by the Thunders to be their son and given unique abilities and powers, you leave the arena today as a new being with a new spirit warrior name."

Turning toward the people and holding the lightning-struck wood up over his head, he said, "I give you Thunder Child!"

Hoots, hollers, lulus, and "a-hos" resounded from the gathered crowd as the elder presented the boy with the long piece of burnt wood.

"This is the warrior's staff, your Lightning Lance, you will carry with you into the battle, which is coming soon!" Cecil announced.

Several members of the Intertribal Medicine Council, though elders, worked together to raise Billy up and above their heads. Six of them carried him aloft as they moved to one of the arbors where a cot had been set up.

As Billy lay on the cot, his mother and Cecil's sister tended to the wounds, cleansing them first to prevent infection. A poultice made of ground-up medicinal herbs was smeared over the cuts, and then gauze bandages were applied over them.

"You'll be good as new in a day or two," Josephine said to Billy.

"Your body has experienced more physical abuse than anyone I know," Billy's mother said as she saw Lisa approaching. Whispering in Billy's ear, Rebecca added, "Don't do anything to aggravate those wounds."

Then she winked and stepped away.

"I've never heard anyone scream as loud as you did," Lisa said with a smile as Billy lay on the cot. "You'd think you were dying or something."

Billy began to sit up when he saw his grandfather approaching. The elder rested a hand on the young man's shoulder, saying, "Don't get up." Then he pulled a small item from a bag he'd been holding and presented it to his grandson.

"I've been saving this until the right time presented itself. That time has arrived. I present you with the most powerful warrior medicine known to the Cherokee Nation. I collected it the day we resealed the Horned Serpent in the cave by the river."

Wesley revealed a medium-sized deerskin medicine pouch tied to a deerskin strap and placed it around the young man's neck.

"What's inside the pouch?"

"Only a scale from the skin of the Uktena," Wesley said.

Billy could hardly believe it. "But how did you get it?"

"After the creature was recaptured, I saw it wedged between some rocks on the side of the cliff below the cave entrance. I was just fortunate enough to notice it and know what it was."

"Thanks, Grandpa," Billy said. "I can always count on you to do something extraordinary."

The teen paused as a realization hit him.

"This is all very real now," he said. "All the things Grandma said are coming true. The things you told me about the ladder with thirteen steps at the stomp grounds. The part the Sun Priest said I'm to play in the scheme of things—all of it."

"I said you were becoming the teacher, and I'm the student," Wesley replied. "We're moving quickly in that direction, so you'd better get some rest. We've got a big meeting to attend later. All hands on deck and all that."

The elder patted his grandson gently on the shoulder and said, "Lisa, why don't we give the boy wonder here a chance to rest?"

She patted Billy on the head and said, "See you later, boy wonder."

After a nap, Billy met with the ITMC, which Wesley was now a part of. Cecil led off the meeting with a list of tasks the council and Billy needed to accomplish.

"Here's our to-do list," Cecil said. "And it's long." He read from a page where he'd scribbled notes.

"First, we must help Shakuru break free from the bondage spell cast by the Snakes. We'll need his abilities and experience in the coming standoff. Second, we must recover the missing piece of the Sky Stone and the Sun Chief's original staff and cape. As you know, the crystal on the staff fits in the center of the stone to activate the soul incarnation spell. Third: we've got to get Thunder Child trained in the medicine practices of all members of the ITMC. We don't know which tribe's medicine will be most effective in the coming conflict or which spell he may need for any given situation.

"Finally, when the time comes, Thunder Child will begin his attempts to block the efforts of the Owls and Snakes to raise up an army of Underworld entities, as foretold in the prophecy. This includes his thorough understanding of the tribal beliefs found in the American Indian *Book of the Dead*."

Billy was having a hard time registering the fact he was the Thunder Child person Cecil was talking about, and the to-do list included many tasks for him to accomplish. In his own mind, he was still just Billy.

Are people supposed to call me Thunder Child now? That seems, I don't know, sort of phony or like I'm putting on airs.

He put it out of his mind for the time being as the meeting continued for several hours.

Both Wesley and Billy met and visited with all the members of the Intertribal Medicine Council. During the session, the teen recounted his out-of-body meeting with Morningstar at the new base camp in the nonphysical realm.

"We'll set up a training schedule that will include a personal visit with every member of this council so you can begin learning their most guarded secret medicine practices," Cecil told the teen. "Each one, as you know, has a specialty, an enhanced ability in one area."

One of the Medicine Council members stepped forward from the seated circle.

"This is Andrew Blackbird of the White Earth Reservation in Minnesota," Cecil said. "Because of the recent unusual tornado event, we've asked him to work with Thunder Child first, since his medicine affects weather patterns."

"*Aaniin,*" Blackbird said. "That means 'I see your light' in the Anishinaabe language, but it's usually just translated as 'hello.'"

The elder shook Billy's hand and then returned to his seat.

After the meeting ended, the newly crowned Thunder Child requested a private meeting with Cecil.

"I don't know what I was expecting, but I don't really feel like a Thunder Child," the teen said. "Am I supposed to call myself that now? Are other people supposed to call me that? It makes me sound like, well, I think I'm special or better than everybody else."

"To activate your gifts and powers, you definitely have to speak as Thunder Child, address all supernatural forces using that title—with authority," Cecil replied. "I think it'll feel more natural once you begin calling on help from the Upperworld and you see some real results in the physical world. Give it a little time."

Cecil knew that Billy's physical body also needed a little time to heal, so he delayed the beginning of the teen's first training session a couple of days. Waiting a couple of days also ensured that all nonessential guests had left the ceremonial grounds. The last to leave were the Buckhorns and the Lookouts, except for Lisa, whose motorcycle and sidecar would provide transportation for her and Billy.

Cecil also knew that the word *training* wasn't exactly accurate for what Billy would experience with each of the thirteen members of the Medicine Council. The process was going to be more like a transference of power, facilitated by Morningstar. What Blackbird, and indeed all the medicine makers, would demonstrate and share were well-guarded secrets that no one outside of their immediate families or tribal healers was privy to.

After two boring days of rest and relaxation, Billy felt ready to take the next step, learning how to control weather from the Anishinaabe medicine man. Before beginning the process, Billy offered him a gift.

"My grandfather taught me to always present a gift to anyone who is going to share traditional tribal knowledge with me," he said. "Please accept this bundle of tobacco, sage, cedar, and sweetgrass as a token of my appreciation."

After accepting the gift, the medicine man said, "Your grandfather taught you well."

The man placed the bundle of four sacred medicines in the leather case he'd brought and removed a beaded eagle feather fan and rattle from it.

"In my tribe I'm known as a weather maker," Andrew said. "Every generation of my people has had one as far back as anyone can remember. The weather event we just witnessed a few days ago, the straight-line tornado, has all the telltale signs of being the work of a weather maker, probably someone in Oklahoma."

Blackbird spent the day demonstrating all aspects of his weather-altering capabilities, including the songs, words, and hand gestures involved.

"How am I ever going to memorize and master all of that?" Billy asked the elder when he was finished.

"Cecil assured me that Morningstar is taking care of that part."

"Morningstar," Billy said, gratefully understanding how it was all going to work. As if summoned, an apparition began becoming visible in front of Billy. Andrew, however, was unaware of what was taking place.

"At your service," the spirit being responded as a voice in Billy's mind. "Who do you think taught the Sun Chief how to transfer messages and abilities to you to begin with?"

"I never really thought about it."

"Stand next to Andrew, and the transfer of knowledge will begin," the spirit man said.

Billy explained to Andrew what was happening and followed Morningstar's directions.

The teen immediately felt a flow of energy moving into and through him. Within a few seconds, it was finished, and Billy felt simultaneously exhilarated and drained.

One down and twelve to go, he thought.

No Bones About It

Chigger noticed that the Buckhorns had been absent from their home for quite some time. He noticed this because he drove by the log house every day. He wasn't sure why he was doing this, but it seemed like something he was supposed to do. He'd always report his findings to his mentor, Carmelita.

He had begun receiving more serious, detailed instruction in Cherokee medicine practices from her, but the boy eventually realized she never saw any patients. That seemed odd for someone who was supposedly a traditional Native doctor. Billy had said that there was always a line of Indians waiting for treatment outside Wesley's house.

During today's lesson, Carmelita had praised Chigger for his recent progress before giving him another cup of her favorite herbal tea and engulfing him in a puff of smoke from her funny-smelling cigarette. He knew it wasn't marijuana she was smoking, because he'd sampled that more than once during parties at a friend's house. This was some other herb.

Now he was on a new mission, this time back to Wesley's house. He'd visited the medicine man's home once before on his teacher's behalf but had failed to achieve his goal then. This time would be different, he hoped. He was to leave a pouch of herbs in several rooms of the house and retrieve the old medicine book created by Benjamin Blacksnake.

Carmelita had explained that the local police had given the book to Wesley after the Raven Stalker incident, because they said no one else would want it. But the book of course should've been passed on to Benjamin's family, and she had assured Chigger that she'd take care of that little mistake once the book was in her possession.

Chigger was double lucky today. First, because the hidden key to Wesley's front door was exactly where Billy had said it would be during one of their many discussions over the years. Second, because the book was so easy to find.

Billy's grandfather originally stored Blacksnake's medicine book in the old bank safe in back of his house. But since Billy had learned to read Cherokee, the teen had been looking through it to see if it contained any out-of-the-ordinary spells that warranted closer study. He'd marked a few pages with Post-it Notes and left the book right out on Wesley's kitchen table for further review.

Carmelita will be so pleased, Chigger thought as he grabbed the weighty tome and exited the house. Little did he suspect that she had a different plan for the book than the one she'd shared with him.

Back at the ceremonial grounds, a caravan of vehicles and a motorcycle departed from that ceremonial field in central Missouri, headed for different points in southeastern Oklahoma. Rebecca drove the family Jeep back home to Park Hill as James drove Billy's truck to the same destination. Both of them had to get back to their jobs.

Ethan, in his Indigenous Archaeology Alliance van, was going to the university campus in Tahlequah to see Augustus Stevens. Cecil and Wesley, in Wesley's truck, made their way toward Tuskahoma, while Lisa and Billy, on Lisa's bike, headed for Spiral Mounds. Would any of them be successful in their quests? None of them knew for sure.

Lisa and Billy carried a small tent, sleeping bags, and some food in the motorcycle sidecar on their six-hour trek that took them to a camping spot on the Arkansas River downstream from the Spiral Mounds. That was where they would spend the night before entering the mounds site in the morning. It wasn't an official public campground, but no one would bother them there.

Billy, not used to riding on the back of a bike, was rather stiff when he dismounted and removed his helmet. Two small spots of blood on the front of his shirt told Lisa it was time to change the bandages over the wounds on her boyfriend's chest.

Before setting up camp, she re-dressed the lesions, noticing once again that Billy's shirt also looked a little tighter on him than it did a few days ago.

"Did you bring any bigger clothes?" she asked.

"No, we'd better find a Walmart or something nearby." Thinking about their objective at Spiral Mounds, he added, "I hope the park director, Langford, remembers me. Otherwise, the people who work there may think it odd that I'm lying on the ground in front of the burial mound with my eyes closed."

He surveyed the clearing and the nearby waterway. He took Lisa's hand and led her to the river's edge. The gentle sound of the slow-moving water reminded him of the previous time he'd been in the area.

"The last time I was here, our team of four with the silly name put a mythological beast back to sleep in a forgotten cave upstream," he said. "Chigger and I were best friends then."

Lisa picked up on the tinge of sadness in Billy's voice and moved closer to him. "When this whole thing's over, maybe you can rekindle your friendship."

"Maybe," he replied as he pulled her to himself and kissed her.

As their bodies pressed up against each other, he released a groan of pain and pulled away, placing a hand on his chest.

"It's a good thing you're wounded, mister, or I might not be able to restrain myself," Lisa said as she walked away from him. "We'd better set up camp."

The following morning, just after nine, the pair presented themselves to the park director, Peter Langford, at the interpretive center. During a brief interaction, Billy reintroduced himself and then introduced Lisa.

"Lisa's father is archaeologist Ethan Lookout," Billy said. "Their family—"

"I know who the Lookouts are," Langford said rather abruptly. "A rather persistent pain in my posterior. It wasn't enough that your grandfather stopped in unannounced earlier this month? You've come to harass me too?"

"But—" Billy said but couldn't finish.

"I'll tell you the same thing I told him," Langford continued angrily. "NAGPRA is meant to create a dialog between museum sites and Indian tribes. It's not an excuse for you to show up anytime you'd like and make demands about your ancestors."

NAGPRA, the acronym for the Native American Graves Protection and Repatriation Act, was a law passed by Congress in 1990 to protect Native American human remains and require agencies operating with US government funds to consult with Indian tribes about returning burial items to the tribes they originally came from.

Billy stepped between the director and his girlfriend.

"That's not why we're here!" he said forcefully. "We just want to spend some quiet time near the burial mound without being disturbed. Is that too much to ask? Or do I need to call my good friend Augustus Stevens at the university? He and Lisa's father are quite close."

Langford immediately calmed down.

"No, no, no," he said, suddenly becoming more friendly. "No need to call anyone."

He straightened his tie and adjusted his suit. Opening the top drawer of his desk, he pulled out a couple of passes and signed them. He handed one to each of them.

"I apologize for my reaction. I've been under a lot of stress lately. These annual passes will get you into the park without cost for a full year. Please be my guests."

"Thank you," Billy said curtly. "That's more like it."

The pair walked out of the interpretive center and headed down the path toward the Sun Chief's burial mound, which was farthest from the park entrance. When they were sure they were out of the director's sight, the two broke out laughing.

"Or do I need to call my good friend Augustus Stevens at the university?" Lisa said, imitating Billy. "He and Lisa's father are quite close," she added, with great bravado.

"Did you see how fast his attitude changed?" Billy said with a chuckle. "I thought he was going to get whiplash the turn was so fast."

"But he was acting a little strange, don't you think?" Lisa observed.

"Yeah, I wonder what that was about."

The pair fell silent as they casually strolled along the winding path that led deeper into the park.

The day before, Cecil and Wesley had driven to the Tuskahoma area to follow up on the search for the missing piece of the Sky Stone. After spending the night in a nearby mountain cabin called Eagle's Nest, the two elders arrived at the historic Choctaw Nation Council House early in the morning before it opened for the day.

Cecil showed Wesley the bronze Red Warrior statue he'd visited before but hadn't been able to access. This time they'd brought a stepladder to help them climb the brick wall that skirted the sculpture. Because of his bad knee, Wesley declined to climb the ladder but instead held it steady while Cecil clambered up a few steps, and then kept watch.

"You're sure this is where Elmore hid it?" Wesley asked as Cecil dug in the dirt at the foot of the statue with the small spade he'd brought.

"'Peace waits for those who know,'" the Osage elder said, reciting a line from Elmore Proctor's clue. "'Take counsel at the house to the north. Kneel at the foot of red warrior. Leave no stone unturned.' This council house is north of Elmore's place, and here is the red warrior, plain as day. What else could it mean?"

Wesley thought about it as Cecil continued to dig. Then the spade struck something metallic and hard, making a loud *clunk* sound.

"Aha!" Cecil exclaimed as he quickly scraped dirt away from the buried object.

Casting the spade aside and dropping to his knees, the elder began removing handfuls of dry dirt from the hole. What came into view was an unadorned little metal box whose lid was held shut with a simple metal clasp.

"What is it?" Wesley asked. "What did you find?"

Lifting the box out of the hole, Cecil carried it carefully over to the edge of the wall and handed it down to his compadre.

"Don't open it until I climb back down the ladder," Cecil requested.

"Hey, old man, what are you doing?" a voice rang out from the museum's open front door as the Osage reached the bottom step.

"Uh-oh," Wesley said. "We gotta go."

He tucked the box under one arm and headed for the red-and-white truck sitting in the parking lot. Cecil was right behind him, choosing to leave his spade and stepladder behind.

Thankfully, Wesley's truck engine started immediately, allowing the partners in crime to escape southward in the early morning foggy mist. With verbal directions from Cecil, they headed for the home of Elmore Proctor's widow across the Kiamichi River with their prize.

Yimmi admitted the pair readily, offering cups of coffee to her unexpected guests. Taking seats at the woman's dining table, the elderly men eagerly tackled the task of opening the dusty container.

Taking turns between sips of coffee, and using a borrowed butter knife, Cecil and Wesley pried and prodded the rusted clasp until it ultimately released its grasp.

"I'll let you have the honor of opening the box," Wesley told Cecil as he slid the box across the table.

"But you're now the Keeper of this piece," Cecil countered. "You should have that honor."

Wesley shrugged, accepted the offer, and opened the lid. Peering inside, he saw a jagged-edged piece of light-colored stone covered in a fine layer of grime. He removed the piece from the box, but Cecil immediately grabbed it from the elder's hand.

"This is not a piece of the Sky Stone!" he declared. "This is . . . this is I don't know what!"

Wesley was dumbfounded. "What could've happened to Elmore's piece?"

Cecil ran a hand through his grayish-white hair. "Yimmi, are you sure no one else has seen Elmore's clues?" he called.

The woman came in from the kitchen. "No one I know of," she replied. "I told you about the person who came here pretending to be Elmore's assistant and what I told him."

Wesley had a thought. "Has anyone else ever worked with or learned from Proctor in the past?" he asked.

"Years ago—and I'm talking ten or more—he had a Choctaw apprentice for a while," the woman said. "But they had a disagreement, and Elmore fired him."

"What was his name?" Wesley asked. "Maybe he did something with the piece."

"What *was* his name?" Yimmi said, trying to remember. She rubbed her forehead as if that would cause the name to pop out. "James something. No, James was the last name." Another pause. "Willy James—that's it! His name was Willy James."

"Willy James," Cecil repeated. "We'll have to check with the other Medicine Council members to see if any of them know of this guy." He reached out and shook Yimmi's hand gently. "Thanks for the coffee and your hospitality. Please don't talk about any of this to anyone, all right?"

"All right," she said. "I'll do whatever you say. Elmore always had the utmost respect for you. Come back for a visit anytime."

After leaving the ceremony in Missouri, Ethan Lookout made a beeline for Dr. Stevens's office on the university campus in Tahlequah. Since they last spoke, Augustus was to have contacted the radiocarbon dating lab at the university in Athens, Georgia, to find out the location of the chief's staff and status of the testing.

"What did you find out?" Lookout asked as he burst into Stevens's office.

"Nothing good, I'm afraid," he replied with a frown. "Someone broke into the lab and stole the items. I just found out this morning."

"Holy crap!" Ethan exclaimed. "We've got to get those back and fast!" His mind whirred in panic mode for a moment. "Did they notify the authorities? The theft of Native American burial objects is a federal offense."

"Yeah, I know," Stevens replied. "The lab called the FBI, and a pair of agents began an investigation this morning."

"Who would do this?" Ethan asked of no one in particular.

"Private collectors with lists of potential illegal buyers in black markets all over the world."

Ethan hadn't expected Augustus to answer his rhetorical question, but both archaeologists knew this was the correct answer.

Back at Spiral Mounds, Billy and Lisa had taken their time walking along the path that led to the farthest burial mound located at the back of the park. As they approached the mound, it became obvious to Billy that more digging had taken place since the Uktena had hastily attempted to access the Sun Chief's cape and staff. A larger area of dirt had been disturbed and then replaced. He explained to Lisa what had transpired when the Paranormal Patrol arrived at the site, including his interaction with Shakuru.

Then the pair got down to business. Using one of the rolled-up sleeping bags as a pillow, Billy lay down and got as comfortable as he could on the grass. Meanwhile, Lisa kept a watch out for tourists who might interrupt his out-of-body excursion.

Billy began humming the song that would cause his cells to begin to vibrate and, in turn, allow him to separate. When the separation came, he began projecting a mental signal meant to call Shakuru. He pictured the Sun Chief's energy body in his mind, expecting that to bring him to the spirit man, or bring the spirit man to him. But nothing happened.

Billy moved around the Spiral Mounds site, hoping to find him somewhere within the ancient grounds. Still nothing. Only a few days ago, Shakuru had revealed his situation, tethered to his own bones and unable to escape. So, Billy reasoned, if the bones were in the burial mound, then the Sun Chief's spirit would still be here somewhere.

Since he didn't seem to be here, it must mean that the bones weren't here either! Billy quickly returned to his physical body and reported his discovery to Lisa.

"The Sun Chief isn't here," he told her. "I think somebody dug him up and moved him! I've got to confront Langford and call Dr. Stevens."

The pair grabbed their gear and rushed back to the interpretive center. Bypassing the receptionist, they barged into the director's office. He was on the phone.

"What have you done with the Sun Chief's remains?" Billy demanded. "His bones aren't here anymore."

"Get out of my office!" Langford replied. "I don't have to put up with this."

Lisa took out her cell phone and began dialing.

"I'll call you back," the director told the person on the phone and hung up. Then, to Lisa, he said, "Who are you calling?"

"My father," she said as she finished dialing. "And you know who he is."

Billy took his phone out and began dialing.

"Who are you calling?" the director asked Billy.

"Dr. Stevens at the university."

Langford picked up the phone from his desk and punched a button. "Security," a man's voice said through the phone's speaker.

"I've got two unruly people in my office who need to be escorted from the premises," he said. "Get in here immediately!"

The two teens didn't wait for the security guard to show up. They exited the building while simultaneously leaving voice mail messages for the two parties they'd called.

A few minutes later in Tahlequah, Lisa's father immediately called Cecil in Tuskahoma, which was only an hour and a half by car from Spiral Mounds. Then he called Augustus, with whom he'd just met and whom Billy had just called. Everyone involved agreed to drop what they were doing and get themselves to the Spiral Mounds site.

An hour and a half later, two Indian elders, an Indian college professor, an Indian archaeologist, and a sympathetic non-Indian digger converged on the mounds to join Billy and Lisa. The squad of seven barged into the interpretive center and marched toward the director's office. The lone security guard made the expeditious decision to step aside and allow the determined intruders to go wherever they pleased.

"Now see here, what's the meaning of this?" Langford yelled. "I'll have the state police—"

"I'd be happy to see you make that call," Augustus said as Ethan stepped over to the director's desk phone and picked up the handset.

"We'll even dial the number for you," the Osage archaeologist said and began to dial.

"All right, all right," Langford said. "Put down the phone."

"What have you done with my ancestor's bones?" Cecil asked in a demanding tone.

"I allowed a collector friend to access them," Langford replied sheepishly.

"Do you know how many federal laws you've broken?" Ethan asked.

"I . . . I didn't think anyone would know the difference," the director admitted nervously. "How did you know?" he asked Billy. "It's not that obvious from the surface."

"Ancient Native American secret knowledge," Billy said confidently and smiled. "It's above your state salary pay grade."

"Give us the name and address of your collector friend or I *will* call the FBI right now," Augustus threatened.

"Okay, okay," Langford said eagerly.

He pulled out a pad of paper with the Spiral Mounds State Park logo printed on each sheet and wrote down a name, phone number, and address in Texas. He ripped the page off the pad and handed it to Ethan. Everyone but the director headed for the door.

"Do yourself a favor and don't call this guy to warn him," Ethan told Langford on his way out. "I'll let the feds know you were helpful when I call them."

"But you said you wouldn't—"

"Dr. Stevens made that deal, not me."

After the group left, Langford sat down in his big, overstuffed office chair and buried his head in his hands. He knew his days as a free man were numbered.

Out in the parking lot, Ethan made the call. He had the regional FBI office on speed dial because, as a Native archaeologist, he'd come across the illegal sale of stolen Native American artifacts and remains a few times. It was one of the reasons he did what he did, to help track down sacred tribal objects and get them returned to their rightful owners, the tribes that the items were stolen from.

When he finished the call, he took charge of the situation and made a few decisions. "If you don't mind, I have an idea about who needs to do what next," he told the Buckhorns, the other two Lookouts, and the university archaeologist.

No one objected.

"Cecil, I think you and Wesley should get back to Tuskahoma to continue the search for the missing piece of the Sky Stone. James, you and Augustus should get back to campus and follow up on the stolen cape and staff from the lab. Billy, you and Lisa should think about going with me to Texas, in case I find Shakuru's bones. That way you could get right to work on freeing him."

Nodding heads from everyone in the group told Ethan his plan was sound.

"One other step I can take is to contact Morningstar and ask for his help in finding both the bones and the stolen staff," Billy offered. "I can do that from just about anywhere."

Ethan nodded and, for the first time, studied the piece of paper Langford had given him. "The Reverend Doctor Samuel Miller, Red River Ranch, Rural Route 3322, Limestone, Texas," he read out loud and then looked up at the group gathered around him. "What are we waiting for? Let's get to work. We've got a world to save."

Lisa's map app showed that it was about a three-hour drive almost due south to get to Limestone, Texas. Ethan pulled a ramp out of the back of his Indigenous Archaeology Alliance van. After detaching the sidecar, he and his daughter wrestled her bike up the ramp and into the vehicle. The sidecar was nestled in beside the bike up against one wall of the van.

Lisa rode shotgun, while Ethan, of course, took the driver's seat. That left a turned-over egg crate for Billy to sit on just behind and sort of between the other two.

He hoped to use some of the time during the drive to learn more about the Mound Builders from one of the foremost experts in the field, his girlfriend's father.

"What happened to the mounds and the people who built them, anyway?" he asked. "I've been reading that book you gave me, and I had no idea there used to be thousands and thousands of platform mounds."

"The Spaniards happened, to begin with," the archaeologist said. "Hernando de Soto arrived in Florida in the 1530s looking for gold, the usual reason the conquistadors came here. With an army of six hundred men, they swept through the Southeastern United States stealing food, enslaving people, burning villages, and slaughtering the inhabitants."

"But wait, there's more," Lisa said sarcastically.

"Everywhere the Spanish and other Europeans traveled in America, they left a trail of diseases that Indigenous people had no immunity against," Ethan continued. "Between the warfare, diseases, and increased European encroachments, Mound Builder

Indians had to abandon their elaborate communities and flee to other lands."

"But the cultures of several tribes seem to have preserved some of the wisdom and beliefs of the Mound Builders," Billy observed.

"That's true," Ethan said. "Traditional Cherokees have maintained parts of the original teachings, as have Osage traditionalists like our family. A close study of many tribal cultures reveals remnants of the original spiritual teachings, if you know what to look for."

That gave Billy much to think about, but all of a sudden he felt very tired. He managed to locate his sleeping bag. Using it for a pillow, he lay down on the carpeted floor of the van as the vehicle continued moving southward.

"I'm just going to catch a little shut-eye," he said, and almost immediately fell asleep.

A few minutes later the teen was able to roll out of his sleeping body and move upward through the roof of the van. A moment after that, he pictured Morningstar in his mind and began hurtling toward his nonphysical base camp on Level Four.

"Time for your next lesson," the spirit man said as Billy landed in the dome-shaped space he'd been in before.

"What is this place called?" he wondered.

"Call it whatever you like," Morningstar replied. "It exists solely for your use."

"How about My Home Among the Stars?"

"And so it shall be."

"And so it shall be," Billy repeated, still in awe of the whole nonphysical experience.

"Now to the task at hand," Morningstar said. "Freeing Shakuru from the Snake Cult spell. Again, thanks to you and Awinita for discovering his whereabouts."

"I still don't quite understand how his situation remained a hidden mystery to you and his own tribe for a thousand years."

"That's a side effect of the Shadow Zone and part of the power of the united forces of the Owls and Snakes. The amount of hate the Snake Priest felt for his own brother was so strong it allowed him to strengthen his negative powers while, at the same time, causing him to become a disfigured soul."

Billy remained silent for a long moment as that information sank in.

"Accessing the Sun Chief is actually easier for you coming from the physical domain, but freeing Shakuru is going to require a group effort much like was used to free you from the House of Bones," Morningstar said. "You and your girlfriend will need to perform certain actions out-of-body while your grandfather and hers will need to perform certain actions and incantations from the physical domain."

"But Lisa told me she can only do the Spider Woman thing to free someone from the skeleton jail and nothing else," Billy protested. "She doesn't really do spirit travel."

"You must teach her," the spirit man said. "And fast—because you two will have to work together to make this happen."

"We have to find Shakuru's bones first," Billy replied.

"I'm confident you will, and after he's released, you can see to it that his remains are returned to his descendants for proper reburial in their rightful place."

"You don't expect much, do you?" Billy said as he began to feel a tug from his physical body.

"See you again soon," Morningstar said as he faded from Billy's view.

Billy slipped back through the layers, awoke in his body, and discovered that, once again, he needed to pee.

Again with the peeing—how annoying.

"Can we stop somewhere?" he asked of his two traveling companions. "I need to find a tree or a bush on the side of the road."

After a brief pee break and some lunch at a nearby roadside diner, the trio made it to the tiny town of Limestone, Texas, late in the day. Using Ethan's onboard supercomputer, they found a detailed topographical map of the Red River Ranch that showed several buildings on the large property.

During lunch, Billy had explained what Morningstar said about him and Lisa working together to free the Sun Chief.

"I need to teach you to do spirit travel with me," the teen said. "If I can do it, I'm sure you can do it. You can already do something like it in your Spider Woman mode."

"If you think so," Lisa replied. "It can't hurt to try."

"First, I'm going on a reconnaissance mission onto the reverend doctor's property to see if I can locate the Sun Chief's remains," Billy said. "If I find them, I'll come back and teach you the spirit travel song, along with the 'lift-off' maneuver I use to escape the physical."

After getting Lisa and Ethan to agree to the plan, Billy left his physical body lying on the van floor and darted off to infiltrate Miller's ranch real estate. Billy remembered that the Sun Chief had traveled however far it was from the Spiral Mounds burial site to the cave on the river when they'd recaptured the Uktena. Apparently, that was the farthest distance the supernatural tether would allow him to go. That meant the spirit could now be anywhere within about a one-mile radius.

Instead of looking for bones, Billy decided to picture the Sun Chief in his mind to see if that would take him to the spirit's location. For an instant an image flashed in the teen's mind. What he saw was a long thin wooden box lying on a shelf next to the storage tube that held the Sun Chief's staff and cape. Just as quickly as it appeared, the image disappeared. Unsure what that was about, Billy again pictured the spirit body of the Sun Chief in his mind.

The teen's energy body was immediately propelled across the rural landscape. He came to a stop just above a large reddish-brown barn that sat away from the main house and the road. Billy drifted down through the barn's roof to take a closer look at the inside.

What he saw shocked him. The well-lit space was filled with row after row of folding tables, and on those tables sat hundreds of assorted Native American artifacts, ceramic pots, woven baskets, blankets, and rugs. Billy dropped down even closer and saw that the walls were lined with glass-front cases containing collections of arrowheads, turquoise jewelry, bows, arrows, and more pots and baskets.

And the objects appeared to be not from one tribe but from several different tribes.

Then Billy detected some movement in one corner of the barn. He looked in that direction but had trouble understanding what he was seeing. There appeared to be an elderly man, a physical human, surrounded by gray, agitated, shadowy figures.

On the table in front of the man were several long thin wooden boxes like the one he'd seen in the quick flash vision he'd just had. The lids were off a couple of the boxes closest to the man, but Billy was unable to see what the boxes held. He moved a little closer until, to his further shock, he saw human skeletal remains inside.

"What the—?" Billy said or thought or exclaimed.

"What the hell is exactly the right question," a woman's voice from behind him said. Turning his attention 180 degrees, Billy found his grandmother Awinita's spirit floating up near the rafters of the building.

"Grandma!" Billy exclaimed. "I've missed you so much! Where have you been?"

"After getting your uncle Frank settled in, I had to attend to some other pressing business in another segment of the nonphysical realms."

"What does that mean exactly?"

"I can't tell you exactly, but think of it this way," she replied as she floated down closer to her grandson. "You don't have to necessarily always think of the nonphysical realm in spiritual terms. It is just another dimension of reality, which your spirit self is part of at all times."

"What? I don't think I've ever heard you say anything like that before," Billy replied. "I'm a little confused."

"Sorry," Awinita said. "Now that you've met Morningstar and learned a little about the layers over here, I thought it was time you started seeing the bigger picture of how things work. But let's deal with the situation right here right now. Maybe we can delve into the other topic another time."

She drifted closer to the activity in the corner of the barn Billy had reacted to earlier. "What you see here is a good example of what can happen when the remains of our dead are disturbed, when burials are desecrated. The man who owns this ranch has been digging up and collecting the bones of Native American peoples for decades, and now he's enmeshed in an ocean of restless ghosts."

"But the night of the last stomp dance, Little Wolf said that ghosts don't linger around the places their bones are buried," Billy objected.

"That's right—usually. But when their graves are broken into and their remains aren't allowed to disintegrate naturally, their spirits may rush back to see what has happened. You see, there is still a weak connection to their earthly existence."

"Is that what happened to Shakuru, the reason he was hanging around his physical remains at Spiral Mounds? That's the reason I'm here, you know—looking for him."

"Why aren't you looking at Spiral Mounds, where he's been buried for a thousand years?"

"Because he isn't buried there anymore," Billy said. "Langford had him dug up and gave his bones to this guy." He indicated the old man surrounded by ghosts.

"I wasn't aware of that," Awinita said. "I've really been out of touch at this level."

"I need to free the Sun Chief from the tether that keeps him tied to his physical remains," Billy continued. "But I have to find him first. I thought he'd be here."

Awinita contemplated the situation for a moment before speaking again.

"I'll see what I can do here to free these poor entities," she said. "You must continue your mission as Thunder Child, and by the way, I'm so proud of you for stepping up to take your place in the larger scheme of things."

As his grandmother's spirit moved toward the sea of ghosts, Billy stretched and returned to his physical self and opened his eyes.

"Well, did you find him?" Lisa asked, noticing that her boyfriend was back in the flesh.

"No, he's not here," Billy replied. "But there are plenty of other Native American human remains here, and hundreds of artifacts, in a big barn hidden away farther back on the property."

Ethan shook his head in disgust. "There are over one hundred thousand skeletal remains of Native Americans held in storage by universities, museums, and private collections in spite of the NAGPRA law," he said. "I'll make another call to notify the feds about this collection, but in the meantime, what are we going to do about finding Shakuru?"

"What if there's some unknown person out there who has both Shakuru's bones and the Sun Chief's staff and cape?" Billy said.

That left Ethan and Lisa speechless.

"What would make you say that?" Ethan asked.

"You had a vision of it, didn't you?" Lisa said.

Billy nodded. "It was just a brief flash, though."

"Can't you just go out-of-body again and track him down?" Ethan asked.

"Morningstar said I need to train Lisa to do spirit travel to help me," Billy replied. "I think we should get back to Tahlequah so I can do that."

"Yeah, and I need to follow up with Cecil to see how the search for the missing Sky Stone piece is going."

North of Tahlequah, at about that same time, Chigger handed Blacksnake's medicine book over to Carmelita, and the old *skili* felt like a young girl again, like someone had given her a bag of delicious candy. She hugged the book to her chest and thought of a more pleasant time when she and her lover had last been together in the flesh.

"What now?" Chigger asked, interrupting her reverie.

"You're dismissed!" Carmelita barked. "I'll let you know when it's time for another lesson, boy."

Chigger's disappointment was obvious, and Carmelita knew she needed to keep the teen appeased for a while longer. That was when a new idea hit her.

"I'll tell you what," she said. "If you come regularly, you can begin learning the medicinal properties of plants. But you'd need to come almost every day."

"But what about school?"

"It's choosing time," she said with a sharp tone. "Time to decide which direction you'll take, the difficult path of the *skilis* or the easy path of the Mundanes."

"The Mundanes?"

"Everyday people," the old woman said. "Dull. Ordinary."

"I'm tired of ordinary," Chigger said.

"Good, good," Carmelita replied. "Now off with you. See you tomorrow morning."

She turned away from him and busied herself with grinding herbs with a mortar and pestle.

On the drive home, Chigger decided just how he'd handle the situation. Every morning he'd get up, get ready, and pretend to go to school. His parents wouldn't be the wiser. He'd come home every afternoon as if he'd been in school all day.

Back at her cabin, Carmelita was feeling pretty proud of herself.

"Won't Benji be so glad that I got his medicine book back!" she said to herself.

Then another idea struck her. She would share the good news with him through her Aztec mirror. Retrieving the device from her safe, she set the polished round, flat black object on its stand and took a seat in front of it. While rubbing its surface with a dab of the special concoction created for the job, she recited the spirit vision incantation.

After finishing with the polish and the recitation, the old woman closed her eyes, held tight to the mirror with both hands, and pictured her beloved Benjamin in her mind. Thankfully, she felt vibrational energy emanating from the black glass, a sign that the mirror had been activated.

Opening her eyes, she gazed intently on the flat surface and then projected her thoughts into the center of it, concentrating on a mental image of Benjamin's face. Suddenly, she found herself seemingly standing in an undefined gray space. She had broken through! It had been quite a while since the black mirror had allowed her mind to cross over.

She knew this land of gray fog provided a buffer to prevent dwellers of the Middleworld from accidentally stumbling onto the path to the Underworld. Having passed this way before, Carmelita knew she only had to wait calmly, and the mist would eventually dissipate. Most souls who found themselves in this land immediately began to panic, which perpetuated the fog and made it even harder to escape.

As the murky haze faded, the familiar and dark Forest of Dread came into view. Also, from past experience, she knew it was the entrance to the second of the Underworld's nine levels, which were first identified by Aztec priests in ancient Mexico. The pack of wolves she sometimes called on resided in these woods, available to be invoked with the incantation she'd learned from Blacksnake.

And just beyond this forest ran the River of Fear, a difficult barrier that needed to be crossed in order to descend any lower into the dark world. The Shadow Zone lay just beyond the river, and she had to project herself across it to connect with Benji.

But first, the wolf pack detected her presence in the forest. They approached cautiously, possibly expecting a hapless stranger who would provide an energy meal for them. Coming from five different directions, as they'd done with Lisa in the material world, they quietly crept toward the old woman's projected presence.

"*Unalii,*" Carmelita said, offering the Cherokee word for friend.

When the animals failed to respond, she repeated the word more forcefully. "*Unalii!*"

The wolves backed down, lost interest, and retreated deeper into the forest. Through the power of the black mirror, Carmelita continued deeper into the woods, eventually coming to the River of Fear. The dark, choppy waters splashed and crashed fearsomely before her as if some storm raged overhead.

Through the watery mist, a burning torch first came into view, and soon afterward, the bow of a canoe. The unsettling figure of a red skeleton wearing a Plains Indian feathered headdress paddled the craft toward the witch. She knew it was his job to keep the Mundanes from crossing the river.

"*Tecolotl! Tecolotl!*" she called out, using the password she'd learned from Benji.

With this, the Nahuatl Aztec word for "owl," she identified herself as a member of the ancient Owl Clan, one with permission to cross the river.

Bitter winds blew directly into the face of Carmelita's projected presence as she struggled toward the opposite shore. She knew better than to gaze down into the River of Fear's choppy waters, for the creatures that lurked there had the power to pull one under.

Straining her vision, the old woman finally caught sight of the water's other edge, and within a few additional moments, she arrived on the far shore. Mentally, she called out.

"Benjamin, are you there? Benji?" Waiting a few moments, she heard no reply. "It is I, Kituwah, Night Wolf, your beloved."

"I am here," a familiar voice, at last, replied from nondescript blackness beyond. "I am coming."

In another few moments, her beloved Benjamin finally approached from deeper in the Shadow Zone. The joy her consciousness radiated intermingled with the energy Benji emitted, and, for a brief moment, she could pretend they were embracing in the flesh. She allowed the moment to last as long as possible, but it soon faded.

"If only I could come with you back to the Afterworld," she said, her longing quite strong.

"If only I could go with you back into the Middleworld so our passion would blossom again," he said, seemingly projecting his longing toward her.

But his mood shifted suddenly, as the reality of their situation intruded.

"But of course, neither of us can do either thing," he continued in a blunt tone. "We know what's coming and what's expected of each of us."

He moved back from her a couple of steps.

"What progress are you making against the Buckhorns and the Lookouts?" he asked, sounding like an employer displeased with the results of a job review.

"Still not as much as I'd like," she answered. Then she smiled. "But I do have some good news. I have your medicine book in my possession now. And with your help, I'm sure I can deal deadly blows against those who are against us."

"Finally!" Blacksnake exclaimed. "Won't Monkata be pleased!"

At the sound of the Snake Priest's given name, Carmelita's anger flared.

"Why do you have to bring him into this conversation?" she roared. "You know I'm jealous of the time he gets to spend with you! I swear I'll kill myself just so we can be together."

"My dearest, you're forgetting the importance of what's about to unfold," Benjamin said, mustering all the patience he could. "You know that after the Great Reckoning is complete, we'll be back where we should be, in control of Middleworld. In the meantime, we each have our part to play, and yours requires you to remain in the flesh just a little longer."

Carmelita regained control of her emotions.

"Of course, I know that," she said. "But it's just so hard to wait for the plan to unfold."

"Now that you have the book, I can reveal its greatest secrets to you."

Carmelita's spirit brightened at the thought. "What are they, my love? I must know them!"

"Okay, but just one for now. I've got much to prepare down here."

"Oh, all right," she said with obvious disappointment in her voice.

"You can reverse the positive effect of any Cherokee formula by repeating the word for 'opposite' in Cherokee," he said, almost in a whisper. "In other words, instead of curing an illness, you can cause someone to contract that illness."

The woman sucked a breath of air in through her teeth and said, "Oh, how delicious!"

"All you have to do is say the Cherokee word for 'opposite' at the same time a medicine person is reciting the formula."

"*Ahnaditlv,*" Carmelita said. "Opposite. That's genius."

"Look on page three hundred and thirty-three of the book for complete instructions," he said.

That should keep her busy for a while, Blacksnake thought.

He had grown tired of dealing with this woman's emotional weaknesses long ago but still needed her to be his eyes and ears in the Middleworld. So he continued to feign interest in her, knowing he wouldn't have to keep up the pretense for very much longer.

Divide and Conquer

When the Buckhorns and the Lookouts gathered back at the Buckhorn house in Park Hill for a strategy meeting, they realized they weren't very far along in their attempts to recover the missing piece of the Sky Stone, the Sun Chief's stolen cape and staff, or the skeletal remains of Shakuru. Someone or something was definitely working against them, and the cosmic clock was ticking.

"Equally important is the fact we haven't begun Thunder Child's training," Cecil observed. "Each of our members of the Intertribal Medicine Council has tribal medicine practices the boy will need to use very soon. And learning medicine ways from each of us also strengthens the spiritual bond we have as a group."

"On top of that, Morningstar said Lisa should learn spirit travel to help me find and rescue Shakuru," Billy added.

"We definitely have a lot on our collective plate," Ethan observed. "Let's decide who's going to do what and when."

"Let me get started with the spirit travel training immediately," Lisa said. "That way I can begin assisting Billy with some of his efforts."

"I can get Billy started making visits to the medicine people when that's done," Wesley offered. "I'll get with Cecil to find out where we start."

"While Wesley and Billy head off to their first stop, whoever else is available can continue helping with our searches for the Sky Stone piece, along with the cape and staff. That's probably the best way to proceed," Cecil admitted. "Divide and conquer."

"I think I'll still be able to contribute to the searches in between medicine training sessions," Billy said. "I have a cell phone, and I'm getting better at doing remote viewings."

"What should we focus on?" James asked.

"Pops, I need you and Mom to write me that letter to the school so I can be excused until further notice."

"That's right," Rebecca said. "We'll get right on it."

Cecil, Wesley, Ethan, and the others continued meeting in the Buckhorn living room to work on follow-up details while Billy and Lisa headed to the guest bedroom to begin Lisa's introduction to spirit travel.

Lisa hadn't returned to the Sequoyah High School dorm since her scare with the wolves in the woods. She was still staying in an upstairs spare bedroom in the Buckhorn house, while Ethan and Cecil had checked out of their Tahlequah motel and moved in with Wesley.

"Lie down flat on your back and relax," Billy said matter-of-factly as they entered the room.

"Why, Billy Buckhorn, if I didn't know better, I'd think you were trying to get me into bed with you," Lisa said with a sly smile.

Billy turned several shades of red and stuttered. "I, uh . . . you know . . . we, uh" was all that came out of his mouth.

Lisa broke out in a boisterous laugh, delighting in her boyfriend's obvious discomfort. "You're so adorable," she said and kissed him on the cheek. Then she lay down on the bed as instructed and got comfortable. "What's next?" she asked.

"We both have to clear our minds of any earthly thoughts or concerns," Billy said. "Just feel your muscles one by one letting go of all tension."

He gave her a little time to accomplish that.

"Now I'm going to start singing and then humming an ancient song," Billy said. "I want you to join in as soon as you pick up the melody and keep humming until I tell you to stop. I'm going to leave my body and then help you escape your body. When you feel my energy underneath you lifting upward, imagine yourself floating."

Lisa silently processed those instructions so she'd remember what to do.

"Got it?" Billy asked.

"Got it," she replied.

Billy lay down beside her on the bed and began singing the song. After a couple of minutes, he switched to humming, and at that point Lisa joined in. It brought to Billy's mind the first time he'd heard the Sun Chief chanting this song. That was the first time Billy had left his body.

A few seconds later he rolled over, heard the Velcro-ripping sound, and fully lifted himself out of the physical. To his surprise, Awinita was standing at the foot of the bed.

"Grandma, what are you doing here?"

"I'm here to help you with Lisa," she said. "I approve, by the way. She is the most perfect mate for you, Grandson."

That gave Billy a warm, glowing feeling throughout his energy body.

"Now, let's get to work," his grandmother said.

Lying on the bed, Lisa had begun humming the tune Billy was humming. It was easy to pick up because it sounded quite a lot like a very old Osage ceremonial song she'd learned from her grandfather. As she hummed, the vibration slowly spread from her mouth and throat into the rest of her body.

At that point, she began feeling very light, as if her body had no weight. She lay in that state for a couple of minutes and then noticed what felt like a pair of hands under her shoulders and another pair under her feet. The hands began lifting her upward, and she sensed that she was somehow floating.

Just as Billy had experienced during his first out-of-body trip, she began floating up toward the ceiling. And just as she thought she'd bump into it, she passed through it and then through the roof. She was out!

Once they were above the roof, Billy and Awinita released their hold on Lisa, and she drifted on her own. Probably because of her previous supernatural experiences as Spider Woman, the girl already knew a little about moving around in the out-of-body state.

"That was much easier than expected," she said.

"You're a natural," Awinita replied.

"You're Billy's grandmother!" Lisa exclaimed. "I'm so happy to finally meet you. Your grandson is so remarkable."

"Welcome into the Buckhorn fold," Awinita said, emitting a warm golden glow. "Now you two run along and have a good time. I am needed elsewhere."

The elder spirit slipped up and away from the couple. To Billy, it almost sounded like she was sending them out on a couple's date, to dinner and a movie or something.

He moved closer to Lisa until their energy fields overlapped. He felt a tingling sensation all through his spirit body. Because of their strong physical attraction to each other, their energy bodies easily attached—like two magnets.

"I feel so free and light," Lisa said, glowing with a happy yellow energy of her own.

"Let's go for a little joyride," Billy suggested, and he pictured his intention to glide northward above the local landscape.

Below them in the night, the roads, houses, and businesses of Tahlequah moved by, all emitting the pale orange glow of artificial lights. The couple passed over the university campus where Billy's former paranormal team met several times the previous year.

"If you practice humming the song loud enough to feel the vibrations and then imagine yourself floating upward, you should eventually be able to break free by yourself."

"I hope so," Lisa replied.

"If you can do it, we can meet like this at night while I'm away on my training trip," Billy suggested.

Lisa liked that idea very much, again emitting a warm yellow-colored glow.

Then Billy moved the pair westward and floated above Tahlequah High School, causing him to remember dark events that transpired there last fall. But he also remembered how he prevented the death or injury of a school bus full of kids.

Turning southward, he guided them over the Cherokee Nation casino on Highway 62 and farther south over the tribe's headquarters. They were almost back where they started, the Buckhorn house located in Park Hill, but Billy decided to do a quick pass over Lisa's school, Sequoyah High School.

That was when he noticed four faint, dark purple glowing spots on the ground. He moved the couple closer to the area and hovered above the nearest building. There was one glowing spot in each of the four directions, with the building in the center of them.

"That's my dorm building," Lisa said. "Why have we come here?"

"Don't you see those four glowing spots on the ground around the building?"

"No, I don't see anything like that," Lisa answered.

"Okay," Billy said. "Wait here while I take a closer look."

He left Lisa "parked" above the dorm building while he moved closer to the glowing spot on the east side. That was when he realized that the glow was coming from under the ground.

Something buried there was emitting the purple glow.

He drifted back up to where Lisa waited and said, "I'll come check this out tomorrow in daylight. There's definitely something very suspicious going on here."

A few moments later, they settled back into their bodies and opened their physical eyes.

"That was incredible!" Lisa said.

Just then, Billy's father knocked on the guest room door.

"We're wrapping up the planning and strategizing downstairs," he announced through the door. "Lisa, your dad and grandfather are heading over to Wesley's house for the night."

Billy opened the door. "We'll be right down," he said, and his father turned away.

"I guess private time is over," Billy said to Lisa. "Let's go hear what they have planned."

Among other things, Billy learned that his first stop on his tribal medicine tour was to be in New Mexico with an Apache member of the Intertribal Medicine Council.

After the joint family meeting broke up, Billy still wanted a moment of privacy with his girlfriend to engage in a more physical activity. The cab of Billy's pickup in front of the house was the best they could do.

"After tonight, it looks like we're not going to have much time to be together for a while," Billy said. "Too bad you can't just come with me. Grandpa said we'd be leaving day after tomorrow."

"You know I'd love to go with you," she said. "But you heard what my dad and grandpa already have planned for me to do here. You and I weren't destined to meet during quiet, uneventful times, I guess."

"You can say that again!"

"You and I weren't destined to meet—"

Billy grabbed her by the waist and began tickling her relentlessly. "Ha ha, very funny," he joked.

When she stopped laughing, Lisa kissed Billy right on the spiderweb scar on the side of his neck. That got his serious attention. He returned the gesture with a kiss on the back of her hand right on the spider tattoo. Then he moved up to kiss her on the side of her neck. Then, just as the situation was about to heat up, Lisa caught sight of Billy's mom coming out the front door of the house.

"Incoming!" she said, pulling away from him. "Your mom at twelve o'clock."

Billy turned and, seeing his mom headed their way, blushed at being caught making out.

So embarrassing.

"Don't stop on my account," she said when she got into hearing range. "I just wanted to let you know you left your cell phone in the house, and you missed a call from your grandfather. When he didn't get you on your phone, he called the house phone, saying he needed to talk to you immediately."

He gave Lisa a look of disappointment and, as he got out of the truck, said, "I guess we *weren't* destined to meet during quiet, uneventful times." After locating his phone, he dialed Wesley.

"Blacksnake's medicine book is missing," the elder said. "I can't find it anywhere. Someone's been in my house while I was away."

"Who would know it was there and would want it?" Billy asked, more to himself than to his grandfather.

"The Night Seers would definitely want it," Wesley replied. "But how would they know it was at my house?"

Both Buckhorns searched their own minds for answers.

"The Owls could be behind all the obstacles we're facing, couldn't they?" Billy said.

"Yeah, I guess so," Wesley said. "That's definitely a real possibility."

"So, my next question is, how do we find out who's in the Owl Clan now?"

"We got some clues from Elmore Proctor's widow. She named a Choctaw man who was Elmore's apprentice for a while many years ago, Willy James. And then there was an old woman who asked to see him who may have poisoned him. Those two are possibilities."

"There also has to be someone close to us, Grandpa, who's been doing some bad medicine," Billy said. "I mean physically close. Think about it. After we met the Lookouts, I got thrown into that skeleton house. Lisa and her family had to rescue me."

"Okay, keep going," Wesley commented. "You were always pretty good at using logic to find answers or figure something out."

"Then Lisa woke up in a confused mental state, a 'fog' she called it. That's the day she rode her motorcycle to the wildlife preserve and was surrounded by a pack of wolves."

"Oh, that's right," Wesley said. "I'd never heard of wolf packs being a problem there before."

"But back to Lisa's fit of confusion," Billy said. "Is there an incantation or doctoring spell that could cause that?"

Wesley searched his own memory banks for anything that might help.

"There's an old treatment to cause conflict and confusion in the standard collection of Cherokee spells," he said. "It was mostly used by warriors against an enemy in battle but could be used for the same purpose on a personal enemy."

"How does it work?"

"In the original form, you'd bury a bundle of specific herbs in two different places in opposite directions somewhere near your enemy's camp. That was supposed to split their attention in two opposing directions, creating a sense of confusion."

"I suppose someone who knew where Lisa lived could do that," Billy observed.

"But the process became much more effective for personal use after the invention of photography," the elder added.

That information struck Billy like a lightning bolt. "Go on," he said. "Explain it in detail."

Wesley gathered his thoughts.

"Say there's a woman who is seeing another man, but you want to break them up so you can be with that woman," Wesley explained. "You'd get a picture of the happy couple and then tear the photo in half. If you could get up to four copies of the photo, it would be even better."

Billy's mind was moving a mile a minute, and he didn't like where his thoughts were going as he listened.

"Then you'd put the torn pieces of the picture in a bundle with the prescribed herbs and bury them in the four directions around where the woman lives. Once the incantation is spoken, the spell is cast."

Billy was silent for a moment before speaking again.

"Lisa and I just took an out-of-body tour around Tahlequah and Park Hill," he said in a quiet tone. "When we floated above her dormitory, I saw four purple glowing spots in the ground, placed in the four directions outside the building."

"That's astounding," Grandpa said. "You can perceive evidence of a negative spell that's been cast. You seem to discover new abilities on a regular basis now."

"I can't believe I'm just now getting this," Billy said. It took him a few moments to build up the courage to even say out loud what he was thinking. "Chigger took a picture of me and Lisa the day before the wolf incident."

"Could be a coincidence," Wesley said.

"But he's been acting kind of funny for days," Billy went on. "He said he'd become the apprentice of a Cherokee medicine woman."

Now it was Wesley's turn to go silent.

"I didn't think much of it at the time," the boy continued. "He said he was tired of living in my shadow. It was time for him to strike out on his own."

"I can see how a boy his age might begin to feel that way," Wesley observed. "But his exposure to the Uktena crystal might have also left some residual negative effects—leaving him open to darker impulses."

"But here's the red flag I ignored when Chigger told me about his new apprenticeship," Billy continued. "He said she turned into an owl right in front of him."

"How come I'm just now hearing about this?"

"I was preoccupied with my own issues and events," Billy answered. "I'd just gotten my own cell phone and I was eager to use it to connect with Lisa. I quickly forgot about Chigger."

"Did he give you the name of the woman he was to apprentice himself to?"

Billy thought back to the phone call. "Carlotta or Caramel something or other," he said. "A name with a lot of syllables." He thought more on it. "Touchy-Feely . . . ah, that's not it. Caramelized Touchy-Feely can't be right, but close."

"Never heard of anyone with a name like that, and I think I know most of the traditional Cherokee doctors."

"Maybe it's an alias," Billy suggested.

"Maybe you're right," Wesley said. "That used to be quite common among medicine people who wanted to conceal their true identities."

He considered this new information for another moment.

"Maybe it's time you refocused attention on your old pal," he said. "He may be up to something we need to know about."

"But I thought we had to get to New Mexico," Billy said.

"We do."

"What about Lisa?" Billy said. "That's something she could look into while we're gone."

"There you go," Wesley said.

They ended the call, knowing they had a lot to think about.

Billy told Lisa about the possible need for her sleuthing services, and then, exhausted, he told her good night and went straight to bed.

The following morning at breakfast, he informed the rest of the Buckhorn/Lookout crowd about the four glowing purple spots and his unfortunate conclusions about Chigger. James and Rebecca, Billy's parents, were the most stunned by the revelation. They'd known and trusted the boy almost all his life.

Meanwhile, that morning, Chigger was back at Carmelita's cabin ready for more lessons.

But his mentor had other ideas for her apprentice.

"We'll be having a couple of invited guests from out of town staying with us," she told him. "Your job today is putting these medicine bundles in the upstairs bedrooms in the main house and, while you're at it, dusting the furniture. I want them to have a really nice visit here."

She held out an old-fashioned round metal key ring filled with keys and two oblong, leather-wrapped bundles.

"But I'm supposed to be spending my time learning about Cherokee medicine plants," he protested. "Not being your personal assistant!"

The old woman squinted and focused her vision on the middle of the boy's forehead. All of a sudden, he felt an intense burning in that area, like someone was holding up a magnifying glass to focus the sun's rays on that spot.

"Ow!" he yelled, stepping back and rubbing the tender red skin.

"What was that you were saying, boy?" Tuckaleechee asked.

"Nothing," he said more as a whimper than a reply.

"Okay, you want a lesson in medicinal plants?" the old woman snapped. "Inside these pouches are the herbs every Night Seer dreams of. Our guests will be so pleased."

"What does that mean?"

"There's deadly nightshade that'll give you hallucinations before killing you. Then there's henbane, which will cause your lungs and heart to fail. Also in there is some monkshood, a pretty straightforward poison, and let's not forget lobelia. Now that's a really great herb. You want to know what its nickname is?"

"I'm not sure I do."

"Puke weed!" the old woman said with delight. "That'll cause rapid heartbeat, coma, and eventually death."

"Wow, you sure do know a lot about dangerous plants."

Carmelita took a step closer to the boy. "But my favorite one in that bundle is called Buckthorn," she said dramatically. "Do you know why?"

"Because it sounds like Buckhorn?" Chigger ventured.

"Righto, bucko!" she replied with a smile, displaying a mouthful of crooked yellow teeth. "You're not as clueless as I thought."

"And you don't like the Buckhorns for some reason I never really understood," he said.

"That's nothing you need to concern yourself with."

She again presented the key ring and the medicine bundles to the boy. He grabbed the items out of her hand and headed for the Victorian-style frame house.

"The feather duster is in the kitchen pantry," she called to him. "And stay out of the basement. There's nothing for you down there."

Muttering under his breath with every step, the boy marched toward the porch. "I'm sick of the way she treats me," he said. "I'm just a servant, not an apprentice."

He reached the structure's aged wooden steps, which were cracked and rotting. They complained loudly under each of his footfalls. The planks on the porch likewise creaked and moaned with every step.

He had to try three different keys before finding the one that unlocked the ornately carved front door, and the door's rusty hinges protested loudly as the boy moved cautiously inside.

A sharp, musty odor hit Chigger's nostrils like a slap in the face.

"This place looks and smells like a museum," he said out loud. "I wonder if it's haunted."

He wasn't sure why he'd verbalized his thoughts, but he realized that speaking aloud actually calmed his fears somewhat.

"Hello, is anybody here?"

He hoped he wouldn't receive a reply.

He began moving quickly then so he'd have to spend as little time as possible in the place. The set of stairs leading to the second floor lay directly in front of him, and he bounded up them two at a time.

At the top of the stairs, he found two doors, one on either side of the landing. He stepped into the room on the right first, and that was when he realized he hadn't retrieved the feather duster from the kitchen.

"Oh, fudge," he exclaimed.

He placed one of the medicine bundles on the bed and left the room. Crossing the landing, he entered the other bedroom and placed the second bundle on that bed. Quickly retracing his steps, he went down the stairs and began looking for the kitchen.

On the first floor to the right of the staircase, Chigger found the living room. It was filled with one-hundred-year-old furniture, and the word *parlor* came to his mind. Against the back wall sat the biggest grandfather clock he'd ever seen. Then a silly idea struck him.

This place looks just like the Munsters' mansion or the Addams family's house.

He'd seen all the old reruns of those TV shows and loved them, but this house—Tuckaleechee's house—well, it was downright creepy. A shiver went down his spine.

Time to get on with it.

After locating the kitchen and the feather duster, he ran back upstairs to complete his disagreeable assignment. But something within him was changing as he firmly realized he was being used by the old woman. He was coming to the conclusion that she'd never ever intended to teach him Cherokee medicine.

He hadn't come to these realizations sooner because of Carmelita's hypnotic spell. That was wearing off now. She'd been so busy plotting against the Buckhorns and the Lookouts that she'd neglected to renew the spell and have him drink another cup of the tea.

Later that morning, after breakfast, Billy, Wesley, and Lisa rode out to the Sequoyah dorm together. The glowing purple spots were still visible to Billy, even in daylight. Wesley and Lisa just watched as Billy easily located and extracted the four medicine pouches buried around the dorm.

In the bed of Wesley's pickup, Billy opened the leather bags to reveal four torn photos of him and Lisa taken in the Taco Bueno restaurant.

"That confirms it," Wesley said. "Your former best friend is working with an enemy."

Billy tried to temporarily put it out of his mind as he and his grandpa began packing for their drive to Mescalero, New Mexico. They'd be heading to the home of Apache medicine man Clarence Chatto, who lived on a reservation road named Buckskin Trail. His was the last house on the back road and was located on a bluff overlooking the main community.

The pair's twelve-hour drive could be accomplished in one long day, with each of them taking turns behind the steering wheel. During his sessions as a passenger, Billy attempted to repeat the out-of-body travel he'd accomplished during Lisa's encounter with the wolf pack.

His first attempts failed. So many challenges and issues flooded Billy's mind that he couldn't relax or concentrate well enough to allow the vibrations to come. After six hours on the road, they stopped at a cheap diner near Amarillo, Texas, to have a bite.

"Cecil gave me an overview of these intertribal medicine sessions you're going to have," Grandpa said once they were back on the road. "Just so you'd know what to expect."

"I've been worried about how I'm going to actually put their healing practices to use, since each medicine maker operates in their own tribal language," Billy replied. "I mean, thirteen incantations in thirteen different languages? Sounds impossible."

"Cecil says it's more about your ability to absorb knowledge-filled energy than it is about memorizing anything," Wesley replied.

Billy thought back to winter solstice when the Sun Priest projected an information-filled energy ball toward him at the Horned Serpent's cave. Then he remembered that Morningstar had performed a similar process with the weather-making medicine man Andrew Blackbird.

"I personally don't understand how that works, but Cecil said you'd already been through it with Andrew," the elder added.

"Yeah, that's true," Billy confirmed. "I was surprised by how easy it was to master the weather spells he showed me, especially after everything was basically injected into my mind."

It was already dark when the pair arrived in the desert community of Mescalero. Clarence Chatto's wife and two grown children greeted them at the door of their adobe home, inviting them in to enjoy a traditional Apache meal.

Back in Oklahoma that night, Carmelita received two invited guests at her home in the woods near Buzzard Bend. The women, both members of the Owl Clan, had come in answer to the Cherokee witch's request for help in her campaign to defeat the Buckhorns and Lookouts.

Jacki Birdsong from California and Geraldine Osceola from Florida arrived none too soon as far as Tuckaleechee was concerned. She had her hands full trying to control the actions of seven people in two families, not to mention the members of the Medicine Council.

"It feels like we're Shakespeare's three witchy sisters," Birdsong said gleefully after being welcomed into Carmelita's home.

"Double, double, toil and trouble," Osceola responded, quoting a line from the Bard's famous play.

They all laughed, knowing full well that Native American witches were nothing like their European counterparts.

Unlike her cozy little cabin, Carmelita's sprawling old house had plenty of room for overnight visitors. After her guests had settled into their rooms, the three sat down to begin plotting their next moves. Three heads, coming from three different medicine traditions, would certainly be able to do ample damage to these two sets of enemies.

After dinner over in New Mexico, the pair of Oklahoma travelers settled into a couple of spare bedrooms in the back of the Chatto home on the Mescalero reservation. Later, Billy had a brief chat with Lisa on the phone, then went to bed and tried to spirit travel. He experimented with a couple of relaxing visualizations before arriving at one that worked. He mentally revisited his paddling voyage with Chigger down the Arkansas River last Thanksgiving. Only this time, Lisa was in the imaginary canoe with him.

He allowed himself to experience all the sensations he went through on that trip. He felt the warmth of the sun on his skin, heard the sound of the water flowing in the river, and smelled the natural fragrances of the landscape around him. On top of that, the smell of cider and pumpkin pie reached his nostrils, just as they'd done on that journey.

That did the trick. He hummed the song he'd learned from the Sun Chief, and soon the vibrations spread from his chest to his toes and fingertips. Then he heard the rip of Velcro that signaled his escape, followed by the sensation of floating up and out of his body. He half expected to see Grandma Awinita because she'd surprisingly appeared when he and Lisa had traveled. But she was nowhere in sight this time.

He focused on the task at hand: checking in on Chigger. Billy pictured his friend's face in his mind and, as expected, was immediately propelled to a position floating just above the Muskrat family's mobile home.

The first thing he noticed was a purplish-colored glow coming from the area where Chigger's bedroom was located. He drifted down and toward the bedroom but was met with resistance. Some kind of energy barrier prevented Billy from passing through the roof and reaching the bedroom. He pushed and prodded along the invisible surface of the barrier looking for a seam or vulnerable spot. Nothing.

He considered his options. From the out-of-body experiences he'd already had, there should be some clue about how to break through. He tried shrinking himself down to the size of a spider as Lisa had done. He succeeded only in making himself the size of a chipmunk. Still too big to find an entry point.

Then he simply tried envisioning himself already in Chigger's room, and voilà! He was in!

But what he found puzzled him. Chigger's physical body was asleep in bed surrounded by a kind of purple haze. Across the room, inside some sort of purple bubble, Chigger's spirit body anxiously paced back and forth while muttering something incomprehensible. The energy body was jagged edged and distorted in ways Billy found hard to understand.

Suddenly, Chigger stopped pacing and ran toward Billy. There was recognition on the boy's spirit face that quickly changed to desperation and panic, but try as he might, he couldn't communicate with Billy.

Then Chigger tried to communicate through a series of hand gestures, but he wasn't making any sense. Then an idea struck him, and he began demonstrating something. First, he mimicked the action of trying to enter his own physical body but couldn't accomplish it. Then he launched himself from the floor in an attempt to escape through the ceiling, but the purplish barrier around the room prevented that.

Billy understood that Chigger's spirit was trapped in his own room, and nonverbally communicated that idea to Chigger, who used the classic charades gesture of touching his nose with his index finger to indicate that Billy had arrived at the right answer.

Billy asked his friend how this happened, but Chigger's only reply was a shrug of his shoulders and a puzzled look on his face.

Billy detected a tug of discomfort coming from his own physical body, and he signaled Chigger that he had to go but promised to work on this problem as soon as possible.

After rejoining his body, he was certain Lisa would have to physically follow up on the comings and goings of Chigger's physical body. He sent a lengthy text to her describing what she needed to do.

Within a few minutes she replied: *Lisa Lookout, private investigator, at your service. I'll find out where this witch, Carmelapple Whachamacallit—whatever her name is—lives.*

The next morning, Billy described to Wesley the puzzling experience he'd had at Chigger's mobile home the night before.

"What you saw might just validate the Cherokee traditional belief in two souls," Wesley said.

"What? I don't remember hearing anything about two souls."

"It probably didn't make sense a few years ago when I first mentioned it, so you may have just forgotten about it."

"If you say so," Billy replied. "Please explain it again."

"Well, first, there's the free-soul," the elder said. "This one is the true soul, your true spiritual self. Then there's the body-soul or breath-soul. This one connects the physical body to the free-soul and is sometimes the part of a person that hangs around for a short while as a hostile ghost before dissolving."

"So, I was seeing Chigger's free-soul, his true self, trying to re-connect with his body-soul and his physical body?" Billy asked.

"Sounds about right."

"Does that mean Chigger isn't really responsible for what his breath-soul and physical body are doing right now?"

"Again, sounds about right. He could be under a hypnotic spell."

Billy pondered the implications of that insight as he prepared to receive what Clarence Chatto called Geronimo's "supernatural gift."

That same morning, Lisa woke to a bright Oklahoma winter day. She drove her motorcycle to a spot not far from Chigger's mobile home east of Tahlequah.

I do feel like a private eye, Lisa thought as she parked her bike behind a tree, took off her helmet, and pulled a pair of binoculars out of her side bag. Checking her phone clock, she saw it was about the time Chigger would probably be leaving for school.

The stakeout has begun, the girl texted her boyfriend.

Then she focused the lenses at the Muskrat front door just as it opened. A Native man who must've been Chigger's dad stepped out on the sunlit porch and held the door. A Native woman who must've been Chigger's mother stepped out next and proceeded down the steps. In a hurry, each sped toward a separate automobile, him to a dented blue pickup and her to a well-used beige economy car.

Ten minutes later, Chigger stepped out the door. He perceivably winced and turned away as rays of sunlight hit his face, looking every bit like a vampire shrinking from the deadly sun.

Holding a school notebook up to block the rays, the teen slunk down the steps and toward his own pickup.

After putting her helmet on, Lisa allowed him to get a decent head start before pursuing at a safe distance. She was pretty sure Chigger hadn't seen her motorcycle before, so there was a good chance he wouldn't recognize who was behind him.

Rather than head south toward Tahlequah High School, Chigger steered his truck northward on Highway 62.

He's definitely not going to school today, she thought.

When he turned down a gravel drive off the highway near Buzzard Bend, she got excited. Maybe he was headed to the witch's house! Instead of turning where Chigger had turned, Lisa kept going northward so as not to raise any suspicions. After a minute, she pulled over and sent a text message to Billy: *Chigger didn't go to school. He just turned on a long gravel driveway near Buzzard Bend.*

Then she turned back and pulled up to the intersection where Chigger had left the main road. Looking down the gravel road the boy had just traversed, her sensitive intuition told her it was not a road to travel lightly.

When Chigger arrived at Carmelita's cabin, the old woman introduced him to her visitors and then sat him down at her corner desk, telling him to organize all the loose papers in alphabetical order in a folder.

"What about studying medicinal plants?" he asked, disappointed in this latest chore.

"We'll get around to that eventually."

Then Tuckaleechee's own trained and heightened sensitivities suddenly told her danger lurked at the edge of her domain. Grabbing her favorite purple quartz crystal, she touched the flat end to the middle of her forehead, site of her psychic eye. That, coupled with the spirit vision incantation, allowed her to view the perimeter of her wooded property as if she were looking through a submarine periscope.

How lucky am I, the old woman thought when she saw Lisa Lookout lurking at the edge of her bearded forest.

"Come on now, girl," Carmelita said in a loud whisper. "Come closer. Let your curiosity guide you." Then she yelled at Chigger, "Quick, boy. Get me the *Ulasigi Svnoyi* herb blend from the top shelf! It's in a green jar with a black lid."

"Huh?" the boy responded, not in the mood to be barked at.

"The Dark Night herbs!" the old woman yelled. "You're gonna have to learn your Cherokee words!"

Chigger reluctantly got up and ambled across the room.

"I said be quick about it!" she thundered as she rubbed her hands together to create an energy ball. She hurled it at him like a baseball, and it struck him in the back of the head, knocking him forward. To stay on his feet, Chigger took three rapid steps and came to a stop right at the back wall filled with jars of dried herbs.

He rushed the jar labeled *Dark Night* back to the old woman, who was waiting with a small opened leather pouch in her hand. Grabbing the jar from her apprentice, she shoved a pinch of the blend of dried plants into the pouch and hobbled as fast as her wobbly legs could carry her out the cabin door.

Meanwhile, Lisa had begun creeping through the forest parallel to the gravel road Chigger had used. As the boy had experienced when he'd first entered these woods, the Spanish moss increased the intensely eerie element of the landscape as she moved through it.

Adding to the creepitude was the unexpected screech of an owl that pierced the silence. A second screech told Lisa the bird was coming her way, so the girl quickly crouched behind a nearby tree. However, within a few moments, the bird landed on a branch right above her, clutching a small leather pouch in one claw.

Prying the pouch open with her beak, the owl allowed the contents to fall right onto the girl below, all the while singing a soft owl song at a low volume. The bird watched as the dried leaves and twigs of the herb rained down on her target's hair and face.

Lisa ran her hands through her hair, trying to brush away whatever it was that had fallen in it.

Too late, Carmelita thought. *The deed is done.*

The owl flew back to the area outside her cabin and transformed into the old woman. "Quick, boy, drive me out toward the main road!" she yelled into the cabin. "Jacki, why don't you come with us. I may need some extra help."

Chigger and Jacki both came out of the log structure and climbed into the cab of his truck, and Tuckaleechee slid into the passenger seat.

"What are we doing?" the boy asked.

"Teaching a trespasser to mind her own business," the old woman said, and then to her guest, she added, "This is the Lookout girl, Billy Buckhorn's girlfriend. She must've followed my jughead apprentice here."

"Damn, you're lucky," Jacki said. "She just fell into your lap."

Chigger drove the two women down the gravel driveway toward Lisa's location.

"There she is," Carmelita said, pointing a crooked finger out the open passenger window. "Get over there as close as you can."

The apprentice medicine man veered off the gravel and into tall grass. Carefully, he picked his way through the underbrush until the truck was within a few yards of Lisa, who was slumped over against a tree.

"What did you do to her?" Chigger asked with genuine concern.

"Nothing serious. She's just asleep—for now. Pick her up and put her in the bed of the truck. I've got plans for her."

"I don't know," Chigger said. "Maybe we should just drop her off somewhere, like at the hospital, or back at the Sequoyah dorm."

Carmelita's anger flared into rage, but she realized she needed to take a different tack now. She calmed herself.

"What do you think is going on right now?" she asked her apprentice.

"What do you mean?"

"I mean . . . do you have the slightest idea of what Jacki and I and the other Night Seers are doing and why?"

"Not really," the boy said honestly. "You really haven't told me much."

"We're making them pay."

"Huh?"

"The generations of white people who ruined our lives," the old woman said in a quiet tone. "And all the Indians who compromised with them rather than stand up to them."

"Okay."

"Their day of reckoning is coming, and we're working to help make it happen."

"Who's 'we' again?"

"The Owls and the Snakes, united against a common foe, taking back control of the Middleworld, especially here on Turtle Island."

"Wow, that's amazing!" Chigger exclaimed, genuinely excited.

"And you're becoming an important part of that reckoning," she lied.

"It does feel good to be a part of something so important."

"So, are you with me, boy?" the old witch asked.

"One hundred percent," the naive apprentice replied.

"So, let's get on with it."

"Yes, ma'am."

Chigger jumped out of the truck and traipsed through the tall grass. Reaching Lisa, he tried to pick her up but couldn't manage it. Seeing that she was needed, Jacki climbed out of the truck and joined the boy in picking up Lisa's unconscious body. The two of them were able to place the girl in the bed of the pickup.

"Make 'em pay," Chigger said with an empty smile as he jumped back into his truck.

CHAPTER EIGHTEEN

Secrets Revealed

Billy had not seen any of the text messages Lisa sent as she followed Chigger that morning, because the Apache medicine ritual began at sunrise.

"Remember," Clarence told him before things got started, "for the duration of the ceremony, you are no longer Billy Buckhorn. The gifts you will be receiving during your training are being conferred on Thunder Child. In order to access the powers and abilities, you'll have to identify yourself as Thunder Child."

"Yes, Cecil told me the same thing," Billy replied. "But it takes some getting used to. I still don't feel worthy or capable."

"Give it time, nephew," Clarence advised. "Give it time."

The teen was made to stand in the center of a ceremonial area set up in Clarence's backyard. He was surrounded by a small group of singers who stood ready to play small traditional hand-held Apache drums with curved willow drumsticks.

As the ceremonial songs began, Clarence explained that he would be transferring a certain secret Apache medicine power to the boy warrior, the power to cause arrows and bullets fired toward him to always miss their mark as if he wore a deflecting shield.

"Wait, what?" Billy replied with a stunned expression.

Such a thought hadn't occurred to the teen until this very moment. He would need protection from bullets and arrows? He would need the ability to dodge deadly projectiles intended to kill him?

Clarence noticed Billy's reaction.

"You can do this," he said, looking into the young man's eyes. "You can do all of it, and we'll be with you every step of the way."

Billy nodded in understanding and took a deep breath.

"I can do this," he said, trying to demonstrate the same determination Clarence had. "I'm ready."

The highly secretive ceremony lasted from sunrise to sunset.

At the end of the day, the teen wasn't sure who he was. He didn't feel like Billy anymore, but neither did he feel like someone worthy of the name Thunder Child—yet.

A thought popped into his mind.

The confidence in yourself will come.

Billy appreciated the encouragement he assumed came from Morningstar.

When he decided to check in on Lisa, he found the text messages she'd sent that morning.

He called her but got no answer. Then he texted. No reply.

He texted both his father and mother next to see if they'd seen her. They hadn't. When neither Cecil nor Ethan knew her whereabouts, the boy worried.

"No one has seen Lisa all day," Billy reported to Wesley. "I'm worried."

"What did her last text messages say?" the elder asked.

"That she followed Chigger northward toward a place near Buzzard Bend. He didn't go to school."

The mention of Buzzard Bend seemed to mean something to Wesley.

"Tell everybody to drop whatever they're doing and go search for Lisa," Grandpa said firmly. "I'm going to call Wilma Wohali—you know she helped free Chigger from the dark crystal's spell—to see if she can get some of the medicine people to help too."

After a flurry of phone calls, both Buckhorns realized they couldn't continue their visit in New Mexico. They had to get back to Tahlequah as soon as possible. A quick explanation of the situation to Clarence and the Chatto family was all that was needed. The core of the ceremony had been completed, and the second day of planned activities was more of a cultural formality.

As they drove back toward Tahlequah that evening, Billy questioned his grandfather about the significance of Buzzard Bend.

"I saw a strong reaction on your face at the mention of Buzzard Bend," he said. "What was that about?"

"It reminded me of certain suspicious events surrounding your grandma's death."

"I don't remember hearing anything about that."

"You wouldn't," Wesley said. "You were only six years old, and we didn't talk about it when you were around."

They drove in silence for a few moments as Billy processed the information. "What suspicious events?" he asked finally.

"A tattooed medicine woman named Svnoyi Waya lived near Buzzard Bend back then."

"Night Wolf?" Billy said. "I don't think I've heard that name before."

"She was rumored to be a *skili*," Wesley replied. "And from what your grandma and I heard from others, she made bad medicine for anyone who would pay her—usually to hurt someone else. So your grandma studied up on how to undo the bad medicine done by someone like this witch."

"You told me Grandma had a reputation for blocking bad medicine, even reversing the effects of negative spells," Billy commented.

"She was the real healer in the family," Wesley said. "I was more like her apprentice than anything when she was alive. Anyway, this Night Wolf woman, who a long time ago used to be with Benjamin Blacksnake, began spreading lies about your grandma to discredit her."

"That's terrible!" Billy exclaimed.

"That, thankfully, backfired on her, which apparently made the woman even madder than before. One night not long after that, your grandma and I heard some noise outside our house in the middle of the night. I went out with a flashlight to see what was going on but didn't find anything."

He paused as his eyes became red with the tears of sudden emotion.

"Next morning, your grandma awoke with muscle spasms and tremors. She couldn't stand up, much less walk, so I rushed her to the Indian hospital. They gave her medicine and put her to bed. I went back home, checked the outside of the house, and found that a circle of little white snakeroot flowers had been spread completely around our property."

"Snakeroot?" Billy said, remembering what Wesley's medicine book said about the plant. "Isn't that used to treat snakebites?"

"Yeah, as a poultice, but if you eat it or drink it in a tea, it causes all the symptoms your grandma had. Or if you surround someone's home with its flowers and recite one of the formulas for the destruction of life, the targeted victim gets the same symptoms."

"Why couldn't the medical doctors at the hospital cure her?"

"They said she had cardiac something or other," Wesley said. "I forget the medical term. So they installed a pacemaker and sent her home, saying she'd be all better in a few days."

Billy could see it was painful for his grandfather to talk about these events. He waited to see if the elder would say more.

"Of course, the docs couldn't do anything about the real reason Awinita was sick," Wesley said finally. "She got worse—the tremors, fluttering heart, stumbling when she tried to walk, weakness in her muscles."

"That must've been hard to watch," Billy said sympathetically.

"I visited a few reputable medicine men to see if they could help, but no one seemed to have the power to block the bad medicine. So I began learning everything I could to cure her, but I was too green, too inexperienced."

"So, you thought it was Night Wolf who spread the snakeroot," Billy said. "What did you say happened to the old woman?"

"I read her obituary in the Cherokee Nation newspaper a few years later," Wesley said. "I figured that was that."

The pair rode in silence the rest of the way to Amarillo, where they had to stop for the night to get a few hours' rest. In the meantime, the remaining Lookouts and Buckhorns back in the Cherokee Nation had organized a search party. And in their different locations, members of the Intertribal Medicine Council got busy using their skills to help remotely locate the girl.

In the Amarillo motel, even though he was exhausted, Billy tried to spirit travel. All he succeeded in doing was falling asleep. After about four hours' sleep, he woke with a start. The clock beside his bed said four in the morning.

What am I doing? My girlfriend is in trouble, and I'm just sleeping!

He jumped out of bed.

"Grandpa, wake up! We've got to get to Lisa!"

Wesley moaned from his bed across the room and tried to sit up. But he couldn't move. "Grandson, I need your help," he said in a barely audible voice. "I can't seem to move."

Billy leaped to his grandfather's side.

"Uncover me and help me sit up," the old man said.

Billy threw the covers back and pulled on Wesley's arms. Then he turned the elder so his feet rested on the floor beside the bed.

"Now rub my shoulders and arms like you're trying to warm them up."

"What's going on?" Billy asked as he carried out the instructions.

"I didn't want to alarm you, but my arms and legs have been getting more and more stiff every day. Thankfully, I've been able to loosen up all by myself—until now."

Billy rubbed and patted the elder's extremities until he could move them on his own. Finally, Wesley could stand up by himself. Billy just stood there with a concerned look on his face.

"I'll have a medical doctor check it out when we get home," Wesley said. "Now let's get back on the road."

Exhausted, Billy and his grandfather pulled into Park Hill at ten in the morning. In spite of their fatigue, both were ready to join in the search for Lisa. Of course, the best use of Billy's time was to do his searching while out-of-body, and Wesley consulted with Cecil to find out how he could best help.

"I did a little searching around your house while you were gone, Wesley, and I need to show you what I found," Cecil said.

The two drove to the elder's house and went in the kitchen. Sitting on the kitchen table were four small leather pouches much like the ones found in holes around Lisa's dorm.

"I found these tucked away in various rooms of this house," Cecil said, "possibly placed there by the same person who stole Blacksnake's medicine book."

Wesley peeked inside the bundles and found they all contained the same ingredients: a piece of flint rock, a tuft of squirrel's fur, a few stems from the wolfbane plant, and a short length of black rope tied in a knot. Wesley immediately recognized the collection as the elements used by medicine makers that were up to no good.

Overwhelming fatigue, combined with shock, suddenly overtook Wesley, and he fainted, hitting the floor hard.

Cecil rushed to fill up a glass with water, which he splashed onto Wesley's face. The elder slowly opened his eyes and looked up at his friend.

"We need to cleanse your house, and your body, to rid you and your home of bad medicine," Cecil said. "Someone's trying to harm you."

When he was feeling a little better, Billy's grandfather gathered up some fresh clothes, stuffed them in a grocery bag, and left the house, again locking the door behind him.

"Back to the Cherokee Inn," Cecil said. "I'll come back and do the smudging once you've settled in there and lain down to get some rest."

Billy, also exhausted, had gone straight to his bedroom to try another session of spirit travel, but again he fell asleep instead. After a two-hour nap, he awoke and tried the relaxation steps again. This time he was successful in separating.

He envisioned Lisa's face in his mind and headed north to the general vicinity of Buzzard Bend. Above the tree line, he scanned the forested area for signs of her, but nothing pulled him in or appeared to him. Upon closer inspection, the entire forest seemed to be under some sort of camouflage veil.

While his son rested, Billy's father called Chief Swimmer of the Tahlequah Police Department to report that Lisa was missing, while Ethan called Sequoyah High School to do the same.

When Swimmer, whose officers had killed the Raven Stalker last fall, heard about another missing Native girl, he said, "Oh no, not again," and immediately sent anyone he could spare to assist with the search.

What no one knew was that Carmelita, with the added powers of Osceola and Birdsong, had indeed cast a camouflage spell around her house, her cabin, and the spot where Lisa's motorcycle had been parked. This was similar to the spell cast by the Snakes a thousand years ago to conceal Shakuru's location from anyone that might be looking for him.

Lisa was now being held captive in the dungeon basement of Carmelita's Victorian-style house, which stood across the clearing from her cabin. The house also served as an archive of her life, including mementos from her years as Kituwah and Night Wolf.

Lisa regained consciousness a couple hours after being locked in the musty, dust-filled subterranean room. Her mind was a bit foggy from the spell Carmelita had cast and the herbal blend the old owl-woman had dropped on the girl's head.

Where am I and how did I get here? Lisa asked herself. *I was hiding behind a tree when I heard the screech of an owl, and then something landed in my hair.*

That was when the answer clicked in her mind. She must be in the witch's basement!

So much for my private eye skills! I wonder if Billy can find me.

The girl rose from the stack of old blankets where she lay and began to look for an escape route. Thinking her cell phone was still in her back pocket, she made a quick search. No phone in any pocket. A dim bulb in the ceiling lamp provided enough light for some exploration of the space.

Finding a set of stairs at one end, she climbed up to discover a locked metal door. Her side of the door was badly marred with several sets of scratches that seemed to have been made by some animal.

Back down the stairs, Lisa took a tour of her prison. First, she ran across a stack of yellowed old copies of the *Cherokee Phoenix* newspaper printed in the Cherokee language. Scanning the top copy, the only thing she could read was the date, 1906, and a caption under the front-page photo of a man named Principal Chief Frank J. Boudinot standing next to a young woman with a diagonal tattoo on her face, who was identified as Kituwah Redbird.

Lisa moved on, coming to a table covered in old, faded photographs and newspaper clippings. Picking up the top picture, she saw the same tattooed face looking back at her. This time the woman was identified as Night Wolf, a medicine maker famous for doctoring Cherokee stickball teams.

Underneath that picture, she found yet another news clipping with a photo. The news article announced the death of medicine woman Night Wolf, and the accompanying photo showed the same tattooed face.

Behind the table, hanging on the wall, was a pair of ball sticks, a set of women's turtle shell rattle leggings, a ribbon shirt, and a bandolier-style beaded bag. All were covered with a thick layer of dust.

Suddenly, Lisa felt a draft of dank air on her shoulders and face. It came from the opposite end of the basement, farthest from the stairs and the metal door. Squinting into the darkness, she could just barely make out what looked like a set of metal bars.

Another breeze of dank air, with a hint of damp animal fur, met Lisa as she moved in that direction. Finally, what came into view was an entire wall of metal bars that stretched across the front of a cave opening.

This house was built partially over a cave entrance.

However, looking every bit like the door to a jail cell, a closed and locked gate blocked the entrance to the cave. The difference here was that this jail cell door was unexpectedly about ten feet tall!

This really is a prison, but was it created to keep something in this room or to keep something in the cave?

Just then Lisa heard noises outside the metal door at the opposite end of the basement. Quickly, she jogged back to her bed of blankets.

With the help of her cane, Carmelita hobbled down the stairs carrying a key ring and made her way over to Lisa. The old woman's leather pouch hung at her side.

"You rescued your boyfriend from one of the lower belief zones," the old woman said. "Now it's his turn to rescue you. Only he doesn't know what I've got in store for him!"

Lisa pretended to just be waking up. As the witch reached Lisa's makeshift bed, the prisoner caught sight of the woman's tattooed face, the same face in the one-hundred-year-old photo! The same face of the woman who supposedly died!

What the—?

The girl successfully concealed from her captor the shock on her own face. "Who . . . who are you?" Lisa asked, faking grogginess. "Where am I?"

"Oh, how rude of me," the woman answered. "I'm known as Carmelita Tuckaleechee, and you're my uninvited guest."

Lisa didn't say anything as the medicine woman pulled something from her pouch with a wrinkled hand.

"But I know all too well who you are, Miss Lisa Lookout," Carmelita said. "My apprentice, young Checotah, told me all about you."

Then she opened her hand and blew the purple powdered contents right into Lisa's face. The girl coughed and gagged and tried to wipe the stuff off her face.

"Go back to sleep and dream a little dream," the woman said. "I've got quite a surprise for you, and your boyfriend too!"

That was the last thing Lisa heard before drifting off. The witch cackled with delight as she hobbled over to the gate and unlocked it using one of the keys on the ring.

Calling into the mouth of the cave, Carmelita shouted, "Tsul 'Kalu, awaken!" She repeated the words three more times. "Tsul 'Kalu, awaken! *Ulisaladodi!* Rise and come forth! A pretty young sleeping maiden awaits your embrace."

Of course, the Osage teen had never heard the Cherokee legend of Tsul 'Kalu, the hairy giant with sharp, slanted eyes. She did not know that he was said to have six fingers on each hand, to be bigger and hairier than a Bigfoot, or to have once fathered children with a Cherokee maiden, much less that he was blamed by many Cherokees for all their troubles.

"Now I've got to get back upstairs," Carmelita said to the unconscious Lisa. "Getting rid of these pesky Buckhorns is such hard work!"

Back in the cabin, the first thing the witch did was cancel her camouflage spell. She wanted Billy Buckhorn to see what was coming next for his girlfriend.

"The trap is set," she said to no one in particular.

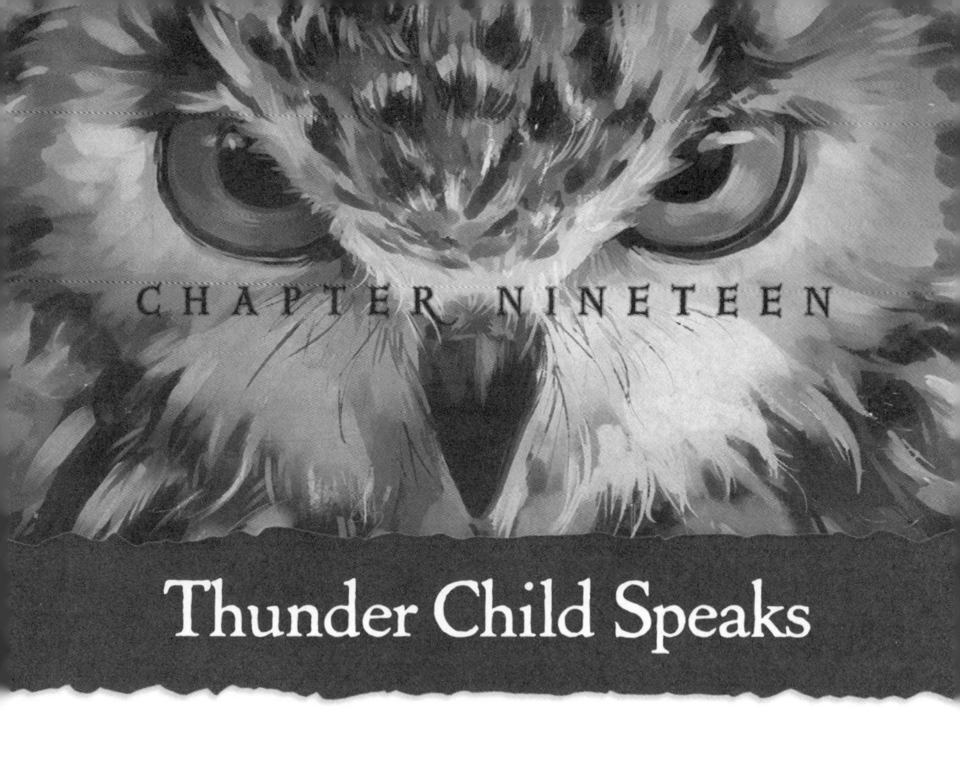

Thunder Child Speaks

After smudging Wesley with sage and cedar and leaving the elder to rest in a room at the Cherokee Inn, Cecil took his medicine satchel to Wesley's house to perform a ceremonial cleansing. He wafted the herbal smoke into every corner of the old wood-frame house.

"That should do it," he said, as if the house was able to hear him.

Later in the day, after a nap, a shower, and a change of clothes, the elder Buckhorn returned home feeling renewed. As soon as he stepped through the front door, he immediately felt the improved energy in his home as well.

News of the medicine man's return spread rapidly via word of mouth, and people with all manner of physical and mental complaints flocked to his house once again. First in line on the front porch waiting to see him were two elderly Native women dressed in rather shabby clothing. They introduced themselves.

"We're so happy you've come back home," the first woman said. "I'm Geraldine and this is my sister, Jacki. We've come a long way to see you and have brought a gift of *hakchuma*, natural Choctaw tobacco."

She handed the medicine man a tightly wrapped bunch of dried natural tobacco leaves. Wesley held the bundle up to his nose and took a whiff.

"The real deal—straight from the ground," he said. "Where did you get it?"

"From our own garden down in Choctaw territory," Geraldine said. "We used to cultivate the plant for the Choctaw medicine man who doctored us for many years, Elmore Proctor."

Wesley didn't expect to hear that name.

"We heard that you've taken on some of his work since he passed," Geraldine said. "We hope you can help us today."

"I'd be honored to help any of Elmore's patients if I can." He turned and stepped back inside the house, and the women followed. "Now what can I do for you today?"

Jacki went first.

"Sometimes at night I get chills and fever, and my bones ache," she said. "When I wake up in the morning, I am so tired, and there are dark circles under my eyes."

Wesley considered her symptoms for a moment and reached a conclusion.

"I'm going to grind up a leaf of the tobacco you've brought and doctor it some," he explained. "Then I'm going to take a couple of medicines from my garden out back and put them in a bag for you to take with you."

"Okay. Then what?"

"You'll put the doctored tobacco in a pipe and smoke it three times a day for three days, and then brew some tea with the herbs and drink that three times a day for three days."

"That seems easy enough."

"Wait right here while I make this up for you."

Jacki nodded, and Wesley pulled one leaf from the tobacco bundle. Then he headed toward the back of the house. While he was gone, the two women talked among themselves in quiet tones.

"Do you remember what symptoms you're going to tell him?" Jacki asked Geraldine.

"Of course," she snapped. "I'm not new at this."

Soon Wesley returned with the items he'd promised and handed them to Jacki. While both of their hands were on the bag of plant cuttings, he recited the Cherokee verbal formula that would activate the spell. As he was speaking, Jacki whispered the Cherokee word for 'opposite' repeatedly under her breath as she'd been taught by Carmelita.

"Now what about you, young lady?" he asked the elderly Geraldine. She pretended to be flattered.

"Oh, you're such a tease," the woman replied with a smile and then composed herself. "Well, to begin with, sometimes before I go to bed, my back feels like it's crawling with ants that sting a little and just keep moving around," she said, using a hand to rub between her shoulder blades. "And then I wake up in the morning and my intestines feel like there are snakes moving around inside me. It's so creepy!"

Wesley, again, considered the woman's symptoms for a short while and then consulted his own medicine book, the one he'd had since his days of doctoring with Awinita. He found the formula titled "To Doctor for Insects" and the one named "When Intestines Come Alive." The names of medicinal plants to accompany the incantations were, of course, also listed.

"I'll have to go to the woods behind the house and gather the wild plants needed for these treatments," Wesley told the women. "If you come back in about an hour, I'll have the blend ready for you. But I can recite the formula now."

"Oh, that's wonderful!" Geraldine said. "Thank you so much!"

Again, as the medicine man repeated the Cherokee words in the formula, Geraldine whispered *"ahnaditlv"* under her breath, setting the reversal spell in motion a second time.

Afterward, the pair, walking and acting like two physically impaired elders, left Wesley's house in a very good mood. They would not be returning in an hour to pick up their medicine. They'd already achieved their purpose for visiting the healer.

"Won't he be unpleasantly surprised when the 'opposite' formula takes effect," Geraldine said when they were far enough away not to be heard by anyone else waiting on the porch.

While Wesley was seeing patients, quite by chance, Billy decided to make another out-of-body journey over the Buzzard Bend area in search of Lisa at about the same time Tuckaleechee lifted her camouflage veil. As he'd done several times before, he first pictured Lisa in his mind, hoping to home in on her location. This time, lo and behold, he was drawn to an old two-story frame house that hadn't been visible before. Next to the house sat an old log cabin.

Why haven't I been able to see this until now? Lisa must be inside somewhere.

Swooping down and penetrating the upper story of the house, Billy found two older Native American women packing suitcases, apparently getting ready to leave. As he moved near the pair, they seemed to become vaguely aware of his presence.

"Did you feel that?" one asked the other. "I think there's a spirit in here with us."

"Yeah, I detect a cold presence," the other one replied. "Who's in here with us?" she called out, looking up toward the ceiling.

Intent on his mission, Billy moved down to the lower levels of the structure.

Nothing on the first floor.

He sensed some movement at a lower level and floated in that direction. Breaking through the basement ceiling, he was shocked at what he saw next. A large, hairy "thing" was gently picking up his unconscious girlfriend from a pile of blankets. He recognized the creature from traditional stories told by his grandfather.

Tsul 'Kalu? That can't be! It's impossible!

As Billy watched from his nonphysical vantage point, the beast cradled Lisa in one arm and bolted into the cave. The teen immediately rushed after them, intent on rescue. But once he caught up with the pair just inside the cave entrance, he realized he was unable to complete his objective. Tsul 'Kalu now existed in the physical world, so Billy would have to confront him in physical form.

Gotta get back to the flesh!

In a flash he was back at his house and back in his body. Up he jumped, ready to return to Buzzard Bend, this time in physical form. Suddenly, an urgent message appeared in his mind. Was it his own memory or was it Morningstar? He didn't have time to find out.

"Billy Buckhorn won't be able to accomplish anything, but Thunder Child can. And he'll need his Lightning Lance."

Reaching up to the top shelf of a built-in bookcase, Billy took down the lance, which had been carefully wrapped in a bolt of deerskin. Wasting no time on the doubts that swirled through his mind, this grandson of a Cherokee medicine man knew the time had come. Would he be able to rise to the challenge he faced, or was it all just a massive fantasy?

"This is about to get very real, Buckhorn," he said aloud.

As he raced out of the house and into his truck, the adrenaline began pumping through his body. Pushing the aging pickup beyond its limits, the boy sped toward Buzzard Bend. He hadn't bothered calling the police—or anyone else, for that matter—to tell them of Lisa's whereabouts, because he knew they'd all just get in the way.

Having mapped the route to the old house while out-of-body, Billy turned down the gravel drive that led to it. The truck came to a skidding halt at the front of the house, kicking up a cloud of dust from the gravel parking area. Grabbing the Lightning Lance, he bounded into the house and began looking for the door to the basement. Surprisingly, the home's owner, no doubt Chigger's medicine woman mentor, was nowhere in sight.

The cell phone in his back pocket rang, but he ignored it and continued the search.

Running from room to room and down a maze of hallways, he couldn't seem to find the elusive doorway to the underground.

It must be hidden or camouflaged.

Retracing his steps, he reexamined all the rooms and hallways on the first floor of the house. Finding nothing, he then began opening cabinets and searching for hidden passageways. As his search continued with no results, his sense of urgency was quickly becoming a feeling of outright panic.

Suddenly, a mental prompting caused him to look more closely at the oversized grandfather clock that sat against the back wall of the home's front room. Something was odd and out of place about it. He studied the ornately carved wooden features of the clock's cabinet and then focused on the clock's face. That was it! Instead of the usual clockface with twelve numbers in a circle, this timepiece displayed phases of the moon.

That's not a normal clock!

On the front surface of the tall, antique moon clock, a much wider than usual cabinet door provided access to the clock's inner workings. Billy opened the door and discovered there were no inner workings. Instead, at the back of the clock, there was another door, a metal door. A simple deadbolt lock held the door shut, and Billy easily opened the portal.

A set of stairs led downward into a pool of darkness. Without hesitation the teen jettisoned himself into the unknown below. At the bottom of the stairs, once his eyes became accustomed to the lack of light, he scanned the space. His eyes came to rest on the bars in the back of the room—a cage with an open door leading into an even darker cave.

He quickly moved closer to the cave as a wave of damp, dank air washed over him.

"Lisa!" he called into the blackness, but only a faint echo of his own voice returned. He looked down at the five-foot length of burnt wood in his hand.

Here goes nothing.

"This is Thunder Child," he said in a loud voice, looking upward and holding the Lightning Lance over his head. "I call on the Upperworld, the Thunder Beings, and Morningstar to ignite the powers of my warrior medicine, to grant me the strength of a spirit warrior. Light my way in the darkness ahead!"

To his great surprise and relief, he felt a ripple of vibrational energy begin to develop in his body—starting, oddly enough, at his feet and working its way upward through his outstretched arm. Finally, the upraised piece of twisted wood began vibrating as visible sparks radiated from it, and as the energy dissipated, the end of the lance lit up, projecting a beam of light from the tip.

Billy felt a sense of power he'd never felt before, and the cells in his physical body seemed to morph and stretch and grow. The Sun Chief's energy had started that process weeks ago, and now the teen knew why. It had all been part of his future role as Thunder Child.

This is really happening!

With newfound strength and energy, Thunder Child charged into the cave, the light from the lance leading the way.

I sure hope there are no bats this time!

The cave's main passage sloped gently downward for a distance before curving sharply to the left. After the turn, a large chamber came into view, a tall space that someone or something had lived in for a long time. The partially gnawed bones of cattle and chicken were scattered about. Tufts of long brown fur had collected in nooks and crannies of the area.

"Lisa!" Thunder Child called, but again, only the echo of his own voice came back. So he pressed onward and downward until he came to a fork in the passageway.

This feels familiar.

The right corridor continued downward into the cave at a steep angle, while the left path appeared to head upward. A faint glow of light emanated from that direction. In the dim light, Thunder Child caught a glimpse of a strand of brown fur tangled around a short stalagmite protruding from the floor.

Upward it is!

Several quick, long strides brought him to a cave exit point. He emerged from the ragged, rocky opening and found himself in a clearing surrounded by a forest of dead and dying trees. True, it was the middle of winter, but the condition of the timber was worse than anything cold weather alone would produce. Disfigured limbs and branches jutted this way and that, giving the area a sinister look.

Again, the cell phone in his back pocket rang, but he ignored it. Nothing could deter him from his primary objective.

"Lisa!" he called out.

The only reply was the sound of wind blowing through brittle dead branches. It seemed odd that he hadn't come across this piece of parched landscape while he was conducting his out-of-body search for Lisa earlier.

A full examination of the edges of the clearing allowed Thunder Child to locate a break in the woods along its southern border. There, again, was a tuft of brown fur stuck to a twig and, just beyond it, a winding path.

The sound of a breaking branch in the distance alerted the boy hunter to the possible presence of his prey. The lightning speed with which he was able to bolt down the path told Thunder Child that he, indeed, had enhanced abilities. He hoped to put those powers to full use very soon.

He didn't have long to wait, because the path ended in another clearing, where sat a crudely constructed hut tall enough to house the Tsul 'Kalu.

"Lisa, are you in there?" Thunder Child called.

"Billy, is that you?" a weak female voice replied from within the hut. "Where am I? What's going on?"

Just then, the giant stepped out of the hut carrying a traditional Cherokee war club in one hand and the jawbone of a cow in the other. His grimacing face, menacing eyes surrounded by dark circles, bared teeth, and drooling mouth presented quite a threatening sight.

"Are you all right?" Thunder Child called to his girlfriend. "Did this big fella hurt you?"

"No, I don't think so," Lisa answered. "I've been unconscious. Night Wolf or Tuckaleechee or whatever her name is gave me something that knocked me out."

"Okay, just hang in there," Thunder Child replied. "I've got to deal with this guy first."

The creature released a deafening roar as he stepped away from the hut. Then, in a deep-toned, gravelly voice, he began speaking some language Thunder Child didn't understand.

Slowly the giant made his way across the clearing, intently focused on his small adversary.

Then the screech of an owl pierced the air, grabbing Tsul 'Kalu's attention. Fear registered on the beast's face as he dropped his weapons, kneeled on the ground, and buried his face in his hands. Thunder Child watched as the oversized bird swooped down out of the sky and over the giant.

The hairy, now-submissive creature's thoughts registered in the boy's mind: "Yes, master. Will carry out your commands. The young medicine man is as good as dead."

Satisfied with her slave's response, the owl returned to the sky and flew to the east in the direction of the old house. Back on the ground, Tsul 'Kalu grabbed his weapons and stood up.

He roared again and charged toward Thunder Child.

As threatening and menacing as the giant was, the teen really didn't want to harm him. It seemed quite miraculous that the beast, whose legend had been passed down through untold generations, stood here before him. On the other hand, if immediate action wasn't taken, Thunder Child's skull would be crushed in the next few seconds!

"Anagalisgv adeyvasgv digvwalosv ayv!" Thunder Child commanded in Cherokee, holding his Lightning Lance aloft. "Lightning flow through me!"

An electrical charge coursed through the boy's body, then collected as stored high-powered energy in the lance. Taking aim at the charging beast, Thunder Child propelled the charge toward him. A bolt of electricity crackled through the air just as the beast threw the war club.

With no time to think, the teen froze in place as the monster's weapon raced toward him.

But an invisible barrier diverted the projectile harmlessly off at an angle.

The Geronimo spell works!

At the same time the war club missed its target, the lightning bolt hit the creature squarely in the chest, knocking the Tsul 'Kalu to the ground. The strong odor of burning fur reached Thunder Child's nostrils as he approached the beast.

Is he dead or just unconscious?

The answer to the question came as the beast's body shriveled and shrank to about one-fifth its original size. When the transformation, which reminded Thunder Child a little of the Raven Stalker's demise, was complete, what was left was a dead raccoon lying on the ground.

What strange spell is this?

"Billy, is everything okay out there?" Lisa called from inside the hut. "Come untie me, please."

The boy sprang into action.

"I thought I'd never find you," he said as he untied his girlfriend.

They hugged each other tightly for a brief moment, then kissed. Lisa broke away to ask a question that had been burning in her mind.

"What do I call you?" she said. "Are you Billy or are you Thunder Child?"

"I don't even know what to call me, so you can call me whatever you're comfortable with."

"I'll have to think about it," Lisa replied.

"If you start calling me Thunder Child all the time, I'll have to start calling you Spider Woman all the time."

"Billy it is, then," she said with a smile.

Billy noticed that the power, the electricity, and the increased size he'd felt just a few moments ago were dissipating.

Back to normal, he thought.

He gave Lisa one more short kiss and then broke away.

"I need to call off the search," he said as he pulled out his phone and dialed.

He made a quick call to Chief Swimmer, gave a quick summary of the situation, and finished by saying, "I'll give you all the details later."

After ending the call, he remembered something.

"My grandpa has been trying to reach me, but I've been a little too busy to take his calls," Billy said, dialing Wesley's home number.

There was no answer.

"My intuition says we need to get over there right away," he said. "I left my truck in front of the old house. There must be another way to get there besides through the cave."

Knowing the house was east of them, Billy grabbed Lisa's hand and headed in that direction. Little did either of them know that the old Night Seer was watching from a distant tree, still in her owl form. When the lightning bolt struck down the prize creature she'd conjured, she was shocked and angered.

I've got to come up with a new strategy to take down this damn junior Buckhorn, she thought. *His abilities are much greater than expected.*

Back on the ground, the couple raced down a pathway through the dead forest. In a matter of a few minutes, they came to a clearing. To their dismay, it was the same clearing they'd just left.

"How is this possible?" Lisa said. "We're right back where we started!"

"Let's try a different path," Billy suggested and led the way again.

Again, they sprinted through the craggy trees only to emerge back in the same clearing.

"I can't believe how powerful this woman, this witch, actually is," Lisa said. "What are we going to do?"

Billy thought quietly for a minute. "Maybe our only way out *is* through the cave and back to the basement," he said.

Off they went in that direction and, fortunately, located the path to the cave. Billy discovered that a little of the power still lingered in the lance, so it still functioned like a flashlight. The pair was able to reach the mouth of the cave back in the basement, but the doorway in the iron bars was closed and locked.

"Now what?" Lisa said. "The key is on an old key ring, but who knows where that is."

Billy shook his head, not able to see a solution to their problem. Then a hopeful look spread across his face.

"You followed Chigger here, right?" he said.

"Yeah."

"He might still be here on the property somewhere, and he might know where the key is."

"So? He hasn't been acting like much of a friend lately," Lisa observed. "I doubt he'd be much help now."

"He's my oldest and now my second-best friend," Billy said. "Grandpa thinks he's been under a hypnotic spell. Maybe I can appeal to our old friendship."

Lisa didn't respond.

"I think it's worth a try."

"I suppose," Lisa said with a shrug.

Billy pulled his phone out of his pocket and began texting.

I'm in trouble and desperately need your help, the message read.

No response came.

If I did something to offend you, I'm sorry.

Still nothing.

"Okay, what's our plan B?" Lisa asked.

Just then, the three little dots on Billy's phone screen began dancing.

What could I possibly do to help you? Chigger's message read.

Lisa and I are trapped behind a set of bars in the basement of the witch's house and don't know where to find the key.

There was no immediate response to that message. After a pause, the dots danced again.

By "the witch" I suppose you mean Carmelita Tuckaleechee, Chigger's response read.

Exactly.

Another pause in the typing.

She really is a witch, isn't she? Chigger replied. *Not a healer.*

She murdered my grandmother and may have done something to harm my grandfather.

Something in Chigger's subconscious mind broke through at the mention of harm to Billy's grandfather. The boy had a nagging feeling that he somehow may have been involved in causing that harm. His memory regarding recent events was very foggy.

How do you get to the basement? he texted.

Through the grandfather clock in the front room of the old house, Billy replied.

Be right there.

Chigger grabbed the key ring that hung on a peg near the desk. Stepping out of the cabin, he looked around to see if his mentor was watching. No sign of her. He darted across the open space between the cabin and the house and went straight for the front room.

He made it through the grandfather clock, down the stairs, and to the cave door in record time, fearful that the old woman would catch him.

"Boy, am I glad to see you!" Billy said. "And that set of keys."

Chigger began going through the keys to see which one would work. The fourth one fit the lock and clicked it open.

"Awesome!" Lisa said.

"This must be the famous Lisa," Chigger said as the couple stepped out of the cave.

"Of course it is," Billy said. "You met her at the Taco Bueno when you took our picture."

Chigger gave them a blank stare.

"I bet you're just pretending you don't remember," Lisa said.

"I'm sorry. I honestly don't."

"We'll talk about this later. We've got to get to my grandpa's house," Billy said. Then he thought, *What about Chigger?* "Are you coming with us or staying here?" he asked his old friend.

"Staying," Chigger said. "I've got some loose ends to tie up."

Leaving Chigger behind, the couple raced to the truck and sped away down the gravel drive. Lisa tried calling Wesley's house again as they drove, but still got no answer.

Things at Wesley's house were strangely quiet. No patients waited on his porch for treatment. No cars filled with ailing Natives lined the road near his house.

After rushing through the front door, the couple searched the home. No sign of the elder.

Frantic, Billy dashed out the back door. He remembered another time he'd found his grandfather covered with gashes and blood in the garden.

Much to the boy's horror, that's where he found Wesley again, lying on the ground. "Grandpa!" he yelled as he and Lisa reached him. "Grandpa!"

The elder moaned faintly.

"Grandpa, what happened?"

"The sisters," Wesley said with much effort and then he passed out.

"Call an ambulance!" Lisa shouted.

"Takes too long," Billy said. "Get some blankets from inside the house and meet me back here."

The Cherokee teen knew he needed to access his Thunder Child abilities again, but this time a thought popped into his mind telling him he didn't have to call out a prescribed set of words. All he had to do was think it, just as he did when operating without his body.

He visualized himself as Thunder Child being energized with the superhuman powers he needed, and to his great relief, this image manifested in the physical. This time, without the lance in hand, the vibratory power began in the middle of his chest and spread outward, seemingly activating every cell of his body.

He ran through the house as fast as his legs could carry him, which he realized was faster than he'd ever moved before. He pulled his pickup around to the back of the house, as he'd done when his grandfather had been attacked by the Raven Stalker, and backed it as close to Wesley as he could. Lisa spread the blankets out in the bed of the truck.

"How are you going to get him up here?" Lisa was asking as her boyfriend, now in Thunder Child mode, stooped down, picked up the elder without effort, and gently placed him in the back of the truck.

"Like that," he said.

Thunder Child now knew for certain that increased speed and strength had come along with his new title. But a new concern hit him. Would his physical body be able to withstand repeated transformations from Billy to Thunder Child and back again? Only time would tell.

"Let's go!" he said, jumping in the truck cab and tossing his phone to Lisa. "Call my mother and tell her to meet us in the ER."

CHAPTER TWENTY

Holy Road

With Rebecca's assistance, emergency room doctors were able to revive Wesley enough for him to have a few visitors for a short period of time. The first to have a turn was Billy, who was quite aware that he was just Billy again. He was able to get a few minutes alone with his beloved elder and lifelong mentor.

"Two Indian women I didn't know came to see me," the elder said in a raspy whisper. "They claimed to be sisters, but I think they somehow put a reverse spell on me. All the symptoms they each described separately are the ones I have now."

"Did they give you any clues about who they were or where they were from?" his grandson asked.

"They said they used to get doctored by Elmore Proctor down in Choctaw country, but I think they're part of the Owl Clan, sent by that wicked woman Night Wolf, who obviously didn't die like I thought she did."

At that moment, Wesley began a bout of coughing that brought their conversation to a complete halt. After several hacking coughs that brought up blood, he winced and grabbed his chest in pain.

"Somebody, come quick!" Billy yelled. "I think he's having a heart attack!"

Rebecca, another nurse, and two doctors rushed into the room and ushered the teen out. Billy joined his father, James, along with Lisa and the Lookout family out in the waiting room. No one spoke. Meaningful looks were all that were exchanged for quite a while.

Finally, one of the doctors came out to speak to the families.

"I'm afraid I'm only here to prepare you for the worst," the man said.

A collective gasp sucked all the air right out of the room, and then a moment later an exhale of extreme sorrow filled it again.

"He seems to be going downhill fast, but we don't understand why," the doctor continued. "None of his symptoms, in and of themselves, should be affecting him this badly."

Wordlessly, Cecil, Ethan, and Lisa moved to console the two Buckhorns with sympathetic words, pats on the back, and gentle touches on the arms.

"You can have some time with him," the doctor added. "But he asked to see his grandson again."

Billy followed the physician out of the waiting area. When he stepped into Wesley's room, the boy rushed to the elder's side.

"Maybe I can cast a counterspell, Grandpa," Billy said as a single tear rolled down his cheek. "Just tell me where to find it in your medicine book. There's still time. There has to be. I can run over to your house and—"

Wesley spoke barely above a whisper. "Give it a rest, Grandson. They really did a number on me, and I'm not coming back from this."

"But I don't know what I'm gonna do without you," the boy said, sounding like a ten-year-old. "You've always been there for me, showing me the way, explaining how our people handled things. You—"

The elder raised one hand as if to say "Enough."

"I'm going to be with your grandma," he rasped. "You're in charge now. You've got more gifts and abilities than anyone I've ever seen. You'll do fine."

The grandson buried his face in the grandfather's chest and began to cry profusely.

The doctor stepped into the room and gently pulled the boy away. "The others want to say goodbye," he said. "Let them have their turn."

Billy tried to calm himself as the physician escorted him from the room. Back in the waiting area, the teen came to a major conclusion. It was time to end the reign of the witch of Buzzard Bend.

Leaving the Lookouts and the other Buckhorns at the hospital, Billy jumped in the cab of his truck, determined to take on all the evil in the world. He first made sure his Lightning Lance was still behind the seat, wrapped in deerskin, along with his hunting bow and quiver of arrows. Then he made an urgent spiritual request.

"Morningstar, Thunders, and Upperworld beings, I ask that you shower your powers upon me as I face a menace that has plagued my family for generations."

Unexpectedly, the spirit of Morningstar came into view in front of the pickup.

"You aren't ready yet," he said. "You've hardly begun your training with the Medicine Council. They have much yet to teach you."

"I don't care," Billy responded. "I can't stand by and do nothing."

"But you're playing right into her plan," the spirit said. "She wants you to attack while you're mad and unprepared like this so you'll make a mistake. Then she can defeat you before you can fulfill the prophecy."

"So be it," Billy replied and started the truck's engine. "One way or another, I'll see you on the other side."

Then, putting the pickup in gear, the teen sped out of the hospital parking lot, headed for Buzzard Bend. Also, a storm began to brew overhead as dark, menacing clouds swirled around the Buzzard Bend vicinity.

"Bring it on!" Billy yelled up at the dark, roiling billows of darkness.

Ignoring all speed limits, he reached Tuckaleechee's gravel driveway in a matter of minutes and hit the brakes only a few yards from the old Victorian home. The witch was waiting on the front porch. Grabbing his Lightning Lance, along with his bow and quiver of arrows, the teen faced off with her.

"Alone at last, Thunder Boy," the old woman said. "It's been a long time coming."

"The name's Thunder Child, and I declare your life on earth is over, old woman. Time to join your mate in the Afterworld."

Wanting to let his adversary know she'd met her match, the spirit warrior looked to the skies and yelled in Cherokee, "I call down the lightning!"

He held his lance aloft, and a bolt of lightning struck the tip, sending a jolt of energy through the boy's body. His whole being glowed with electrical energy as his Thunder Child power was reactivated. He began moving toward his adversary, pointing the rod in her direction.

Tuckaleechee rubbed her hands together, creating a fiery energy ball that she hurled right at the teen's head. Again, the Geronimo spell did its job, deflecting the energy. Instead of striking Thunder Child, the fireball ricocheted off the invisible shield and hit a tree at the edge of the clearing, setting the Spanish moss ablaze.

The eyes of the sorceress flared with surprise and anger, and she reached a hand toward the stormy sky. Closing her hand around some invisible object, she drew her arm down and threw the unseen object in the teen's direction. Gale-force winds hit the boy like a wall of bricks, knocking him to the ground. The bow and collection of arrows were knocked away from him a few feet.

From where he lay, Thunder Child, holding the lance like an orchestra conductor holds a baton, pointed it skyward. Then, directing an unseen force, he aimed the lance at the witch.

Immediately, a bolt of lightning struck the porch behind her, igniting another fire. He realized he'd need some target practice to make the lightning more precise.

"You might want to call down some rain to douse that blaze," the old woman yelled, "since your worthless friend Checotah is locked in the basement!"

Her cackling laugh transitioned to the hoot of an owl as she mutated into her bird form and flew up to a branch in the nearest tree. Thunder Child proceeded to summon a series of lightning strikes, each hitting a tree branch near the owl as she narrowly escaped each bolt and flitted off to another branch.

Grabbing the bow and knocking an arrow, the boy took aim at the witch bird as she launched herself from yet another branch. The hours of archery practice Billy Buckhorn had put in over the years paid off as Thunder Child's well-placed arrow struck the bird through the breast and into the heart.

The unnatural sound released by the animal could only be described as the squawking screech of an owl merged with the death cry of a wounded wolf. The angled thrust of the arrow spun the oversized bird around, causing it to pinwheel through the air as it plummeted downward. It landed with a thud on the roof of the burning house.

The roof's steep angle quickly caused the owl's body to roll and tumble off and onto the ground. Thunder Child approached, arrow drawn, ready to finish the job in case there was any life left in the carcass. To his amazement, the owl began a transformation back to human form, echoing the Raven Stalker's transformation at the moment of his death.

First, Carmelita Tuckaleechee's form became visible, but then her face dissolved into a series of other faces. Thunder Child realized he was seeing the faces of all the people the witch had deprived of life over the years—the faces of the innocent who'd fallen victim to her witchery as she extended her own life.

The final face he saw was the true face of the 174-year-old *skili*, in all its withered, desiccated reality. There was surprised horror in her eyes. Then, in the next few moments, the woman's whole body disintegrated into dust.

Thunder Child watched the entire process as if in a trance, almost disbelieving that a life had just ended. As evil as that life had been, it was hard for him to accept that it was he who had just ended it. After all, the Raven Stalker had died as a result of a volley of bullets fired by armed police officers, not by his hand.

And yet, in both cases, the outcome was necessary in order to set the world right again, necessary for the protection of the innocent. Thunder Child knew this would not be the last time he would be called upon to rid the world of deadly threats. In fact, it was only the beginning.

Suddenly, he snapped out of the trance and saw that the old Victorian mansion was engulfed in flames. The forest surrounding the house and cabin was also fully engulfed in the inferno.

"Chigger!"

Running faster than he'd ever run, the teen charged into the burning Victorian structure and headed for the grandfather moon clock. After throwing the entire clock cabinet aside, he ripped open the metal basement door, pulling it off its hinges.

"Chigger!" he called into the smoke-filled darkness.

No reply.

He charged down the stairs and found his friend collapsed on the bed of blankets. Easily picking up the scrawny kid, Thunder Child carried him up and out of the burning house to safety.

Within a few seconds, after the fresh air hit his face and filled his lungs, Chigger came to. The first thing the boy saw when he sat up was the witch's burning cabin.

"Oh no!" he exclaimed and, inexplicably, ran off toward the blazing building.

"What are you doing?" Thunder Child called.

Chigger didn't answer but darted inside the blaze. Thunder Child began to follow, but before he reached the cabin door, his friend emerged carrying a large item wrapped in cloth. It was Blacksnake's medicine book.

"Since I think I'm the one who probably stole it, I wanted to be the one who returned it," Chigger said, handing the tome to his friend. "It belongs in your family, and from what I gathered from Tuckaleechee, it contains important secrets that could undo the Night Seers."

"Thanks" was all Thunder Child said.

"I'm so sorry," Chigger said. "For anything and everything I might have done while under the old woman's influence. She brainwashed me or hypnotized me and took advantage of all my flaws. I—"

"Forget it," Thunder Child said, holding out his hand.

"Best friends forever?" Chigger said as he shook it.

"Longer than that," his friend confirmed, pulling the boy in for a bear hug.

After a long moment, Chigger broke free of the hug to make a point. "If someone doesn't do something soon, the whole Cherokee Nation may burn to the ground," he said.

"Oh, yeah," Thunder Child replied. "Somebody had better do something."

Billy placed Blacksnake's medicine book in the cab of his truck. Then he looked up at the sky. Using another of the spells he'd learned from weather maker Andrew Blackbird, he gestured upward, moved his arms in a figure-eight pattern, and then pulled downward with his hand as if he were lowering a window shade.

Within a few minutes, drops of rain began falling, and within another few, a torrential downpour soaked the two boys and doused the fire completely.

Soaking wet, the friends made their way to the Buckhorn home, where they found the Lookouts and the other two Buckhorns in a somber mood after Wesley's passing. Both families were shocked to see the boys enter the living room together.

"What is *he* doing here?" James and Lisa demanded, almost simultaneously.

"He's the last person on earth I expected to see you with," James added.

"Chigger's been under the witch's hypnosis spell and wasn't responsible for his actions," Billy replied. "He doesn't remember much, if anything, of the things she had him doing."

He escorted Chigger over to Lisa.

"Lisa, I want to formally introduce you to my oldest friend, Chigger."

Chigger extended a hand, expecting to shake with Lisa.

Lisa didn't move.

"Like I said before, we already met at Taco Bueno the day he took our picture," she said. "And then he used the photo to help his witch master cast a spell of confusion on me!"

"I'm so sorry for all of it, even though I didn't really realize what was going on," Chigger replied in a remorseful tone.

No one spoke.

"Come on, guys," Billy said, breaking the silence. "Grandpa Wesley would be the first to forgive and the last to hold a grudge.

Anyway, ding-dong, the witch is dead, and now we can move on with all the other challenges we face."

"Have you forgotten that we've got to make arrangements to bury your grandfather?" James said with an accusing tone. "Let's focus on that for the time being. Several years ago, he gave me a set of instructions to follow when he passed."

"I know exactly what Grandpa wants," Billy said, his anger building.

Then the boy caught himself, closed his eyes, and took a few deep breaths. His grandfather's words echoed in his mind.

You're in charge now.

Opening his eyes, the boy said, "Chigger, our family needs time to grieve. I'll call you in a few days."

Chigger nodded and turned to leave.

"For what it's worth, I believe you," Billy said.

That meant everything to Chigger. He smiled a little smile as he left the Buckhorn home, hopeful that his best friend was still his best friend.

Turning back to his family, Billy said, "Of course this is a tragic day, but have you forgotten that Grandpa isn't lost to us? If I've learned anything in the last few months, it's that a whole other journey begins when a life here on earth ends."

He paused a moment as he thought of how to proceed.

"Pops, I'll help you carry out Grandpa's final wishes. That includes maintaining the four-day vigil and keeping the sacred fire burning at the grave site."

"Okay, son, thanks," James replied, calmer now. "Everyone else, please join us tomorrow before sunset at the Live Oak cemetery."

Next morning, James and his son took the half-hour drive from Park Hill to Muskogee to visit the Regal Casket Company. This manufacturer carried a wide array of caskets from the simple to the sublime. Wesley had specifically requested the simplest.

Once that was purchased, the pair drove back to Wesley's house, where a circle of Cherokee medicine makers, including Wesley's friend Wilma, had gathered. Many in this group had known the man most of his adult life. Together, they prepared his body for burial using traditional methods.

Afterward, in a caravan, the group proceeded to the Live Oak cemetery, which sat west of the stomp dance grounds. The graveyard's location was in keeping with the traditional belief that the soul traveled westward to reach the land of the dead.

Everyone in the group took a turn digging the grave, which was located next to Awinita Buckhorn's burial plot. Unlike a church-sanctioned process, this grassroots endeavor was more lighthearted, more in keeping with sure confidence in the reality of the soul's immortality.

Of course, grief would come to all who knew and loved Wesley, because his physical presence would be deeply missed. But the process of saying goodbye and sending his soul off to a higher level of the Afterworld was a hope-filled activity.

As the sun sank low in the western sky, the Lookouts and Rebecca arrived at the cemetery, greeted by those who'd spent the day there. The coffin had already been lowered into the open grave, and some of Wesley's most cherished possessions had been placed on top of it: his clearest quartz crystal, the coffee mug he drank from every morning, the turquoise-inlaid pocketknife Awinita had given him, his wedding ring.

Four logs, aligned in the four directions, had been placed near the grave, and assorted kindling, branches, and firewood had been piled on top. Billy set the wood ablaze, giving the people and the nearby woods a dancing orange glow. Enough wood had been gathered to keep the blaze going for four days.

Each mourner then took his or her turn speaking a few words of remembrance for the man who'd made such a positive difference in so many lives. And finally, one at a time, each passed by the burial pit and dropped a handful of dirt, along with a pinch of tobacco, on the coffin.

Thanks to an unexpected inner prompting, Billy sang one of Wesley's favorite songs from the stomp grounds. Those who knew it joined in as the remaining dirt was shoveled in the pit. When the pit was filled, the shoveling ceased, and everything went quiet.

For a few minutes, the only sound was the crackling and popping of the fire. Smoke from the fire rose into the night sky, wafted westward, and then disappeared. Every so often a burning orange cinder shot upward from the fire to dance and float in the darkness like a spirit that had been freed from its physical prison.

James and Billy shook hands with everyone and thanked them for coming, and then the mourners began to disperse. Lisa, Cecil, Ethan, and Rebecca lingered a little longer, sitting near the fire with the son and grandson of the celebrated medicine man. Finally, they left too, leaving father and son alone to keep the vigil.

After setting up their tent by the harsh glare of the pickup headlights, the professor and his son, the Chosen One, gazed up at the quiet night sky. The campfires of the ancestors burned as bright as ever.

"I envy you a little, son," James said. "The lessons in Native history, culture, and spirituality you are learning and will learn, the experiences you're having, the depths of human knowledge you'll gain . . ."

He searched for words.

"I don't think there's ever been anyone or anything like it," he said.

"You could write a book about it all, but no one would believe it," Billy replied. "But really, you should write a book. It all needs to be recorded."

Those were the last words either of them spoke for the next four days. They'd committed to keep a silent vigil, stoking the fire from time to time to keep it alive. In traditional beliefs, the fire was meant to guide the spirit of the deceased on its four-day journey to the land of the dead.

Because of his out-of-body journeys, his conversations with Upperworld beings, and his own near-death experience, Billy had ceased to believe in those concepts. However, he was now honoring his grandpa's final wishes, respecting his Cherokee people's cherished beliefs, and strengthening the connection to his own father.

Each was reason enough itself for practicing the tradition.

Billy wondered each of the four nights if Grandma Awinita would visit him or bring Grandpa for a final goodbye. He hoped she would. Awinita had been strangely absent from his life recently, and he was sad about it but knew there was probably a good reason for it. He missed her visits just the same.

On the fourth night of the vigil, Billy decided to sleep beside the fire instead of in his tent. It was a clear, crisp night. The starfield overhead was especially bright and seemed closer to earth than usual. He was about to fall asleep when a rift between the physical and spiritual worlds began opening near the foot of his bedroll. The edges of the portal emitted a golden glow as it grew taller and wider.

Sure enough, Awinita stepped through the portal, appearing more glowing, radiant, and powerful than ever before.

"Grandma, I'm so glad you came," her grandson said. "I've missed seeing you so much."

"I'm sorry for not being more available to you," she replied. "I've been called on to perform more and more duties in the Afterworld in recent times.

"And Grandpa? How is he doing over there?"

"It's quite an adjustment, even for someone as connected to the spirit world as he has been," Awinita said. "But more about him in a minute."

She paused before changing the subject.

"Remember your ladder vision during the Labor Day stomp dances last year? Well, we all have our ladders to climb, and I'm moving up a rung or two on mine."

"What does that mean?" Billy asked.

"It means I won't be your spirit guide anymore, but someone else you're familiar with is taking my place."

She looked over her shoulder and gestured to someone who wasn't visible on the physical side of the rift. In another moment, a second figure stepped through the opening.

"Grandpa!" Billy yelled. "I'm so happy to see you!"

It was obvious that Wesley was unaccustomed to the whole spirit phenomenon. His energy repeatedly flickered and wavered, dissolving in and out of focus like the poorly projected image of a movie on a screen.

"He's a spirit guide in training," Awinita said. "He has several more lessons to master before he can come through consistently."

"At least I know what the four-day vigil is all about now," Wesley said with a smile. "I'll tell you all about it sometime, but I—"

Suddenly, he disappeared from view.

"Give him some time," Awinita advised. "He'll improve with practice. Meanwhile, you've got a lot of challenges ahead, don't you, Grandson?"

"Don't remind me," Billy replied. "I get exhausted just thinking about it: finding the Sun Priest's physical remains, locating the southern piece of the Sky Stone, tracking down the Fire Crystal . . . Oh, and let's not forget battling whatever Underworld creatures and disasters materialize here in the Middleworld!"

"All by the time you turn the ripe old age of seventeen," his grandmother said.

"Wait. What?"

"The attack of the Underworld seems to be set for spring, and the final outcome will be known by summer solstice. Quite an early birthday present, huh?"

"The Siege Before Solstice," Billy said, doing his best impersonation of a boxing match announcer. "Be there."

"On that note, I'll leave you so you can get some sleep," Awinita said. "Remember, even though you won't see me, I'll still be there for you in spirit. Good night and good dreams."

As she faded from view, Billy couldn't help but wonder again if he was really the right guy for the job.

BIBLIOGRAPHY OF SOURCES

Conley, Robert J. *Cherokee Medicine Man: The Life and Work of a Modern-Day Healer*. Norman, OK: University of Oklahoma Press, 2005.

Diaz-Granados, Carol, James R. Duncan, and F. Kent Reilly III, eds. *Picture Cave: Unraveling the Mysteries of the Mississippian Cosmos*. Austin, TX: University of Texas Press, 2015.

Garrett, J. T. and Michael Garrett. *Medicine of the Cherokee: The Way of Right Relationship*. Rochester, VT: Bear & Company, 1996.

Jefferson, Warren. *Reincarnation Beliefs of North American Indians: Soul Journeys, Metamorphoses, and Near-Death Experiences*. Summertown, TN: Native Voices, 2009.

Kilpatrick, Alan. *The Night Has a Naked Soul: Witchcraft and Sorcery among the Western Cherokee*. Syracuse, NY: Syracuse University Press, 1997.

Kilpatrick, Jack F. and Anna G. Kilpatrick. *Friends of Thunder: Folktales of the Oklahoma Cherokees*. Norman, OK: University of Oklahoma Press, 1995.

Little, Gregory L. *The Illustrated Encyclopedia of Native American Indian Mounds and Earthworks*. Memphis, TN: Eagle Wing Books, 2016.

Little, Gregory. *Path of Souls: The Native American Death Journey*. Memphis, TN: ATA Archetype Books, 2014.

Mooney, James. "The Sacred Formulas of the Cherokees." *Seventh Annual Report of the Bureau of Ethnology*, 1886, 301-397, Bureau of American Ethnology.

Monroe, Robert A. *Ultimate Journey*. New York: Doubleday, 1994.

Pauketat, Timothy R. *Cahokia: Ancient America's Great City on the Mississippi*. New York: Penguin Books, 2009.

Zimmerman, Fritz. *The Native American Book of the Dead*. Self-published, 2020.

ABOUT THE AUTHOR

Gary Robinson, a writer and filmmaker of Cherokee and Choctaw Indian descent, has spent more than thirty years collaborating with American Indian communities to tell the historical and contemporary stories of Native people in all forms of media.

His most recent books include *Native Actors and Filmmakers: Visual Storytellers* and *Be Your Own Best Friend Forever*, both published by 7th Generation in 2021.

His historical novel series, *Lands of Our Ancestors*, portrays California history from a Native American perspective. It is used in many classrooms in the state, and has been praised by teachers and students alike.

He has also written several other teen novels, including *Billy Buckhorn and the Book of Spells*, *Standing Strong*, *Thunder on the Plains*, *Tribal Journey*, *Little Brother of War*, and *Son Who Returns*. His two children's books share aspects of Native American culture through popular holiday themes: *Native American Night Before Christmas* and *Native American Twelve Days of Christmas*.

He lives in rural central California.

Look for *Billy Buckhorn and the War of Worlds*, the exciting conclusion to the Thunder Child Prophecy Series. Available September 2024.

"I think it's beginning," Billy told Morningstar, the Upperworld being who'd been guiding the teen in his role as Thunder Child. "It seems the Underworld has chosen strange weather to start things off. What should I do?"

"Volcanoes, earthquakes, and atmospheric phenomena probably aren't the main events," the spirit replied. "You already know this at a deeper level, and you'll need to rely more on your innate intuition for the turmoil ahead."

That wasn't the response Billy had hoped to get.

When the Owl Clan and the Serpent Society renew their ancient evil alliance, they launch a series of supernatural events meant to usher in a new age of horrific Underworld dominance. Bizarre weather patterns produce raging floods. Fantastic beasts from Native American legends roam North America once again. Multiple fabled Horned Serpents slither forth from their Underworld abodes.

Can Billy Buckhorn, aka Thunder Child, and his dedicated and gifted team—his oldest friend Chigger; Osage girlfriend, Lisa; the Intertribal Medicine Council; and his allies in the Upperworld—prevent this apocalypse from happening?

For more information, visit: **nativevoicesbooks.com**

Book Publishing Company • PO Box 99 • Summertown, TN 38483 • 888-260-8458

Free shipping and handling on all orders.